Praise for *Precious Thing*:

'Keep your eyes peeled this summer for an astonishing new talent . . . *Gone Girl* but with a Brit voice'

David Mark, author of *Dark Winter*

'Fantastic and beautifully chilling'

Imogen Robertson, author of *The Paris Winter*

'A brilliant, chilling debut. Psychopathy has never seemed so attractive'

Ali Knight, author of *Wink Murder*

'Dark, intriguing and full of unexpected twists'

Lynn Shepherd, author of *Tom-All-Alone's* and *A Treacherous Likeness*

'The plot of *Precious Thing* is like a Catherine wheel, spinning faster and faster as it approaches its final twist . . . It is a fine debut from Colette McBeth. Roll on her next'

Clio Gray, author of *The Brora Murders*

'[A]n excellent debut, well-written, gripping and tense, which skilfully weaves an unfolding nightmare with a dark past'

Cath Staincliffe, author of the *Sal Kilkenny Mysteries* and the *Scott & Bailey* novels

'[T]his psychological thriller had me gripped from start to finish. [Colette McBeth] has a unique voice'

Mari Hannah, author of *Deadly Deceit*

precious thing

colette mcbeth

precious thing

First published in Great Britain in 2013
by HEADLINE REVIEW
An imprint of HEADLINE PUBLISHING GROUP

1

Cataloguing in Publication Data is available from the British Library

ISBN 978 1 4722 0593 3 (Hardback)
ISBN 978 1 4722 0594 0 (Trade paperback)

Typeset in 13/17pt Bembo by
Palimpsest Book Production Limited, Falkirk, Stirlingshire

Printed and bound in Great Britain by
Clays Ltd, St Ives plc

Headline's policy is to use papers that are natural, renewable and
recyclable products and made from wood grown in sustainable forests.
The logging and manufacturing processes are expected to conform to the
environmental regulations of the country of origin.

HEADLINE PUBLISHING GROUP
An Hachette UK Company
338 Euston Road
London NW1 3BH

www.headline.co.uk
www.hachette.co.uk

To Paul
and Finlay, Milo and Sylvie.

September 2007

OFFICIALLY, I DON'T think of you any more. I am one hundred per cent focused on the future. When anyone asks how I'm doing – and they do regularly – I'm fond of using the terminology of war – it adds drama don't you think? *I am conquering my demons; I am battling the dark thoughts that have been twisting inside me.* Sometimes, if the situation lends itself to it, I'll lean forward, fix them with a steely look and say with as much reverence as I can muster: *I am a survivor, I will beat the past.* In return I get a sympathetic nod, a concerned smile. I can almost hear the *whissh* of relief blowing through them. I can see the checklist of worries being ticked off in their minds. *She's making progress.*

In reality I'm doing nothing of the sort. I can't empty my head of you in the way I would spring-clean a cupboard. People don't seem to understand that no matter what has happened between us we will always have each other encoded in our DNA. I don't want to move on, quite the opposite. I want to go back to the very beginning. To the time when you made me smile a smile that reached all the way to my eyes and tingled in my head; when we laughed about the little things that only we found funny, when we traded the knowing winks, the in-jokes, as if they were our own personal currency. To the days when we were always together because it was the only way we made sense.

Your absence is an ache in the pit of my stomach, a hunger that is never satisfied. Even when I close my eyes I can't escape you. I see you everywhere. Yesterday, the late-afternoon sun slanted through the window and fell into the room. I closed my eyes to bask in the warmth of it. I imagined I was sitting under a vast, endless sky, staring out to sea. I focused on the horizon, the reds and yellows and greens of the fishing boats moving on the swell of the waves; the blue of the ocean dancing under the sun. For the briefest moment my mind stilled and emptied. I breathed deep. I was freed from my thoughts. Then I glimpsed you, jumping over the waves, dark hair in ringlets from the water, laughing as a breaker pulled you under. I ran down to the water to see you, straight in. Only when you emerged the hair and face weren't yours.

These are the cruel tricks my mind plays.

I can't rest until I reach you. Oh, what I'd give to see you one last time, to have you look me in the eye and know, without a flicker of doubt, that I have only ever loved you, that everything I have done was driven by a fierce desire to protect you.

I don't blame you for thinking otherwise. I blame the people who've poisoned you with their lies. But listen to your heart. Trust your instincts. Think of the beautiful, precious thing that we have shared. Know that something so pure could never be bad.

That's why I'm writing to you. So you'll understand. I don't know how it will reach you, but I'll find a way. No one knows about the letter; its content doesn't fit with my 'moving on' narrative. Let it be our secret. Just imagine me close to you, whispering it in your ear – our story, in my words. And maybe at the end we will work out how we lost each other and how we can find each other once more.

Chapter One

MY STORY STARTS on a Monday morning in January because it's the obvious place to begin. I used to think, *Oh, that was the day when everything changed,* but of course it's never that simple. The seeds of what happened then were planted years before.

In my box of memories from January the twenty-second 2007 these are the things you'll see: a single sunflower in a garden, the waves; the huge yawning jaws of them thrashing under ripe clouds. And the violet of the sky, the way it looked electric, like it had been plugged into a vast source of negative energy.

But the mind plays tricks. So does the memory. What we see is not necessarily how things are. I do believe, though, that the sky and the waves were as I have described them. But the sunflower, in winter? I can see it as clearly now as I can see my hand in front of me. But it doesn't mean it was there. Maybe I see it because the flower has always reminded me of you, of us. Of the beginning of the end.

It was a one-way conversation, the kind that often marked the start of my working day. Robbie, my news editor, barking his orders down the phone. 'Some woman has disappeared in Brighton, police are holding a press conference. I'll e-mail you the rest,' he said before hanging up. That was as much as I knew.

I left London in the freezing rain and by the time I reached the outskirts of Brighton the snow had begun to fall, in giant fuzzy felts on my windscreen. In the city a film of slush coated the roads. I drove up Southover Street, weaving in and out of the rows of squashed terraces to John Street and the police station, a boxy construction in white and beige with dirty brown windows, not far from the sea.

I was late so I pulled up on the kerb – a parking ticket always preferable to a bollocking from the news desk for missing a story. A blast of icy air hit me as I got out and reminded me why I hated Robbie. The flimsy mac, the heels, the skirt, the air-stewardess chic. It was my attempt to appease him after being told to *make more of an effort.* Not that the viewers gave a damn if I wore the same coat three days in a row, but he did.

Outside the police station the TV vans were lined up, satellites pointing to the sky and humming. Our own with its National News Network logo, a mangle of Ns, was next to the Global Broadcasting Corp truck. Through the half-open door I caught a glimpse of the monitor feeding pictures from inside the press conference. Relief: no sound yet, no one had started talking. I reached for my BlackBerry to read Robbie's e-mail and fill in the blanks of the story, winging it as usual, when Eddie the engineer emerged from the sat van, barely recognisable in the bulk of his North Face jacket.

'They've just given us a two-minute warning. Should have worn your running shoes, Rachel.'

The smell hits you first in police stations. It's the stench of lives unravelling, of drink- and drug-fuelled chaos, of people crossing the line. It's the same in hospitals and old people's homes, the way it clings to you. The one in Brighton was no different. I could feel it catch my throat as soon as I went through the automatic doors.

There was a man in front of me at reception in a grey shell suit that was a shade or two darker than his skin. Gunmetal next to putty. His dark hair shone with grease and he was chewing fingernails that were thick with dirt.

'What the fuck you looking at eh?' he snarled. 'You got nothing better to do?'

'Pipe down, Wayne,' said the woman on reception. Her name badge said she was Lesley. She had big gold ovals hanging from her ears, stretching her ear lobes, dark circles round her eyes.

I flashed my press card.

'They're just about to start, darling. Fill this in.' She tapped the visitors' book with her right hand so I could see that she wore gold rings on three fingers, excluding her thumb and pinkie. One said MUM, as if she needed to be reminded, and the other spelled out LOVE.

'You,' she pointed a finger at shell-suit man, 'you sit down and someone will see you in a minute. You, come with me, I need to buzz you through.'

We walked through a double door into a long corridor to the conference room. Inside was the usual smattering of local newspaper journalists, huddled together in their cheap suits, a wall of chatter surrounding them, cameras set up ready to go live the moment the police started talking. A clutch of microphones was propped on the table and sitting behind it were four people: two police officers, the press officer Hilary Benson, and a young woman. Jake Roberts was there too. But I didn't see him until later. I wouldn't see any of this until later. Instead, as soon as Lesley opened the doors, my eyes locked on to a poster, about two foot by two foot, hanging next to the table. It was a photograph of a woman. A photograph of you.

Those blue eyes of yours, they sucked me in, deep deep down where it was cold and dark. My lungs inflated, my whole body screamed for air. I was drowning, Clara, and all the time I could hear the sloshing and swirling of water in my ears and the muffled sounds of the media circus gearing up for a performance. No one saw what happened to me in that moment, no one noticed that I had been sucked from the outside of the story right down into its murky depths. No one could have guessed that the story was part of me.

I felt like I had hit the bottom. Everything stopped.

Then I heard a voice louder than the rest, reaching above the chatter. And finally I came back to the surface, greedy for air.

'We're just about ready to start folks,' the voice said. It was DCI Gunn, announcing the start of the press conference like he was about to introduce an act in a show.

'Thanks for coming', DCI Gunn said in his West Country twang. I noticed he was looking straight down the barrel of the camera lenses. 'We want your help in finding the young woman you can see here.' He nodded to the poster of you. That smile, so beguiling. 'Her name is Clara O'Connor. She's twenty-eight years of age and her disappearance is completely out of character.'

I should explain that DCI Gunn and I had what you would call a professional relationship. He was a contact I had cultivated three years before when I first landed the job of crime correspondent at National News Network. We'd have lunches, drinks-on-me and after a while the information began to flow. Tip-offs on stories on his patch, a few leaks here and there. And an unspoken pact: he'd make me look good if I returned the favour. It's the kind of cosy relationship journalists rely on and this was the moment ours began to unravel. He had never met you and yet suddenly he was an expert on your character. The blood rushed to my head, my teeth sunk deep into my lips.

'She was reported missing by her friend and flatmate Amber Corrigan. Amber was staying at a friend's on Friday night but had planned to meet Clara the next day for lunch.' He paused, looked over at the girl sitting two people down from him at the table. I had heard you mention her before but this was the first time I had seen her – she was a tiny, fragile little thing. The seat almost swallowed her up. I thought if she took a step outside she'd be blown away by the gathering storm. But she was pretty, and TV cameramen and photographers love a pretty girl crying. Your story would get more coverage that way.

DCI Gunn cleared his throat, 'Clara was supposed to spend an evening with friends last Friday, January the eighteenth in Brighton city centre. They had arranged to meet but she was late and from what we can gather she only turned up briefly. She was seen leaving Cantina Latina on Marine Drive around eleven thirty p.m. and told her friends she was going back to her flat. Unfortunately she has not been seen since.' He paused and looked around the room for effect. I tried to grab the information he was giving and process it in my head. It was like trying to catch water in my hands.

Looking back it's hard to explain my behaviour that day. In truth I don't understand it myself. I can still hear the voice in my head that screamed at me to stand up and shout as loud as I could that this account of Friday night was all wrong. I wanted to holler to DCI Gunn that I was your friend, your oldest friend, and if anyone knew you it was me. I wanted to reach out and press pause, to bring everything to a standstill for a moment and allow myself to think. Every muscle in my body was straining, willing me to do something, say something. But nothing. I was anchored to the spot, pinned down by a force greater than me. I had no voice, my body was paralysed. So I just sat watching events run away from me until it was too late to catch up with them.

'I'm grateful that Amber Corrigan has come today,' said DCI Gunn. 'You can appreciate that this is a very traumatic time for her, but she wanted to do everything she could to help us in our search for Clara.'

My eyes turned to focus on Amber. She was your flatmate but I doubted she knew you very well. And yet here she was, face mottled, eyes emotional, red. Later, I would wish I could cry like her but my tears would be slow to come.

'I just want to say to Clara . . .' She paused and gulped. Her voice was quiet but she enunciated every syllable of each word, like she'd practised her lines. 'Clara, if you're listening, please get in touch, we're worried sick. I know this isn't like you and we're all scared something awful has happened.' She began to sob and used the back of her hand to rub away the tears that fell down her cheeks. The sound of the cameras zooming was inaudible but I heard it all the same. 'Please, Clara, let us know where you are.'

I wished she had said something more original, something more fitting of you.

DCI Gunn stepped in, 'I'd like to thank Amber for coming along today and I'd ask that you all give her some privacy.' Everyone nodded in agreement, knowing that the first thing they'd do would be approach her for an exclusive.

He talked about how they had already begun to contact your friends and colleagues (would I be the last because I was under W in the address book?). About you being a promising artist, which made me raise my eyebrows a little.

Then finally he asked: 'Does anyone have any questions?'

My head was full of questions, each one screaming and shouting and taunting me. But still I had no voice and the ground around me was crumbling away. If I moved I would surely have slipped into the dark hole that was forming beneath me. So I sat there, rigid, as others raised their hands and their questions floated in the air above my head.

I wonder now if there was something else at play that day; if I realised even on a subconscious level that DCI Gunn couldn't help me. If somehow I already knew that I had all the answers, I just needed to search for them.

Chapter Two

Three days before

EVEN THROUGH THE phone I can hear it in your voice. The spark I had forgotten existed. And your laugh, loud and contagious, ricochets through me like a charge. This is how we used to be, I think. I've missed you, Clara. I've missed us.

'Honestly Rachel,' you say, 'I haven't had so much fun in ages. We went to this club that was so tacky but hilarious. I even had a snog at the end of the night, although God knows what he thought of me.'

'I wish I'd been there,' I say, not mentioning the fact that you didn't invite me because I don't mind, not really. I understand. You need to broaden your circle of friends and that means doing things without each other; after all, my life has moved on too. The career, the boyfriend. And Jonny isn't just any boyfriend, he's everything I thought I couldn't have. His dark eyes twinkle when he laughs, which he does a lot. When he kisses my neck it tingles all the way through my body. He understands me, totally, just being around him makes me calm. Sorry if that all sounds a bit corny but I love him. Now we just need to work on finding you someone too.

'Are you seeing him again,' I ask. I'm five leaps ahead already. I'm turning into one of those smug people who want everyone else to couple-up and share the happiness.

'I very much doubt that very much.' You are giggling so much you can't get your words out. 'I had to break off mid-kiss to puke in my handbag.'

'You are not serious?' I ask in my big-sister voice. 'I'm protective, Clara. It used to be the other way round, I know, but for a long time it's been me looking out for you.'

'Well, what was I supposed to do? I wouldn't have made it to the loo, and I didn't want to do it on the floor, so the bag was the next best place. He didn't see me either. Though the bag was in a terrible state and the keys . . .'

'Stop! I don't want to hear any more,' I say, but I am laughing too. 'So who are the new friends?'

Your laughter is replaced by a cough. I imagine the smile slipping from your face.

'Just some people from school,' you say finally.

'Really? Who? Do I get to meet them?'

'I didn't realise I needed your approval on everything?' Your mood has changed and your words slap me down.

'Jesus, Clara, I'm only asking, I'm curious, that's all . . .' I let my sentence trail off. *Don't bite, don't rise to the bait.*

'Well since you ask, Sarah Pitts and Debbie Morton.' You sound out the names slowly, for effect I think.

Those names carry with them bucketloads of memories. In an instant I'm transported back to school, I can feel their hockey sticks on my shins, their elbows sharp in my ribs during netball. But that's nothing compared with the time Lucy Redfern pushed me in the water on the PGL school trip in Shropshire. I see myself emerging from the lake; the whole class is laughing at me but Sarah's cackle is the loudest. Lucy jokes that I needed a wash anyway, and her twin James leads the boys in a round of applause. You were there, Clara, you saw my face turn beetroot with the shame of it all.

Then again it was a long time ago. Maybe they've changed, I think.

'Does Debbie still smell of chips?' I say. I don't even ask about Sarah.

'Fuck off, Rachel. You're so up your own arse.'

'Jesus Clara, I'm just joking. They ruined my last year at school but you know me, move on, never hold a grudge.' You give something that sounds like a snort. 'Though now I can see why I wasn't invited,' I add.

For a moment neither of us speaks and the elation I felt at the beginning of our conversation is sucked out of me by the silence. I wonder if it will ever be right between us again.

And then you say something that surprises me.

'We're going out again on Friday.' Your voice is softer. You pause as if considering your words. 'You could always come. Stay at mine afterwards. You might even change your mind about them.'

I am about to say no and then I think about it for a moment. The first thing that occurs to me is that Jonny will be away, travelling out to Afghanistan to film a documentary, and I will be alone. The second thing I think of is this: Sarah Pitts was my high-school nemesis but who's laughing now? I have the job, the boyfriend. She can't touch me.

'Why not,' I tell you. 'I might even enjoy myself.'

On the roads there is an edge to the traffic, a hint of menace. Corporate boys bloated on expense accounts are tailgating in their Audis and BMWs, shining their lights too close to my Mini. I blink to clear my vision but the rain falling on the windscreen blurs it again just as quickly. Occasionally I question the wisdom of agreeing to meet you and Sarah and Debbie. Given the choice I would be at home, snuggling up with Jonny on the sofa, with a Thai takeaway and a bottle of wine. I think you've guessed I'm having second thoughts. You've called three times this week to check I'm still coming, which is unusual to say the least. Lately you rarely call or return mine.

Anyway Jonny is staying at Gatwick tonight to catch an early flight so I'm not going to cry off. Our flat is cold and empty without him. It feels like we are two halves of the same person these days. With every other guy before him it was like they were from one planet and I was from another. And then he spoke to me and we just clicked and I thought *hello, my man from earth*. Before I knew it I was doing all the things I used to frown upon, like peeing in front of someone one minute and then fucking them the next with such an urgency, such a need that makes you want to laugh and cry at the same time. We fill each other's spaces, end each other's sentences and sometimes we just sit in silence because we don't have to hide behind words and gestures. We can just be ourselves. What I'm trying to say is when he's not at home I feel like I've lost part of myself and I'd rather be anywhere than face the flat without him. So here I am on the M23 with the Arctic Monkeys playing on my CD, a Diet Coke and a bag of Haribo, heading towards you and the high-school bitch girls.

I'm a few miles past Gatwick when I get that familiar sinking feeling. The traffic is slowing, the red brake lights are all bunched up on the road ahead. The Haribos are gone, my teeth are aching from the sugar and my bladder is full of Coke. I start flicking between radio stations to get the traffic update and catch snippets of news. The woman on Radio Four says that eleven people died in yesterday's storms in the Midlands and the North. On Radio One there's a breathless girl reading too fast and stressing words in all kinds of weird places. She says the Prime Minister Gordon Brown is in India talking about a racism row on *Big Brother*. Is this what the world has come to?

Ahead, I see flashing lights, strobing in the rain. We are funnelled into a single lane, slowly, slowly. Further up the road there are two police cars, a fire engine and an ambulance. I can see high-vis jackets moving in the gloom. I wonder what they have found but I don't have to wonder for too long because soon I see it myself. To the left of me there is a red Ford, a Fiesta I think, with its roof half off and the firemen are cutting someone out. Either that or they are trying to get into the car to see what is left of the driver. I picture severed limbs and death. There's another car, a silver Mercedes, at a right angle, near the Ford. Its rear and side door have been bashed but it has fared better than the Fiesta. *The beauty of German engineering*. A man who looks like the driver is sitting on the roadside. He has a blanket draped over his shoulders and his head is in his hands. Underneath the blanket he is wearing a suit and black shoes. I shudder. I wish I hadn't seen him, but the image is burnt into my brain now. And I am reminded that we are not in control, even when we think we are. Life is random; anyone who thinks otherwise is a fool.

Slowly the traffic starts moving again. As I pull away my phone beeps. A text message. I'll wait until I stop to read it, I think. I'm not ready for my life to change suddenly on the M23 on a dark Friday night in January.

I open it when I arrive in Brighton. It's from you.

Rach, so sorry, feeling terrible, think I might have flu, still in bed but will heave myself out to make it. Will call later Clara x

When I try to call you back, it goes straight to your answerphone. I don't leave a message. I text you back instead.

Don't leave me on my own with them!! Take some Lemsips. And turn your phone on. X

But you never do.

It is a five-minute walk from the car park on Black Lion Street to Cantina Latina. The wind, sharp from the sea, shaves my skin. I cross the road and walk past the pier, illuminated in the dark. A few arcades are open, defying the January freeze to lure the hardcore gamblers. In front of me a group of girls teeter on high heels, no coats. Don't they feel the cold? Occasionally one of them laughs. The night is full of expectation. Smudged make-up and disappointment will come later.

My work clothes look out of place among the short skirts and shiny shirts. And I realise I'm not part of this now. Jonny and I go to pubs. We talk. You tease me about it, Clara. You say I act like I'm middle-aged and I can't have fun any more but that's not true. Jonny and I are happy in each other's company, we don't need anything else. It's the way *we* used to be, Clara.

I see Cantina Latina across the road from the Sea Life Centre, next to a fish and chip shop. As I approach I notice two bouncers, like fat bald pillars on either side of the door.

'Evening,' says the shorter of the two with a gold-tooth smile. He pulls the door open and I am inside.

The air is liquid. Sticky. It runs down my back, seeps into my pores. The change, from outside to in, is so sudden it sends me swimming. I try concentrating to steady myself but my eyes can't hold on to anything. The room is a sea of blue and pink and green lanterns and fairy lights which nod in and out of focus. I reach for the nearest table to steady myself. I know you won't leave me here with the two of them. But still, I want to turn round, go to your flat and drag you off your sick bed, just to be sure. The only thing that stops me is my bladder, which is ready to burst. And in the toilets, waiting for the two-at-a-time girls to come out and reapply their lip gloss, I give myself a talking-to. *She'll come, she wouldn't dare not turn up. Have a drink. Relax*. That's what you always said wasn't it? 'Relax, Rachel.' So I take your advice.

I'm waiting at the bar. There is no queue to speak of, more of a mob shouting to be served. I can feel the mass of a belly against my back, soft and wide. It pushes and jostles me and it has a voice which shouts above my head, 'Becks, mate,' to the barman, who is busy with someone else and doesn't even look up. The voice tries again, this time louder, angrier. Then the shout stops and is replaced by a yelp not unlike a dog's. The heel of one of my Louboutins has found its way on to a foot and is grinding down. It must be his. You told me I was mad to pay that much for them. I always knew they were worth the money. The barman looks and me and then to the guy behind me and I wink.

'A peach Bellini, please.'

'Happy hour finishes in –' he looks to the clock above the bar – 'in two minutes. You want two of those?' The barman's hair is not unlike a cloud around his head, thick and long and bouffant with curls.

'It would be rude not to.' I smile. The voice behind has started shouting again. I think he will miss happy hour. I think he knows it.

I take my Bellinis and move down the bar away from the crowds. I drain the first glass in minutes and wait for the alcohol to soften my edges. It does, quickly. I breathe. Deep. My shoulders sag, the tension in my head is released by degrees. I look around, my eyes seeking you out at tables, in dark corners of the room. I look to the door. I think I see your shape coming through it countless times only to realise it is someone else.

I'm trying to call you again when I'm interrupted by a voice so loud it reaches above the music and thunders across the room. All of a sudden I'm back at St Gregory's and the same voice, powering across the school yard, makes me small. I look around again and see her and suddenly I am glad I came. Sarah Pitts, the prettiest girl in the school, has moved a few dress sizes in the wrong direction. I laugh to myself, remembering how she used to swear blind ice cream had no calories in it because it melts. If I'm honest it looks like someone has taken her old school face, pumped it up with a balloon and covered it in thick, orange make-up. Her bobbed hair is bottle-blond and ends abruptly at her jawline. 'Ghosty' she used to call me and told everyone you could see through my skin to my blue veins. Oh I remember that now and I'm smiling inside. I'm smiling inside and out.

'Oh my God, Rachel, it's you.' She gives me a prod. 'We've seen you on TV so much, and now you're here. We couldn't believe it was really you when we saw you, you looked nothing like you used to. You're so polished these days and you are TINY, isn't she Debs, how did you lose all that weight? I need some tips,' she says and with her thumb and her index finger she pinches a roll of fat on her stomach to prove her point. I remember how that felt, the desire to be thin. Now we have swapped places.

Sarah doesn't stop talking but I notice Debs is looking down at the floor refusing to make eye contact with me.

My shoulders stiffen again. I am the one supposed to be here under duress, am I not? I don't dwell on it though because Sarah pulls me towards her in an awkward embrace, burying my face in her neck. She smells of 1991. Calvin Klein Eternity. I am left thinking (with even more satisfaction) that she hasn't come very far at all.

'How do you do it? Standing up there every night on the TV in front of millions of people? So professional. I could never do that. Does someone tell you what to say? Or do you think of it all yourself?' She doesn't pause for breath. But her eyes are flitting about, she can't hold eye contact for more than a second. I think she must be nervous. My job has elevated me in her eyes. I'm worth talking to now. She removes her pink coat and scarf to reveal a purple top which isn't up to the job of containing her enormous boobs.

'I wish someone did tell me what to say, it might make more sense,' I laugh, surprised to find myself enjoying her attention. It seems the schoolgirl in me still wants to be liked. 'I can't get through to Clara,' I add.

Her eyes dart towards Debbie, who is looking around the bar, and then she laughs, a forced, jangling laugh.

'Scared to be all alone with us?' She nudges me. 'She'll be here, trust me. At least now we get to pump you for gossip about her new man.'

Something catches in my throat, a bubble from the champagne, or maybe it's Debbie's perfume. Whatever it is, it brings on a cough. 'Come on, let's sit down and you can tell us all about him,' Sarah says.

A waiter leads us through the crowds to the darker part

of the bar. His orange shirt is unbuttoned revealing a tuft of hair on his olive chest. The dress policy for staff, I note, is to wear as little as possible. He sits us at a table with tea lights which illuminate Sarah's and Debbie's faces in a ghoulish glow. I don't know whether to laugh or cry.

'To old friends,' Sarah says once we are seated. She chinks my glass first then Debbie's like she's been practising it.

'To old friends,' I repeat, and I look towards the door again but there is no sign of you.

'He's probably the one she told me about a few weeks ago, I don't think she's that serious about him,' I say.

It's a bluff, Clara, as you know, because you haven't told me anything about a new man in your life. I'm not angry though, just surprised and a little bit embarrassed because they expect me to know everything about you. We're so close we're almost the same person, that's what they think.

'I doubt that's true.' The voice is quieter, an octave higher than Sarah's, unpunctuated by laughter. It is the first time Debbie has spoken. There is a smugness running through her words. I look at her properly for the first time. She is smaller than I remember, thin and bony next to Sarah's girth. Her mousy hair is cut in a crop. Too severe. And her eyes look like the lights have gone out. I'm willing to bet Debbie's life so far hasn't been all she hoped for.

'She's really into this bloke. I think he's married or something, maybe she didn't want you to know, maybe she doesn't tell you everything after all,' she says.

The tone is the verbal equivalent of her sticking her tongue out at me and the child in me wants to stick mine out at her. I don't, of course. To be honest, I feel sorry for her, the way she is trying to intimidate me, unaware that she doesn't hold that power any more. She fixes me with her eyes and I notice they have little specks of orange at their centre, like pools of fire. I don't blink. Debbie doesn't like me even after all these years. I shouldn't care but I do. I smile. The challenge of winning her over is too much to resist.

'You could be right,' I say.

'Well, we all change don't we, Rachel,' Sarah is giggling again, 'and Clara was away for so long? Was it five years?' Sarah asks.

'Seven,' I say. And I wonder how much you've told her. What gaps you've left in your story. 'She was away for seven years. It's been hard for her, her dad dying and then adjusting to life here again. Mind you, a few more weekends like the last one will put a smile back on her face.'

Debbie and Sarah look at each other and then back at me and cackle in unison. I detect a crack in the ice; it is thawing. 'It was a hoot,' Sarah says. 'Clara is so funny, she completely cracks me up. Don't you think, Rachel?'

'Oh God, you don't have to tell me. Can you remember that home economics teacher . . . what was her name?'

'Mrs Glass,' Debbie says.

'Yes, Mrs Glass,' I say, 'the one with a lisp. Well, Clara is so good with accents and ripping people off, she had her down to a T. She used to creep up behind me and holler in her Mrs Glass voice and scare the life out of me.'

Sarah has to swallow her drink quickly before she spits it

out. 'Ah, you can laugh about it now,' I say. 'At the time she used to make me go dizzy with the giggles. I couldn't stop and Mrs Glass would be saying, "Rachel, stop laughing this instant or I'll throw you out," and that would make me laugh even more. No wonder I always burnt my soufflé.'

I think back to those days, to what we shared, Clara. I had none of your natural timing but God, did I work hard to please you. Did you ever realise that? Those moments when I'd make you giggle or smile, or the ones where I'd do something funny and you'd pat me on the back and say, 'That's why I love you Rachel,' they were my proudest times because it made me believe our friendship was equal. Your laughter was like a drug, you see. It boosted and bolstered me, made me feel strong. I'd have done anything to hear it again and again and again.

I think Sarah may be drunk or at least well on her way because her words are coming more slowly now and when she speaks her eyes look at me rather than darting around.

'I mean, Rachel . . . and don't take this the wrong way, but at school you two were so close nobody else could get near you. Joined at the bloody hip. It seemed a bit, oh God, I don't know what the word is . . . dense, no, intense, that's it,' she says.

Intense is not a word I thought Sarah would use but I run it through my head, against my checklist of memories. I think it just about sums us up.

'What you're really trying to say is you thought we were weird.' My laugh permits them to do the same.

'Well I wouldn't go that far,' Sarah says smiling and

showing the dimples in her cheeks. 'OK, maybe weirdly close.'

'It's all right, I get it. It must have seemed a bit odd from the outside but we just clicked,' I say. 'I felt like I'd met her before, like we were supposed to be friends.' I pause and then bang the table. 'God, would you listen to me, I've gone all Mills & Boon.'

It was true though, even then we knew that what we had was a rare thing, something special to cling to. We were two missing pieces of a puzzle.

I watch Sarah laugh, listening as she talks and talks and talks. Now that she is in her stride I realise that she must have been as wary of me as I was of her though I'm not sure why. I don't bite.

As she talks I watch the door for you and I lose count of how many times I check my phone or search the room for your face. I can't understand why you wouldn't call or pick up your phone. I wonder if it's your idea of a practical joke, to make me suffer a night with them. Well come and see me now, Clara – I'm not so stuck up after all. I can get along with anyone just as easily as you can.

We drain the endless jugs of orange/red summer-afternoon cocktails the waiters bring us. The alcohol smoothes me out, soothes me, and I reach a point where I surrender to the evening and soak up the gossip about people from school, who's had four kids by different fathers, who's going bald, who got rich. Even Debbie seems to have thawed. Only when the pink and orange and green lanterns on the tables merge into a kaleidoscope of colour do I get up to go.

'No way,' Sarah is looking at her watch, 'you can't.' I am surprised by the strength of her grip. Maybe she sees my surprise because it loosens. 'I mean it's only ten o'clock, Clara promised us she would be here. Don't you need to wait for her?' I am aware that I am being moved towards the stairs and a basement I didn't know existed.

'Come on, we haven't even had a boogie yet.'

Before I know it we are in the bowels of the building where the ceilings are too low and the bass is so loud it vibrates through my throat.

'Get this down you.' It is Debbie, who has returned from the bar. She hands me a shot glass, standing over me as if she expects me to throw it into the yucca plant next to us. So I do as I'm told and down it. Tequila. I gag as it hits the back of my throat. It tastes of teenage Friday nights and sends flames burning through my body. I'd like to sit down, to find somewhere to close my eyes, but I'm dragged on to the dance floor where Beyoncé is playing and Sarah and Debbie are moving their hips and waving their arms. My legs seem to be moving so I go with it for I don't know how long, until they give up on me, and I give up on the night. And give up on you.

Sarah tries to persuade me to stay but it is half-hearted this time. 'I don't know what's happened to Clara,' she slurs.

'Neither do I, but I'm sure I'll find out. I'm supposed to be staying with her.' I am putting my coat on, buttoning up for the cold outside.

'Tell her to call me,' she says, holding an imaginary phone to her ear. Her feet are struggling to hold up the weight of her body. 'And let's do this again.' She gives me a kiss of lemons and tequila.

Outside I smell the sea. There is cold and salt in the air. I call you again and when you don't answer I walk along the seafront to buy some chips from the blue-and-white café, just like we used to. All the chairs are on the table, bar one where a teenage couple are sitting holding hands, nuzzling into each other, eyes droopy from a night's drinking. The guy serving is not much older than them. I can't imagine he has a girlfriend. His skin is pockmarked and little white-heads have erupted over his face. It's not his fault, I know, but it's not what you want to see when you're about to eat. I try to order without looking at him too much, though I'm careful to make sure his hands don't touch my chips. After I pay I take them outside and sit on a bench where the winds are fierce and sobering. I stay there until my fingers begin to hurt with cold and get up, putting my gloves on and pulling my scarf tight around me. I've only taken a few steps when I notice a guy on the next bench down, a dog, a sleeping bag and a can of Carlsberg for company. His shoes are worn, his hair grey and matted. I can't put an age on him; he could be sixty or much younger. He could be old enough to be my father, I think, and then remember I don't know how old my father is, or whether he is still alive. A sadness takes hold of me. In my bag I feel for my wallet. There are two twenty-pound notes left. I pull one out and clear my throat so he knows I'm there. He looks up and I hand it to him then carry on walking. I'm a few paces away when he realises what I've given him and he shouts out loud against the wind, 'God bless you.' I raise my hand in the air to wave but I don't look back.

People are spewing on to the street from the late-night bars, black bin liners of rubbish are piled up for collection. Short-skirt girls balance on stilettos, clinging to each other as they're buffeted by the wind. A car drives by, windows down, shaking from the bass of the music. Every taxi I see has its lights off, shadows of people being driven home inside. I don't even try to flag one down. I just keep on walking. To your flat. Brunswick Place, number twenty-five. Top floor. I buzz outside and wait. I am supposed to be staying with you after all. I want to see if you are OK, but most of all I want to be warm and protected from the sea winds that are screaming through me right now. And I am tired of all this. So tired. I buzz again. No answer. I can't give up. You must be there. I buzz on number twenty-seven.

'Hello.' The voice is male and impatient.

'It's Clara, from number twenty-five, can you buzz me in?'

'Where are your own bloody keys?'

'My friend's inside with them, she must have fallen asleep.'

'Lucky her,' I hear the voice say at the same time as the door buzzes. I push it open and climb the stairs to your flat. You used to keep a spare key above the door frame so I reach up and sweep my fingers along it. Nothing. Then

I knock again and again before I slump down and pull my knees into my chest and my eyes close on me.

I don't stay there all night. I wake up, my back cold from leaning against the wall, my bum aching from the hard floor. I call a cab and tell the driver to take me to The Old Ship Hotel because it's the first one that springs to mind.

When I arrive I see the receptionist has nightshift bags under her eyes, yellow-blond hair with dark roots and a red lipstick, too bright for her pale complexion. I wait for her to say hello and when she doesn't I ask for a room.

'What kind of room? Single, twin, double?' The questions are fired like bullets. Her accent is strong, Eastern European. I am about to interject but she carries on. 'Breakfast? Do want a paper? What kind of paper would you want?'

'Just a room thanks, that's all.'

She rolls her eyes and makes a pouf sound through her teeth.

'Sign here. Address. And I will need a card from you.'

I do as I'm told and she throws a key card across the counter. Then I am in the lift and opening a door on room 312 and falling on a bed. I may have glanced at the clock before I closed my eyes. It may have said one twenty-eight a.m. But I couldn't be sure. I'm asleep within seconds.

So I didn't see you that night. I wish I had. More than anything I wish I had. Because I know now that you must have seen me.

Chapter Three

A NOISE DRILLED through my thoughts. A hand on my shoulder shook me gently. I heard a jumble of words. My brain struggled to assemble them in order.

'You need to get ready, Rachel, they're coming to you live in a few minutes, off the back of the press conference.'

I waited. Something turned over in my head, then an explosion. I don't think I screamed, not out loud but inside, that was where it was all happening. I looked up at the figure looming over me. The familiar features, the bitter chocolate of his eyes, the flop of his hair falling down on to his forehead. The 'surfer at work' look. Jake Roberts, my producer. His presence belonged to another day. All the other days when we worked as a team, when I could function and do my job.

He thrust a black rectangle into my hand. 'Get hooked up, they'll be with you in minutes,' he said.

I held it out in front of me. The receiver that connected me to the gallery, to the presenter, and allowed me to hear them. The earpiece attached to it would be fitted in my ear.

It was the equipment I used every day to do my job. He wanted me to go live on air and talk about the disappearance of a young woman. To talk about you.

I couldn't even begin to explain to Jake what had happened. The seismic shift that had taken place. Not there, not in the minute I had before I went on air. How your face had assaulted me in a way all the others didn't. All those women, children, mothers, fathers, blond, black, smiling, scowling, all those people who had 'everything to live for' but didn't live any more. People who had been abducted, murdered, attacked. I'd talked about all of them on TV. Relayed the details of each story clinically, using words like horrific, shock, brutal. They all rolled off the tongue. But I never really thought about the huge craters they left in people's lives. Even when their relatives made desperate appeals from haunted faces all I got was a flutter of emotion that passed like wind. They were stories whose details and circumstances were a thousand times removed from me. You couldn't have been any closer, Clara. You were real.

'I'm. Not. Ready,' I said.

I didn't look at Jake. I stared at the earpiece. It wasn't my own. This one had been used by someone else, the crumb of orange/brown wax told me as much. I couldn't take my eyes off it. 'I can't put this in my ear, look at it,' I shouted.

'For fuck's sake, Rach, there's no time.' I must have been on my feet by then because I could feel the cameraman attaching the receiver to the belt on my trousers.

'Tell them I'm not ready,' I said. I thought I might cry, just fall down on to the floor and curl up and weep without caring who saw me. Instead I sunk my teeth into my lips again, I wanted to hurt, anything but this crippling numbness. The metallic taste of blood filled my mouth but still, I couldn't feel a thing.

'It's the lead story.' He watched me grip a chair, something solid to hold me up. His voice softened. 'Come on, what do you want me to say? They want you on air before Global get their correspondent on. You know, first with the news and all that shit.' He smiled and then bent down and rummaged in my bag.

'Here,' he said, handing me a bulging black purse that contained everything I needed for my TV face, 'put some slap on, don't want you to scare the viewers, do we? I'm going to see if DCI Gunn will do a one-to-one with you.'

I took my make-up bag from him and glanced in the mirror of my powder compact. Blue lips on white, white skin stared back at me, swollen where I had bitten them. My eyes were lined with red. Without thinking I powdered my face with bronzer and then applied a crème blush in one shaky stroke of each cheek. And lipstick too, but my hand wouldn't follow the contours of my mouth, so I wiped it off again. Then I heard sound waves coming through my ear. The cameraman must have slipped the earpiece in. I thought of the wax crumb sitting in my ear and shuddered.

'Nice of you to join us, Rachel,' the director's voice said. And I wondered how I would escape now. 'We have all of thirty seconds before we come to you, after these headlines. Give us a few words for level.'

I looked around, desperate to grab Jake's attention, but I could see he was at the other side of the room talking to Hilary Benson and DCI Gunn. 'Rachel, some level please.' The director's voice was louder, more pissed off now. 'We're coming to you next.'

I was trapped in front of the camera, in this surreal and nightmarish situation. I couldn't run now; somehow I had to get through the next five minutes.

Five minutes, five minutes, just do your job and then it'll all be over.

I tried to move my tongue to form words but it was burnt and brittle and hit my scorched mouth with a click-clack sound. My lips stuck to my teeth. I grabbed a bottle of water from my bag and gulped. It ran off the sides of my mouth without soaking in. 'I'll be talking about this level,' I said, click-clack, wiping the sides of my mouth. And then I sounded your name out. Slowly, each syllable a word of its own. 'Clara O' Connor was last seen . . .' I looked down the lens to focus. I had no idea what I was going to say, what questions they would ask. My breaths were shallow, I tried to regulate them. I thought of foreign correspondents reporting from war zones with bullets whistling around their heads carrying on when everything was crashing down. *They could do it, so could I.*

'That's great,' said the director, interrupting my thoughts. 'Do you have a guest with you?'

I remembered Jake's conversation. 'He's trying to get DCI

Gunn,' I said, wondering what I could ask him, more than he'd already told us.

'OK, we'll just go with the flow then. You'll be talking to Charlie Gregson in the studio. With you in ten seconds.'

I didn't want to talk to any presenter in the studio but I definitely didn't want to talk to Charlie Gregson, a bitter, out-of-favour has-been whose long questions were all about making himself look good and catching the correspondent out. But I didn't have a choice. The next thing Charlie's voice was in my ear.

'Police in Sussex say they are seriously concerned for the safety of a twenty-eight-year-old artist who has been missing for three days. Detectives say it's possible she may have been abducted. Well, let's cross live now to our correspondent Rachel Walsh who is in Brighton with the very latest. Rachel what have police been saying this morning?'

The moment that followed was filled with dead, leaden air. How long did it last? Short enough to be taken for a satellite delay? Maybe. I don't know. I was too busy sifting and sieving one reality from another inside my head, working out what I was allowed to say. My version of events where you had flu and didn't make it out was to be stored away. I was to talk about the alternative one where you disappeared after leaving Cantina Latina. The official version.

Only then did the words come and I said your name as if I had never met you before. For those few minutes on air, Clara, you and I became strangers.

I told whoever was watching why police were concerned, that it was out of character. I trotted out all the journalistic clichés. When my sentence came to an end, I waited, hoping there would be no follow-up question. But there was. You were being used to fill air time, Clara.

'And Rachel, what about witnesses? It was a Friday night when she disappeared; police must obviously be hoping someone would have seen her leaving the bar?'

I opened my mouth once more. Click-clack.

At that moment I became aware of a presence by my side and turned to see DCI Gunn and Jake, standing next to him just out of shot. *My lifeline*. He could do the talking now; I just had to think of the questions.

'Well DCI Gunn has just joined us, so let me put that to him.' I stepped out of shot to allow the cameraman to focus on DCI Gunn. I repeated Charlie's question. Today was no day for professional pride.

DCI Gunn nodded as I spoke. 'That's absolutely right, Rachel,' he said and I cringed at his first-name too-chummy-for-TV address. 'There would have been lots of people leaving bars and clubs in that area on Friday night who may have come across a woman fitting Miss O'Connor's description and we would like to hear from them. We also understand she may have been with a male that evening and we would say to that individual please come forward so we can eliminate you from our inquiries.' I listened to him talk in that robotic police-speak and wondered who the hell had told him you were with a man. How did he know that?

I asked him a few more questions from my stock list gathered over the years of crime reporting: were they looking at

CCTV (yes); what state of mind did they think you were in? (no reason to believe you were depressed) and then I heard the director say, 'One last question Rachel, then wrap up.'

So I asked: 'Why is it you think she may have been abducted?'

I watched DCI Gunn's expression change and his voice grow quieter. 'We have reason to believe Miss O'Connor was worried for her safety.'

Questions screamed through my head.

'Time,' shouted the director so loud it made me jump, 'hand back now.'

And so I did.

Who was out to get you, Clara? The bogeyman? Were you scared of shadows and shapes that came out at night? Domestic violence victims or witnesses in murder trials, I can see why they might be 'worried for their safety'. But not you. What was there to be scared of? You never said.

I'd hoped you told me everything. I'd wanted us to share all our secrets just like we used to. But at that moment the realisation crept over me that maybe I had been deluding myself all along.

I sat for a moment after I came off air, making a play of gathering my things together, but whatever I tried to grab – my notepad, my make-up bag – dropped out of my hands. My body was incapable of carrying out the simplest task.

Around me the TV crews packed cameras away, retrieving cables and microphones. Photographers downloaded images of you, producers shouted into their mobiles to news desks, 'Corrigan . . . no, I said CORR-I-GAN, double R. And GUNN as in a pistol but with a double N.' Reporters sat, laptops on knees, filing their stories for the next day's newspapers. The wheels of the news machine turning as if nothing had happened.

My phone rang with a number it didn't recognise. I answered.

'Hello?'

'Rachel. I've just seen you. About Clara. What the hell is going on?' The voice was screeching, hysterical. 'Has something happened to her?' Sarah Pitts asked.

I didn't even think about how she got my number. I moved away from Jake and the cameraman to a quieter corner of the room.

'I don't know anything else,' I said. 'The police think she came to the bar.' I whispered that into the phone, feeling guilty as if the act of whispering made me complicit.

'She did come, Rachel.' Sarah sniffed and gulped the sobs away. 'Just after you left and then she went to find you. She said you'd called her and you were meeting up because you'd had an argument about her boyfriend.'

I let her finish and listened to the snot and the sniffs. I didn't say anything because I couldn't. I just held the phone with one hand and held my other hand out in front of me. To make sure I was still real since nothing else seemed to be. And when I saw the deep brown of my nail polish and the veins on my hand and the moonstone ring on my middle finger and I was finally convinced this was happening to me, 'I didn't speak to her. I couldn't find her. She wasn't there. I went for chips and then to a hotel.' I kept my sentences short and drew a breath with each one. I wouldn't give in to hysteria.

'But she took the call in front of us.'

'Well it wasn't me.'

'Oh God, I could have been one of the last people to see her,' Sarah said, crying again. I imagined her face, puffy and red.

I looked up. Jake was hovering over me.

'They're throwing us out of here now, Rach.' I nodded and motioned to him that I was winding up on the phone.

'Sarah, I have to go.'

'I should have made sure she was safe.' Her voice begged for reassurance.

'It's not your fault,' I said. 'I'll call you.'

An hour before there had been cars and colours and grass outside the police station. Now there was only white. White under a grey sky. It was quiet too. The snow can do that, can't it? Deaden sounds, silence everything. It felt like the world was standing still, taking a moment to catch its breath. I walked into the car park wishing my footsteps didn't have to leave a trace. Wishing we didn't always have to ruin everything that began so perfect and pure.

I know what you'll be thinking at this point in the story, Clara. Not a word to DCI Gunn or Jake? Why not tell them

I knew you? The answer is nothing and everything. I couldn't think logically. Trust me, you don't in these circumstances. Maybe I believed that if I told someone all this would have become real. And I wasn't ready for that, much as I came to regret it later. Instead I did what was expected of me: I scripted a version of your story for the evening news bulletin that wasn't my own. When we were done we sent it back to London on the satellite. All that guff that people write on their CVs, about being calm under pressure, professional, well it was true of me that day, though even then I knew it might be construed differently.

The trains to London had been cancelled, which is how Jake came to be sitting in my car that afternoon, both of us eager to escape Brighton. If we'd been honest we would have admitted it was hopeless. The traffic backed up around the Old Steine hadn't moved in ages, just exhaust fumes steaming in the cold. The light was failing too, and outside on the pavements only a few outlines could be seen, trudging home, curved in the wind. I stared at the Pavilion, thinking its exotic lines looked so out of place and forlorn that day they could have been blown in from the Orient by the storm.

In the end it was the traffic and travel woman on the radio who pointed out the obvious. The A23 out of Brighton was shut because of the heavy snowfall.

'I'll call Robbie,' Jake said, and I nodded.

⁂

Remember that game we used to play, Clara? The superpower one.

'If you could do anything Rach,' you'd say, 'and I mean anything, what would you do?'

'I'd fly, you know I would,' was my reply every time. 'Sometimes at night I think I can. I go above the rooftops, anywhere I want to go.'

'Wouldn't you want to be invisible, or see into the future? Imagine the possibilities,' you'd say, trying to fire up my imagination.

But I never wanted to see into the future. The power to lift myself up and away from home, from my mum and the mean girls at school, that was all I wanted.

I wished I could fly that day, away from the grey of the sea that loomed over me, up and over the snow-filled Downs. Away from you. Away from what was happening.

Jake and I booked into a hotel, one of those new ones that claim to be boutique and part of a chain at the same time. It was the kind of place I would have come to with Jonny, not a work colleague. Velvet armchairs and low lighting. But I was grateful for the comfort, the log fire in the lounge, the way the smell of it permeated the air. I took in lungfuls, deep-down breaths, and closed my eyes to block out the day.

Laughter came from the far end of the room, frivolous and naughty. I looked up and saw two women. One was in her twenties, probably not much younger than me. Groomed in a footballers-wives kind of way. Candy gloss on her lips, long blond hair, straightened. The woman next to her shared the same jawline and almond-shaped eyes although her features had begun to sag and collapse with age and the years had creased her skin. Mother and daughter. I wondered what it was like to look at someone and see an image of yourself three decades on. Not that I ever would. My image of Niamh Walsh is forever preserved in 1997.

I watched the younger woman sweep her hair back from her face. The huge diamond she was wearing on her ring finger caught the light of the candles and winked at me. I thought of Jonny and the future he'd allowed me to believe I could have. I pulled out my phone to call him. If he answered, I told myself, it was a sign that everything would be all right. I dialled. It went straight to answerphone. 'Call me as soon as you get this message,' I said, speaking to no one. 'I love you.'

'You sure you can force one down?' Jake was back from the bar, pouring two large glasses of deep purple liquid from the bottle.

'We all have off days.' I said, cradling my phone.

'Not the great Rachel Walsh. Don't tell me you're actually human?'

'Fuck off, Jake.'

He leant across the table and touched me. A warm touch that hit the cold of my skin.

'I thought you might have been spooked by another e-mail or letter.'

'I haven't had one for over a week,' I said.

I didn't want to think of that, to introduce another problem into the day.

'Anyway, look on the bright side, you're stranded in your home town. At least you can catch up with old friends.'

'I wish,' I said but he didn't hear me because the barman was hovering over us to take our order.

'I don't suppose you could turn the TV on, just for the news?' Jake asked. The barman looked around at the almost empty room and then nodded.

'I'll have to turn it off afterwards, though,' he said for no discernible reason.

You were in the headlines, Clara. That photograph again. I looked away when I saw it. You weren't the lead story though, you were second up. I heard the words 'manhunt', 'young artist' and then I heard my voice, or the television version of it.

'Here we go,' said Jake, as if we were about to go on a fairground ride.

I didn't want to watch. I never wanted to see that picture of you again. I played with the candle on the table, dipping my little finger into the liquid wax and peeling it off. Only when I heard myself say, 'Rachel Walsh, National News Network, Brighton,' did I look at the screen again.

'Not exactly award-winning, but it did the job in the circumstances,' Jake said, leaning forward to chink my glass.

We ate in silence, and afterwards, leaning back in the chair, a calm settled over me. In the morning you would turn up. This kind of thing happened to other people. Not us.

The sound of my phone beeping interrupted my thoughts. I felt warmer still. I knew it would be from Jonny. Everything would be OK. It was a private number which made sense because he was in Afghanistan.

I opened it.

It read:

Do you wish her dead?

I read the words again and again. A pain stabbed me between my eyes. The phone was hot, too hot, burning my hand. I threw it on the table, startling Jake.

'Whatsup?' he asked.

I said nothing. My face told its own story.

He took the phone from the table.

'What the fuck does this mean?' There was a twitch in his jaw, a flex of a muscle. 'Is this him?'

'I don't . . .' My sentence trailed off. 'How would he have got my number?' I asked, aware that neither of us knew the answer.

The *Oxford English Dictionary* definition of stalking is this: to harass or persecute someone with unwanted and obsessive attention.

Well, Bob had certainly made me the focus of his obsessive attention but I can't say I ever felt persecuted. And he wasn't called Bob, as you know, Clara, though I don't think I ever explained to you why I gave him a name, and that name in particular: a) Because with a name came a personality and a face and when you knew someone they weren't as scary; b) Bob was a cuddly, granddad name, a woolly-jumper, pipe-smoking man whom I had no need to fear; c) As far as my memory served me, I hadn't covered any stories where a Bob had featured as a rapist or murderer which would have precluded him from being the woolly-jumper, granddad Bob of my imagination.

You warned me to be more careful, take him seriously. But I imagined he lived in the suburbs, watched daytime TV and had a comb-over. And when he tired of watching *This Morning* and *Cash in the Attic* and realised he had no one to talk to, probably never would, he wrote letters and e-mails to people like me who came into his living room every evening. He wanted to believe we were his friends. Once he asked me to smoke a pipe with him because he said I looked like the kind of 'girl who would'. And when he craved more than just chat he'd ask me to 'read the news in leather'. He should have known better, a man of his age. A letter a day, e-mails too. But it was low-level, harmless, wasn't it? Still, I went through the motions, reported his correspondence to a woman in Human Resources called Hayley who listened with a serious face and gave me a lecture on what to do and a brochure which said I wasn't to walk home alone if I thought I was being followed. But I knew Bob wouldn't do that.

Now I didn't know what to believe. With one text, he'd crossed a line. When I closed my eyes I couldn't conjure up an image of him any more; he'd disappeared into the shadows.

⤚o⤙

Tiredness came over me, bleeding into my head. I needed the day to end. I said goodnight to Jake and went to my room. Inside it was like a fridge, the air conditioning inexplicably cranked up in January. I found an extra blanket in the wardrobe and got into bed, pulling the duvet around me. It was cold and crisp. All around me was dark, the dark of heavy curtains blocking out streetlights. I closed my eyes and waited for sleep to erase my thoughts. Instead I saw colours and images and light, flashing, speeded up. A film reel playing and no button to stop or pause it. We were the stars of the show, Clara, you and I. On and on it ran. But wait – it was going backwards, taking us to a time where our faces were happier and our smiles more innocent. Then finally it stopped. At the beginning. On the day we first met.

Chapter Four

September 1993

'Now who has a spare seat next to them?' Mrs Brackley has her arm round me. They all do that. It's the bit I hate the most, being a novelty.

A couple of girls raise their hand slowly in the air. 'She could sit next to Gareth, miss,' one says and then I hear a boy's voice pipe up: 'That's if she doesn't mind the smell of his farts.' The class erupts into laughter. I try to block it out. That's how I always deal with it, in these classrooms that all look and smell the same. I am almost fourteen now and Niamh has promised this is the last time we'll move but she has said that before. So why should I believe her?

My eyes are drawn to one girl at the back of the class who isn't laughing. She looks older than her peers, bemused by their behaviour, almost serene. A bubble of calm surrounds her. She is pretty. No, not pretty. I think she is beautiful. I watch her gaze shift from the desk and move dreamily towards the window, like she knows none of this matters because there are better, more important things waiting for her out there.

'That's quite enough of the joking, James,' Mrs Brackley

says, her arm raised in the air as if that gesture alone has the power to silence the laughter. Her face is shiny, hot from the classroom, and her cheeks are bright red. She's wearing a stripy shirt in satin, red, brown and yellow, and there are rings of dark circling her armpits. Through the window I see the September sun, low in the sky, bouncing off the bike-shed roof and sending shards of light across the playground. It makes me squint.

'Rachel.' She turns to me and I get a whiff of tea and biscuits from her breath. Rich Tea, or maybe Hobnobs. Niamh says I've got a great sense of smell. But I'm not so sure, I think anyone could tell when she's been drinking. 'I'm going to let you choose where you want to sit. There are two seats at the front here,' she says, pointing to them, 'or one at the back.' Before she has even finished her sentence I know there is no choice. Like a magnet I am being pulled towards the girl at the back of the class, drawn into her force field.

With my rucksack on my back I walk towards you, aware that there are thirty pairs of eyes trained on my steps. There is a snigger that travels like a Mexican wave around the class when I place my bag on the desk next to you. I don't understand why they are laughing but I don't dwell on it for long, I am too busy looking at you. Your hair is thick and brown, loosely tied back so a few stray curls tumble out on to your face. 'Clara,' says Mrs Brackley, and only then do you look up, 'I'm sure you'll make Rachel feel welcome.'

I have never known a Clara before, I was expecting a

Sarah or Louise or Helen like all the other girls. But then I realise those names would be too ordinary for you. Clara suits you.

'Right class, books out. It's *Much Ado about Nothing*. We'll pick up where we left off last week,' Mrs Brackley says.

There's a collective groan, although no sound comes from you. 'Clara, you'll have to share your book with Rachel for the time being.'

Finally you turn to look at me and I'm struck by your eyes, pierced by the blue of them. I fight the urge to smile because you are not smiling. You are sizing me up, I think, and instinctively I want to pass whatever test it is you have set me. So I find myself holding your gaze and we stay there, unblinking, locked in a moment that seems to go on forever, neither of us wanting to give in. And then, as if it has been synchronised, our eyes snap shut at precisely the same time and when I open mine again I see your whole face has come alive with a smile and the blue in your eyes is rippling and glistening like water. I don't understand the weird alchemy of friendship but I know that in the briefest click of an eye something has happened. A current of excitement, of possibility, is fizzing through me and suddenly the sniggers and the new-girl stigma melt away as if they never existed.

I watch you reach for your bag and pull out your copy of *Much Ado About Nothing*. Instead of putting it on the table you rest it on your lap and give me a gentle nudge. I look down to see two red squares of raspberry loveliness sitting on the page. You take one and press the other into my hand. We unwrap them quietly and slip them into our mouths when Mrs Brackley's back is turned and a moment later we're sitting chewing, the scent of raspberry Hubba Bubba like a cloud around us. 'It's my favourite,' you whisper as you lean in to me.

Somehow I knew it would be because it's mine too.

At break time no one says, 'Rachel, come with us,' they just file out without looking my way. Novelties do that; they wear off quickly. I'm not bothered though. You look around to see if I'm next to you. I am and we slip into step with each other as if it has always been this way.

'It was my mum's idea,' I say when we stop and sit down on the wall that separates the playing field from the playground, 'to move here.'

'Didn't you miss the sea in London? I'd hate not to be able to walk to the beach and hear the waves.' Your eyes are closed as if you are listening out for the roar and the crash of them. I hear the seagulls above and watch as they swoop down and poke at empty crisp packets and chocolate wrappers.

'I've never lived by the sea so I've never thought about it. And my aunt lives here so we used to visit now and then.' I think of the visits to see Laura, what they did to Niamh's mood afterwards. I'd get the silent treatment, or worse, screamed at for nothing.

I tell you I have lived in a lot of places because Niamh is always craving 'a change of scenery', which is shorthand for running away from her mistakes. How long, I wonder, will it be before we're packing up again? 'She says we're not moving again. She says we're here for good,' I tell you.

'Do you believe her?' You take a bag of prawn cocktail crisps from your pocket and put one into your mouth. 'Help yourself,' you say. So I do.

'I've moved school five times and every time it's the last. What do you think?'

'I think your mum's a liar.' You laugh through a crunchy mouth and I am laughing too.

We sit there eating crisps in silence as the playground zooms around us. There's a huddle of girls I recognise from class, all legs and short skirts, and a couple of boys, lanky and greasy. They look at you and then at me before whispering to each other.

'Are they your friends?' I say although I already know the answer.

'Nah, not really,' you tell me as one of the boys from the group swaggers over to you, chest all puffed out like he wants to impress.

'Have you taken pity on the new girl then, Clara?' he asks, ignoring the fact I am sitting right next to you. His tone tells me he is trying to play it cool but his reddening face is a giveaway. A screwed-up attempt at schoolboy flirting.

You give him a smile and I cringe. Have I misread your overtures at friendship? I'm expecting you to laugh along with him, readying myself to shrink away into the bustle of the playground and make myself invisible.

'Her name is Rachel,' you say, still smiling at him, 'although now we're friends I call her Rach.' And you turn away from him to offer me another prawn cocktail crisp.

The boy's face grows redder still. He hangs in front of us for a moment not knowing what to do. You've dismissed him so casually, any semblance of cool has been stripped from him.

'You don't look like you need any of those,' he shouts, swiping the crisps out of my hands and sending them flying into the air in a pouf of prawn cocktail. He cackles as he runs back to join the rest. But even I can see it's an empty victory.

You shrug your shoulders at me and shake your head, as if he's a child to be pitied.

'Who was that?' I ask you.

'James Redfern, class joker. Don't worry about him.' You put your hand on my knee and squeeze it softly.

It's then that I understand the sniggers I provoked by choosing to sit next to you. I realise that everyone in that class would like to be your friend but you keep your distance. And there was me, the fat, ginger new girl, daring to try my luck. They were expecting you to ignore me and reject me. And me to fall flat on my face. But instead I have succeeded where they failed. I don't know why that is, but I do know I can't stop smiling.

A couple of days later you explain you are older than everyone in the class because you had to repeat a year. When I ask why you say, 'Stuff.' I don't pry; I don't want to upset you. I am happier than I have ever been. It's as if someone has turned the colour on in my life. It's hard to explain but I feel like you've been there waiting for me all along. Like we are meant to be. For the first time I have someone on my side who understands me, laughs with me. Protects me.

We've known each other for eight weeks. We both love Take That, though we fight over who will marry Robbie and you always win. We both hate macaroni cheese, especially the one they serve up in the school canteen which is grey and watery and looks like maggots. And we hate games; the trampoline where all the other girls have to stand around and make sure you don't fall off but laugh at the thought of you smashing your head on the hard floor. Or netball because I always get pushed over. But most of all I hate getting changed in front of the girls in our class. The taunts at my pale skin and freckles and ginger pubes; my fat legs, the rolls of blubber on my stomach. And it's no use forgetting your kit because then you have to wear some from the lost property which smells of mothballs and invites even more ridicule.

So when you call me on Sunday and say, 'I've got the answer, Rach, we won't be doing games for a while,' I'm so happy I think I'm going to burst and I'm dying to know what plan you have concocted. But all you say is; 'I will reveal it tomorrow, Rachel,' in a funny voice like you're pretending to be a magician.

At break time the next day we go and sit in the furthest corner of the field, leaving behind the smells of roasting meat in the playground. It is November and the ground is hard and cold but there's still warmth in the sun when it escapes the clouds. I've been begging you to tell me all morning; I think you're enjoying keeping me in suspense.

'So come on, tell me the master plan,' I say.

'First of all you have to tell me how brave you think you are.' You are unbuttoning your red peacoat and taking it off.

I don't know what that's got to do with missing games but I give you my answer anyway. 'In the right circumstances, I think I could do anything,' I say.

'Good, you have passed "Go", Rachel Walsh,' you say and you push my elbow away from me so my body falls on the grass. Then you fling your coat at me. I sit up and watch you take off your shoe, a black patent pump with a small heel.

'Oh my God, what's this, a striptease?' I ask.

'Here. You'll need this.' You give your shoe to me.

'You've totally lost me.'

'Well, no gain without pain and all that. What we need to do is break something and the wrist is easiest, even a chip on it will do. Six weeks in a plaster. No PE.'

I think you have lost your mind and my face must tell you as much. 'My dad's a doctor, remember, he knows these things,' you say as if that makes everything OK. I met your dad for the first time on Saturday. He opened the door to me, surfer T-shirt, jeans and flip-flops, tanned face and arms. I thought he was too young to be your father until he said, 'You must be Rachel. I'm Simon, Clara's dad,' with the warmest Saturday-morning smile I'd ever seen. 'Come in, come in, I'm just making brunch.'

I guessed brunch was something between breakfast and lunch, though I didn't want to say I'd never had it before. Instead I followed him into the kitchen where you were sitting on a stool at an enormous breakfast bar, a glass of orange juice in front of you, swinging your legs and humming along to the radio. The picture of a perfect weekend. 'She's got terrible taste in music,' he said with a wink, 'I hope yours is better, Rachel.' You picked up a satsuma from the fruit bowl and threw it in his direction. But he saw it coming and caught it with one hand. 'Nice try, Clar,' he teased and turned back to beating the eggs. 'I hope you girls are hungry, I'm doing my special sweetcorn fritters,' he said and I found myself thinking your dad was a revelation.

I can't imagine he would tell you how to hurt yourself.

'You mean he told you how to break your wrist so you can skip PE?'

'No, but I've been asking a few questions here and there so he's not suspicious.' You take the shoe from me. 'We need to hit it here.' You bring the shoe down to your wrist gently. 'Thing is, I'd be rubbish doing it myself. You can do it for me and I'll do yours.' You say it like you're suggesting we do each other's hair or make-up. Not taking a shoe to crack your friend's wrist.

'You don't think it's a bit extreme?'

'It's a bit of pain, Rachel, nothing more. I'll do it on your left arm if it makes you feel better, then you can still write your English essays.'

You press the shoe back into my hand again. 'I want to do it, even if you don't so please, you have to do it for me. Think of it as a friendship initiation thing.' You throw your head back and laugh. When you bring it up again I see your eyes are intense, fiery. 'Go on, I'll count to three.'

'I . . . I don't want . . .'

'Come on, for me,' you say, 'do it for me.' Then I hear the words, 'One . . . two . . .' Your eyes are watching me, willing me to do it, and I know I have to, otherwise it won't be the same. 'THREE.' I bring the shoe up above my head and slice it through the air on to your wrist. I close my eyes as it hits but I feel it whack against your bone, like a piece of rock. You roll back and scream a scream that pierces the air. I throw the shoe down and find you writhing on the ground. 'Are you OK, Clara, Jesus, we need to get you inside.'

'Of course I'm not fucking OK, you've just broken my wrist,' you say eventually. You are laughing and crying at the same time and your eyes look like they have sparks coming off them. I think the pain is making you manic. 'Come on,' I say, pulling you up.

'It's your turn.' You pull me down with your good arm.

'Clara, honestly, this was a bad idea, you can't seriously . . .'

'We made a deal, remember?'

I can't remember shaking on any deal but when I see your face drained of colour and your teeth chattering but not from the cold, I know I owe it to you. I take my coat off and roll up the sleeves on my jumper and shirt. 'Here,' I say. I see the run of freckles up my arm. My wrist is thin compared with the rest of my body. I imagine it smashing under the force of your shoe.

You tell me I have to rest it on the grass because you can't hold it still with your bad arm. I do as you say. The grass is cold and damp against my bare skin. You start your count. ONE. I turn away and close my eyes tight shut. TWO. My body tenses in expectation of the pain. THREE.

I hear it first, the crack of a hard object against the bone. Then the pain shoots up my arm like an electric shock. I scream. Your laugh is ringing through my ears. It is distorted, grotesque. I'm on my feet, twisting in agony, about to shout at you when I taste the acid in my mouth and I retch. I bend over and I'm sick all over my shoes. When I'm finished I wipe my mouth with my sleeve and see the ground spinning around me. I think I am going to faint but then I feel your hand on my shoulder, steadying me. It is the same hand that broke my wrist but this time it is gentle and soothing. I look up and see a flush of colour returning to your cheeks. You are still shaking but there is fire in your eyes, making them glisten and sparkle. Throwing my head back I emit a sound from deep in the pit of my stomach. It doesn't sound like me, more like an animal howling, and I hear it echo through the trees. I could get lost in that roar, the way it reverberates through my body and reaches my nerve endings jolting them into life. I don't think I have ever felt more alive. I could go on forever.

And I understand, Clara, it is all so clear to me now – the attraction of pain, how it can be delicious and warm. How it fills you with a power that makes you strong and invincible. How you have to push yourself to the edge to realise what you are capable of.

You have been watching me in silence. Your eyes are wide with surprise. I reach out to you with my good arm and we fall into each other, our laughs and tears mixing together. We don't speak. We don't have to. We know what we have done has set us apart from everyone else and joined us together with an irresistible magnetic force.

Chapter Five

My eyes were half closed, heavy with sleep. A slice of sunlight warmed my face. There was a moment, between dreaming and wakefulness, when I could have been anywhere. On holiday perhaps, where a summer sky, a pool and a day of discovery lay beyond the windows. Then I stretched my leg and drew my foot over the empty side of the bed where the sheets were crisp and untouched and I remembered. There was no pool, no summer sky. There was only a face. A smile. The picture of you.

I reached for my phone. Desperate to see his name; a missed call, a text. And yours too, Clara, of course I wanted to see your name and number. But I needed to hear his voice more because he could make everything OK. The only person who ever could. But you'd guessed that much already, hadn't you?

My inbox was empty. So I scrolled through my recent calls and found the number I was looking for. Her voice had none of the laughter of the other night.

'We need to talk, Sarah,' I said.

'I know,' she said in a way that sounded like she wasn't convinced.

'There's a coffee shop just off Black Lion Street, on the corner, can we meet there?' I asked.

'I'll be there by eleven,' she said and the line went dead.

I was dressed in yesterday's clothes so I left the hotel early to shop. I hadn't felt warm since arriving at the police station the day before. I needed an extra layer of protection. As I turned off the seafront I saw the winter sun sitting low. Beneath it the sea was bleached so white I couldn't tell where it stopped and the sky started. Sequins danced on the water. I blinked and shielded my eyes. After the gloom of the day before, the pier, the buildings, the hotels, the people that lined the seafront, they were all cleaner, brighter under this sun. But what had changed? Nothing had changed at all, Clara. It was a trick of the light. Everything is a trick of the light.

There were pastries and cupcakes laid out on the counter, the kind with more icing than sponge. I was hungry but I knew gorging myself on a muffin wouldn't create the right impression. Maybe Sarah thought the same. Both of us cradled mugs of steaming coffee and shook our heads when the waitress suggested food. Sarah stared down into her mug, refusing to make eye contact with me. I had expected us to hug and hold each other, to show some solidarity in our loss. Sarah had other ideas.

'Have you heard anything?' I asked. This time, as if by

some monumental effort, she lifted her head and stared at me, or through me, because that was how it felt. The shine from her hair, the way it clung to her head, told me it was due for a wash. Her make-up was a shade too dark for her skin. I concentrated on the patch of it that hadn't been blended in. This Sarah was a different person from Friday-night tequila-and-laughter Sarah.

'No,' is all she offered. I could see dark circles under her eyes, escaping from underneath her heavy concealer.

I looked around. The place was almost empty, the coffee-and-croissant office people had been and gone. The only other person was a woman in her early twenties, dressed in wedges, a long skirt that brushed the floor and a sequinned top. She looked out of place with her purple cherry lipstick and pink nails on the end of her long, bony fingers. And she sat fingering her shiny phone. I imagined she was a model or an actress waiting for a call.

I turned back to Sarah, still leaning over the mug, as if it was the only thing keeping her from falling on to the table.

'It's all so screwed up. Why would Clara have come so late in the night, without calling me?' There was a note of desperation in my voice. I couldn't help it. I'd been running different scenarios through my head all morning, and still nothing made sense.

Sarah closed her eyes as if the effort of remembering Friday night was a source of pain. I could tell she was struggling too, so I fought the urge to grab her hand and look deep into her eyes and beg her to help me, *I am literally dying here, Sarah,* but instead I sat on my hands and waited for what seemed like an eternity, listening to her sigh, watching her wipe her tears away with her painted red fingernails, before, finally, she spoke.

'Clara came to the bar just after you'd gone. I can't remember the time.'

'Late,' I said. 'I left at half eleven so it must have been after that.' I pictured myself sitting eating chips on the pier, the cold biting into me and you so close by. If only I could rewind and go back in time, Clara. I'd stay for another drink, we'd meet and everything would be so different now. Tears of frustration pricked my eyes.

'She was looking for you,' Sarah said. Her tone made it sound like an accusation but I let it pass; we were both tired and emotional.

'I was searching for her. I even went to her flat to see if she was OK.'

'You went to see her?' Her voice had quickened.

'Of course I did, I was supposed to be staying with her and I was getting worried because she hadn't answered any of my calls so I walked over to Brunswick Place but there was no answer so I booked myself into a hotel.'

'Alone?' Sarah said.

'You saw me leave, was I with anyone?' I didn't mean my words to sting her. I watched another tear cut a trail through her make-up. 'I'm sorry,' I said.

'Why did you argue?' Sarah asked suddenly. She was sitting upright now as if she'd sprung into action.

'What?'

'Clara said you'd had a proper falling-out. That's what she told us when she came. What did you argue about?'

'I have no idea what you're talking about,' I said. It hit me then, the reason why there was no comfort from Sarah, no hugs, no kind words. Nothing had changed.

'Shall I tell you what she said, then?' Technically that was a question but I knew she didn't need an answer. 'She said that you'd had an argument over a bloke, the one she was seeing.'

There was something slipping in my head again. A shifting of realities. I turned and saw the model holding a slice of chocolate cake in her hand, sizing it up. Then closing her eyes she put it to her mouth and inhaled. She was inhaling the cake. I thought of days, weeks, months of strict diet, self-control. And now she was giving in, as we all do, to the urges we try to suppress.

'Why didn't she just ring me, Sarah? I had been trying to call her all bloody night.'

'So there was an argument?' Sarah said. The teaspoon was in her hand. Shaking.

'No, for fuck's sake. There was no argument. Listen to me,' I leant forward, close to her face. 'I came down on Friday to meet Clara. We didn't fight, not about anything, certainly not about a bloke. I didn't even know there was one.'

'That's not what you said.' Sarah let her hair fall over her face so I couldn't see her eyes, then she pushed it slowly back behind her ears. I trawled through the blur of Friday night to the conversation about who you were seeing. I remembered my bluff. Now it had a consequence.

'That was nothing. Just some one-night stand she mentioned,' I said.

'She was different, Rachel. She looked frightened.' Sarah wouldn't give up. I sat back in my chair and looked at a slice of sunlight falling on the table. I could see the particles of dust floating, phosphorescent in the air.

'Why are you doing this, Sarah, when we both want the same thing? Clara is out there somewhere. Surely we should be sticking together, not fighting each other.'

She shrugged her shoulders.

'How long has it been?' I asked.

'What are you talking about?' Her voice was defensive.

'How long has it been since you and Clara have been friends? Seven, eight months? Has she really told you everything?'

'She's told me enough,' Sarah said. It was clearly not the conversation she wanted to have.

'So you'll know where she was? You'll know what happened to her in all that time she was away? Because if you don't you can't really understand her, not like I do.'

'I don't care what happened in the past. I want to know where she is now.'

'It wasn't my idea to come to Brighton, to meet up with you and Debbie,' I said. Sarah laughed, a cynical laugh.

'You surprise me.'

'I didn't mean it like that,' I said. 'She wanted us all to go out, she wanted to see me. And then she doesn't turn up, appears after I'm gone and doesn't even try to call me. You don't think that's just a little bit strange?'

'Whatever you say?'

'It's the truth.' My voice was louder than I wanted it to be, louder than it should have been in a public place. From frustration, because my words had no impact on her.

It was then I saw the look on her face that brought it all back. Fifth year. The two of us in front of the teacher, wet from the water, out of breath and crying. In the distance the sound of an ambulance siren getting closer and closer though we already knew it was too late for Lucy Redfern; the screams of Lucy's twin James piercing the air. Sarah and I were on the bank shouting our version of events to Mr Payne the PE teacher and even though we weren't listening to each other I knew her words didn't fit mine and mine didn't fit hers. We had blankets placed round us and were told to sip sugary tea which of course we couldn't because we were shaking so violently. And all the time this look of horror, of disbelief, which didn't leave Sarah's face, not for hours, not until her mum came and drove her away in a maroon Ford Escort.

'It was a long time ago, Sarah. An accident.'

'I have no idea what you're talking about.'

'Don't play dumb. It wasn't like that and you know it,' I said.

'Of course it wasn't, Rachel.' Her words were heavy with sarcasm.

I didn't answer. There was nothing to say. She hadn't forgotten the past. Does anyone? I tried to escape it too. But it kept on finding me.

Sarah took her coat from behind the chair and picked

up her bag. I had finished my coffee but waited for her to leave. We didn't have enough conversation to get us to the door.

'Let's keep in touch, you know, if we hear anything,' I said and she nodded. 'I'm sure they'll find her soon.' But my words were lost in the hum of the coffee machine. She was already walking to the door.

I went back on to the seafront and followed the road round to the pier. Against the sea, so dark and endless, I felt small and insignificant and wondered if I was making too much of the situation. Next week, when you'd reappeared, I would see this for what it was – an insignificant little drama. Clinging to that thought I carried on walking up towards the Old Steine, and then I saw it: the headline gracing the *Brighton Argus* billboard outside the newsagent's – FEARS FOR MISSING BRIGHTON WOMAN. You were nowhere and everywhere.

I ran and ran until I got to the bandstand where there were no shops and posters and no pictures of you. I took out my BlackBerry and dialled.

'It's Rachel at NNN,' I said when he answered. There was a pause.

'Rachel, sorry, my hands are tied on this one. And we don't have much to go on. I promise you'll be the first to know when we do.'

'She's a friend,' I said and listened to a deep breath being sucked in through teeth.

'Is she now?' The emphasis was on the 'now'. I thought he would be more surprised.

'An old one,' I replied.

'When can you come in?' he asked.

'I'll be there in twenty minutes.'

Your face was hanging on the wall in the police station, your deep brown hair that fell down in waves, your tanned skin and those eyes, the sharpest, crystal blue. Everyone always said you should have had brown eyes with your colouring; the fact you didn't made them all the more hypnotic. You looked as if you were peering down into the room and smiling in satisfaction at what you could see. Because in that airless office there must have been fifteen or twenty people, and every one of them was searching for you.

Underneath your photo, on a whiteboard, was a timeline with locations. Brunswick Place, Marine Parade, Cantina Latina, King's Road. And then nothing. The point at which you had vanished into the cold night air.

I stood in the middle of the room waiting for DCI Gunn to finish his conversation with a youngish blond woman in jeans and a pink shirt. She must have been all of five foot next to his six foot five. I tried to eavesdrop, picking up enough to work out what she was doing; trawling the CCTV cameras on Friday night to see if you had made an appearance.

A phone ringing on the empty desk next to me disturbed my thoughts. I looked around to see if anyone was going to answer it. No one made a move. On and on it went. Each ring amplified in my head. Couldn't they see it mattered? What if it was someone with information? Or you. And then it stopped.

Finally DCI Gunn led me to through the room to his office. Until now our meetings had taken place in an old boozer in Hove just off Church Road. I'd call him Roger and order him a pint of Poacher's Choice and a Diet Coke for me. By the third pint, when his cheeks blushed from the alcohol, he would be more amenable to sharing information. Not that he was alone in that. How else do you think we got our stories? Coppers, criminals who liked to talk, there wasn't a whole lot of difference in the way you wooed them. Flattery and booze (and the occasional backhander) and before you knew it the exclusives and the tip-offs would be coming your way. It was all part of the game we played to stay ahead of the pack. And getting the senior officers on side meant that when a big story came up you could bypass the press officers and the 'no comment' lines they peddled.

But this inner sanctum was unfamiliar territory for me. I realised my eye was twitching and my eye always twitched when I was nervous. And knowing that made my heart beat faster. I was out of breath by the time I reached his office.

'Please,' said DCI Gunn, pointing to a seat opposite his desk. His voice was starchy, formal. It was not going to be a 'Roger' kind of day.

I sat down and looked at the neat stacks of paper and files on his desk. On each side of his PC were two lines of yellow Post-it notes, almost flawless in their symmetry. The computer was on an angle, away from me, so I couldn't see what was written on them. On his desk a Parker pen was positioned parallel to his keyboard; a stapler was on a right angle next to it. I was struck by the perfection of it.

It's funny, isn't it, what a desk can say about someone. Looking at the papers and the pen and the stapler I saw in DCI Gunn a man beaten by the vagaries, the randomness of his job, desperate to instil order wherever he could. Or maybe he was just tidy.

'So,' he said, making the word last longer than it should, 'it must have come as a shock, yesterday.' He let that hang in the air. My eye twitched again.

'I . . . seeing her face, in that room . . .' I let my sentence trail off and tried to compose myself. 'I'm still waiting for someone to tell me it's all a mistake.'

I'm not sure what I hoped to find in his face, Clara. Hope? Reassurance? I found neither.

He wasn't even looking at me. His gaze was fixed on a red elastic band that he stretched out between his fingers which were thin and surprisingly feminine. He kept his nails long, too long for a man's, and I saw they were thick and yellowing at the tip.

'Good report last night,' he said, finally looking up.

'You saw it?' I asked. I always assumed police had better things to do than watch themselves on the TV news.

'I was around all day,' he said. He took the elastic band from between his fingers and put it in a drawer in his desk. I had his full attention.

'I wasn't really thinking straight. Everything happened so quickly, after the press conference I was straight on air. I tried to tell them . . . I didn't even know what I was saying.' I paused. He was still staring at me. His stare would not let me go. I didn't know where to put my eyes so I rummaged in my bag, pulled out my phone and handed it to him.

'I was in Cantina Latina on Friday night. I didn't want to go but Clara went on and on about meeting up with these girls we used to go to school with. Her new friends. Then she sent this.' I pointed to the phone, which he still had in his hand. 'And that was it.'

'But she did turn up, didn't she?'

He was leaning back in the chair, with his hands clasped behind his back, a pose that stretched his shirt more than seemed wise. *Time to cut back on the Poacher's Choice.*

'So you say, but I don't understand. I tried to call her all night. Why didn't she call me?' I asked.

He made no attempt to answer.

'Clara's my oldest friend. The thought of something happening to her . . . We were always so close.' My voice was quiet, thin.

'Were?' DCI Gunn.

I wasn't sure how to answer that, Clara. You were my oldest friend, you were part of me, that would never change, but we had drifted away from each other. I couldn't deny it. I didn't know you properly any more, not bone-deep the way I used to. That was when I made the decision to tell DCI Gunn about your history in case it had a bearing on what happened. It's not what you would have wanted, but he would have found out anyway and now wasn't the time for secrets. You were missing. The police needed to be armed with all the facts.

'She went away,' I said, 'when she was nineteen, for treatment.' I expected that to cause a ripple of interest, but his face gave nothing away. 'Psychiatric treatment, she had a breakdown.' I stopped, aware that the situation called for tears. My tears. And Jesus, I could cry buckets watching *The X Factor* but for some reason I couldn't cry when I needed to, when DCI Gunn expected me to collapse in a puddle.

'What was the trigger?' he asked, the policeman in him searching for a cause and effect. But not everything happens like that. Some things just are.

'It's hard to say. My mum died and she took it badly.'

'*Your* mum?'

'They'd become close. Clara took her death badly.' That was true wasn't it, Clara? You didn't cope with Niamh dying. You crumbled under the weight of your grief. 'She was away for seven years. I mean she wasn't having treatment all that time. Her dad paid for her to study in Madrid and then she taught English and went travelling. She came back about a year and a half ago because her dad was dying.'

'And did she seem different?'

Does anyone stay the same after seven years?

'Yes,' I said, 'she was different.'

He made a face and motioned with his hand for me to elaborate.

There were so many ways in which you'd changed, Clara.

The things you said, how you behaved. You seemed angry, aloof, distant. But most strikingly the spark in you seemed to have been extinguished. I worried about you, God knows I tried to help, to make it better, but it was never enough.

'It was as if something was eating away at her,' I said, aware that the DCI would have wanted a more solid explanation.

I told him how I went to check on you in your flat on that Friday night of your disappearance but you didn't answer. I described how I walked along and booked myself into a hotel afterwards. And after two hours of explaining and talking I ran out of words, but still I waited, like a schoolchild who needed to be excused before I could get up and go.

'If I can be of any more help, just call me.' I said, inviting him to dismiss me.

'Why didn't you report her missing, Rachel?' he said, smiling at me in the way a shark might before it swallows you whole.

It was a legitimate question. I can see that now, but at the time I was taken aback. The truth is it didn't occur to me that something might have happened to you. I was angry with you. I was being stubborn. I thought you should call me first and apologise for your no-show.

'Clara has been . . .' I searched for the right word. 'Flaky since she got back. You said yesterday her disappearance is out of character and it is. I mean I don't think she has ever gone missing for days before. But sometimes she'll make arrangements and not turn up, or she'll turn up without warning you. Her moods are unpredictable—' A knock on the door stopped my flow. DCI Gunn shouted for whoever it was to wait and walked across the room to open it. I turned to see the petite blond officer from earlier. There was a conversation, too hushed to hear. Then DCI Gunn came back in with a brown file.

'Look, if there's anything I can do, just call me, OK.' I stood up to leave but he raised his hand to stop me.

'There is one thing you can do before you go.' He put the file on the table and took out three pictures. Images, grainy and blurred. Captured on CCTV.

It was you. I could see that much.

And someone else.

Next to you.

You'd pulled the collars of your coat up against the wind and your body was close to his, like you were holding on to him, holding him up. You weren't smiling. Neither was he, I took some comfort from that. His eyes looked like they were closed but that could have just been the shot, the moment the image was taken.

'Do you know who that is?' The DCI pointed to the male figure.

I nodded; my head was heavy on my neck. A fist clenched in my stomach.

'Yes,' I whispered, barely audible.

What else could I say? I'd woken up to his face every morning for almost two years.

Chapter Six

THERE WAS A hole, deep and black and bottomless, in that office and I was hurtling through it. My body was stiff with terror. I wanted to grab hold of something to stop my fall but nothing. There was nothing.

I shook my head. I wanted to shake the image out of it. Jonny and Clara. Clara and Jonny. Without me. Why? What was he doing there? Everything was changing. All the things I thought I could hold on to were being snatched away. I didn't know what I would be left with. I wanted to curl up in a ball and silence the screams inside my head.

'Why would they have been together, Rachel?' DCI Gunn asked. There was a harshness to his question. Surely my face told him everything he needed to know.

How the fuck should I know?

I said nothing.

'Do you have any idea, Rachel, what Jonny was doing there? Were you supposed to be meeting him too?' He leant forward, across the desk, to force me to look at him. His hot spittle landed on my cheek.

'Jonny was staying in Gatwick. He had an early flight the next morning.'

'When was the last time you spoke to him?'

It was an obvious question. I bristled, knowing how he would react to my answer.

'I haven't.'

'You haven't spoken to Jonny since he was out with Clara?' The sound of your name in the same sentence as Jonny's stung me. You and Jonny. Jonny and you. DCI Gunn looked flushed; his upper lip beaded with perspiration. He licked his lips, like he'd smelt blood, ready to swoop down for the kill.

'He's a documentary-maker. He was filming in Afghanistan. It's not unusual for me not to hear from him for days, sometimes a whole week when he's away filming.'

'But you would have expected him to call you?'

'No, I wouldn't have expected him to call me. I've just told you, he's away filming. In Afghanistan. Sometimes it's impossible to get a phone line out.'

He leant back in his chair and folded his arms. I imagined he was planning his next line of attack. I wanted to wake up from this dark dream and find myself back living my old life, the one I inhabited before you disappeared. I tried to find my voice, a calm, even voice to defend myself.

'Look, Roger,' I said. 'I don't know what's happening any more. I'm scared shitless, to tell you the truth. Yesterday I found out my best friend had gone missing and today you show me a picture of her and my boyfriend together on the night she disappeared. I have no idea why they were together; he should have been at Gatwick. But I'm certain of one thing – however it looks, you've got it wrong. Jonny wouldn't betray me and he wouldn't hurt anyone. Least of all Clara. He is protective of her because she's my friend and he knows we go back a long way.' I watched him pursing his lips and stroking his chin. I thought I might have got through to him. He looked up and nodded as if he had taken my words on board.

'Were they having an affair?' he asked.

'Jesus, no! Did you hear anything I said?'

'I have to ask these questions, Rachel. The fact that we know each other doesn't change anything. We need to find Jonny because as it stands he was the last person to see Clara. I don't have to tell you the implications of that.'

'Well, when you find them tell them you're not the only person who wants some answers.' I smiled, half forced a laugh to try to make light of the situation. But even as I said it I knew it hit the wrong note.

'I hope it works out that way,' he said but he wouldn't meet my eyes. He stood up and walked round from his desk so he was next to me, reaching out to shake my hand. His palm was cold and damp like putty. I could feel the grip of his hand crunching mine. 'I'll be in touch,' he said as he showed me to the door.

Outside the police station I slumped down next to the railings. The wind screamed up from the sea. I lifted my face to it in the hope it would wake me from my stupor. Why, Why, Why? Why was he with you, Clara? Why hadn't you met me? Anger coursed through me, tingling as it ran up my spine and down my arms to the tips of my fingers. The idea of Jonny betraying me with you was so alien it had no place inside my head. I would never believe it, not unless I saw it with my own eyes. All I had seen so far was the two of you together. No one knew what had happened. The police were making assumptions that had no basis in reality.

You see Clara, I trusted Jonny. I would have trusted him with my life. But you? I began to wonder if I even knew you. When you came back after all that time away I thought we could pick up where we left off. Naively, I thought I could recreate that closeness again through sheer force of will. God knows I put the effort in. I wanted to be there to look after you, support you. And I thought it was working. The memory of us all on the skiing trip came back to me: you and me and Jonny and his friend Luke, the four of us together at Christmas. It was only a month ago but it felt like it belonged to a different age, when I was someone else and so were you. All day long we had been carving down slopes under a cloudless sky, floating on powder at the top of a mountain, thinking we'd gone to heaven. When we reached the bottom our smiles lit up our whole faces. We were full of life, bursting with it.

'My round,' you shouted as you removed your sunglasses. Your face was tanned and red and glowing. The skin around your eyes was white.

'Panda eyes,' I teased.

'You're just jealous because I beat you on the slopes,

although . . .' and you nudged me so I fell over in the snow, 'you've been getting some practice in my absence.'

You disappeared into the bar and emerged with four large beers in frosted glasses.

We sat on the terrace overlooking the piste and the mountains in the late winter sun and all agreed beer had never tasted so good.

'So Clara, come on, what else can you beat Rachel at?' It was Luke, Jonny's friend who obviously fancied you.

'Swimming, tennis . . .'

'All right, sport wasn't my thing at school. But I do have some skills.' I stood up and held the beer out in front of me.

'Don't tell me you can still do that?' you asked incredulously.

'Some things never leave you,' I laughed, wondering if I could still pull it off, and then I took the beer, threw my head back and downed it. I heard the cheers from Luke and Jonny and you.

'Bloody hell.' Jonny was sitting mouth wide open, eyes laughing. 'I didn't realise my girlfriend had such hidden talents.'

'From my ladette days,' I said, planting a kiss on his lips. 'Now I am a ladee on TV I don't do it so much. And to mark my achievement I think we should have a group photo now.' I handed my camera to a snowboarder next to us. '*Vous pouvez prendre un photo, s'il vous plaît?*' I asked.

'Yeah, no problems mate,' he replied in a thick Essex accent which made us collapse with laughter.

We huddled together, sunglasses on our heads, squinting in the sun. I remember wanting to preserve the memory of that moment forever, to stop it fading in time.

When I got home I printed the photograph out and put it in my wallet. Now I found myself looking for it as I walked away from the police station. It was still there, the shot of the four of us, under a sinking Alpine sun. Then my tears fell on the paper – finally, tears – and the colours leaked into each other so our faces became blotchy and smudged. I could hardly see Jonny any more, I couldn't see myself, but the smile on your face remained.

Heading back to the hotel I called him, ten times over. Each time I listened to his voice, willing it to come alive. But it was only a recording, trapped in time on his answerphone. I had heard it so often I knew where the pause would come, which words he stressed, even the slam of the door in the background.

'Hi, it's Jonny, sorry I can't pick up, leave a message and I'll call you back as soon as I can.'

As soon as I can. When would he call me? I had never wanted to talk to someone so much, to spill out my fears and have them dismissed, gently: *Rach, it's OK, I can explain everything.*

The not-knowing, the waiting, made me want to claw at my eyes in frustration.

Nick, Luke and Sandra. They were the three names that stood out as I scrolled through my contacts book; Jonny's friends and his mother. I needed to call them in case he had been in touch but I wasn't ready to tell them the full story. I wasn't prepared to create a chain reaction, passing my fears and worries from one person to another and giving the situation the oxygen to breathe and grow and mutate into something far more serious than I hoped it was.

In the end I only spoke to Luke.

'Hi, I can't get through to Jonny, I don't suppose he has called you,' I asked, trying to sound light and breezy.

'Rachel . . . eh, no I'm sorry, I haven't heard from him. Look, I'm right in the middle of something at work, can I call you back?'

'No, it's fine, that's all I wanted to know.'

Nick didn't pick up so I left him a message. And Sandra; I couldn't bring myself to call her. Not yet anyway.

I escaped Brighton that evening, exploiting the small window of opportunity before it started snowing again. Jake said he'd come with me and I was surprised to find I was relieved. I didn't want to talk. I just needed to feel a friendly presence close to me after hours of hostile combat with DCI Gunn.

'So where did you get to?' We were barely out of Brighton. Jake's tolerance for silence was much lower than mine.

'Just seeing a few people,' I said.

'I thought you had no family left.'

'I didn't say all my friends were dead too did I?'

'Look,' he said, 'don't take this the wrong way but you've been acting a little off kilter since yesterday. I know you can be a pain in the arse to work with sometimes,' I was looking at the road but I knew he was smiling, 'but for the last day you've just been plain weird. So are you going to tell me what the fuck is freaking you out?'

'You wouldn't believe me if I did.'

'Try me,' he said, and when I turned briefly to look at him I thought maybe that I could. Maybe I needed to offload. And then I heard his voice turn into a yell.

'RACHEL, what the fuck!'

I can still remember the look of terror on his face, as if something had taken possession of his whole body. I can still see his arm outstretched pointing to the road. There was a car coming right at us from the inside lane. How I hadn't spotted it I don't know, but I was going too fast to stop. I heard the sound of metal against metal, a crunch then a high-pitched screech of the cars meeting at high speed. Then I swerved right. The central reservation racing at us at 100 miles per hour. Everything speeded up, then stretched out in time. My foot was hard on the brakes but the car wasn't stopping. I closed my eyes, braced for the impact. And then finally we stopped. About a metre away from the barriers. I waited for the impact of another car crashing into us. Jake shouted at me to drive. I turned the key in the ignition, hands shaking. There was a pain in my chest where my heart was beating so hard. Finally the car moved; I straightened it up and drove over to the hard shoulder, expecting the other car to have done the same. But it had disappeared out of sight. My head fell down on the steering wheel.

'Fucking hell. What just happened there?'

I tried to take a deep breath to slow my heartbeat.

'There was nothing in front of me and then he was right there.' My voice came out distorted as if I was talking through water.

'I saw it,' said Jake. 'Fucking idiot had the whole road and pulled out right in front of you.'

I wiped my eyes and realised I was crying again. And knowing I was crying made me cry even more. Jake found a tissue in my bag and handed it to me. 'I'll drive the rest of the way if you want.'

I nodded my head and climbed into the back so he could move over into the driving seat. I was hollow and lifeless and empty, like a toy with the stuffing removed. I was crying about nearly dying, about Jonny, about you. About everything. But most of all I was crying because I wanted it to stop.

Have you ever been in a place where your thoughts are scorched and the framework of your mind, the nuts and bolts that hold it together and the machinery that keeps it ticking over, has been dismantled? I ask you, Clara, because I thought I was beginning to grasp in some crude way what had happened to you all those years before. I thought I was on the precipice that night. I'm just glad no one told me how much further I had to fall.

I dropped Jake off on the Harrow Road and drove up Chamberlayne Road and into Kensal Rise alone. There must have been snow in London earlier in the day – telltale deposits of grey slush lined the pavements – but the rain was coming down hard now and in a few hours it would be washed away.

I turned into Kempe Road and found a parking space about six doors away from my flat. I can't remember thinking anything, I certainly wasn't glad to be home because I knew Jonny wouldn't be there. I was numb and cold and I wanted to sleep so badly for the escape. I wanted a break from myself.

So I wasn't thinking or looking or taking in my surroundings. I was just walking up the path towards the front door and then I saw it: the light shining out from behind the white shutters in our living room. I looked away and shook my head because I didn't believe what I was seeing. But when I looked again I knew that I wasn't mistaken. Someone was in the flat.

A huge crashing wave of relief engulfed me. I dropped my bag on the ground and started to laugh and then cry and laugh and cry until it became one hysterical noise. *Jonny is home, Jonny is home.* It was all I could think of – you know I never ever leave anything switched on, Clara – so it had to be him. And I must have been so deliriously happy I shouted it out: 'Jonny is home!' because my next-door neighbour Janice came out and said, 'Is everything all right, Rachel?', and I looked down at myself, wet through and shivering, and I nodded and picked up my bag and went inside.

'Jonny?' I called his name softly, like a question I was

asking of myself. He didn't answer. I went into the living room; it was empty. Cushions plumped and arranged in the same way I arranged them every day before I left, the Heal's one with green and blue circles next to the Missoni one which was multicoloured stripes and then the white and black one with an outline of London that I hated but Jonny loved. They were all in order. Nothing had been touched.

'Jonny?' I called again, louder this time, running into the hall and through to the kitchen. All the surfaces were polished and clean. My plants on the windowsill lined up in ascending size.

'JONNY.' It wasn't a question any more but a plea. There was a pulse in my throat. The relief that I had felt only a moment ago had mutated into a cold fear thumping through me. I screamed his name again and again but he wouldn't answer. Then I ran into the bedroom. No light there, still dark. Still dark. My hand was on the light switch. I didn't want to look.

He needed to be in our bed, chest heaving, deep sleep breaths, oblivious to what was going on. I needed to touch and smell him and drink him in. I needed him to wrap me up in one of his hugs and hold me so tight the breath would almost be squeezed out of me. He needed to be there because if he wasn't, nothing was right, nothing would ever be right.

I flicked the switch and kept my eyes closed.

Then I opened them.

Just an empty bed.

Nothing would ever be right.

I was still for a moment, perfectly still. And then I looked around, searching for something. Something had changed. My eyes scanned every corner and crevice of the room. White cotton sheets taut over the bed, cushions propped up against the pillows. Jonny's unread books stacked up on his bedside table. His side was the messiest. An old glass of water. A notepad. Painkillers. Everything was as we had left it and yet something had shifted.

Then a glimpse, and it clicked into place, like a camera finding its focus.

I inhaled. Deep breaths and it was the smell that told me. It wasn't Jonny. It wasn't me. It was someone else. And it was fresh. My eyes took me to the dressing table. There were cleansers, eye cream, hand cream, a candle in green fig, my favourite scent. There was perfume, Dolce & Gabbana Light Blue. Some tulips in a vase, now empty of water. And there was a photograph. Framed in black. A picture that captured the gentle warmth of an evening in Ibiza. Me and Jonny drunk on sunshine. I blinked. That image was coming from memory. It was gone; someone had replaced it with a photograph of a woman and a teenage girl. The woman's dark hair was falling over her face, partially covering one eye. Her freckled cheeks were red from the sun and she had smile lines creasing out like little streams from her eyes. One arm was round the girl whose lips were upturned in a smile that looked contented and warm. The teenager next to my mother wasn't me. It was you. A photograph taken on a warm summer's day ten years ago. The day before my mother died.

Chapter Seven

December 1993

YOU ARE COMING to tea, to my house, which means you'll meet my mum. I don't have friends for tea, not normally, not ever. I don't tell you that you're special, I think you already know. And when I told you about my mum, how she's not like other mums, you just smiled and said: 'At least you have one, mine left me and my dad when I was a baby.' Somehow that makes me feel better. Another thing we have in common: mothers who fuck us up.

We're out of breath from walking up Ditchling Road. It's March but more winter than spring and we're fighting against the wind. 'Nearly there,' I say as we turn into Dover Road. I stop outside a house and search for my keys in my rucksack.

'Is this it?' you ask.

I look and see I've stopped outside Mrs Reagan's house. The neat garden, freshly weeded, and the red front door that has no paint flaking from it and the curtains with the tie-backs arranged just so and picture frames on the windowsill. I can't see the photographs they contain and I haven't been in her house but I know they're of smiling children on sunny days. Happy families. I shake my head and grip my keys. They are slippery in my hand.

''S'a bit further down,' I say.

Our door is blue, faded, paint cracking. It's number twenty-one but the two has fallen off so the postmen always get confused. There are no curtains in the living room, Niamh thinks they're bourgeois, so instead we have an enormous ethnic print sheet that she brought back from India years ago. She hangs it from the window in the same way they do in the student houses on Lewes Road. 'Home sweet home,' I say as we walk up the path.

The air is thick and sweet. Some people's houses smell of Daz or fabric softener, or lavender air freshener, but mine always has the same heady sweet smell from the cigarettes Niamh smokes. I stick my head round the living-room door and see her sprawled out on the sofa in a kaftan, hair held up by a pencil. Her eyes are glassy and she's looking up to the ceiling, blowing perfect circles in smoke. Sometimes I think her face is sinking into itself; her cheeks are hollowed out, her eyes too deep in her head, but still there is no denying her beauty, or at least the shadow of a beauty that has long passed. Oprah is on the TV but she's not watching. Her arm is outstretched, the cigarette suspended from her fingers. I see the ash ready to fall on to the carpet.

'Hello *d a r* ling.' She says it loudly and without looking at me. You don't say anything but you must be surprised by my mother's vowels, which go on forever, unlike mine. I haven't told you she comes from a posh family with a big house and a horse, have I? She threw all the education and breeding back in their faces. My Aunty Laura said my mother told her parents she didn't need their money. How I laugh now when I think of her rich-girl arrogance.

'We're going to get a drink,' I say.

She doesn't look up, just wafts me away with her hand like I'm cigarette smoke in her eyes.

You go a bit quiet, like you're weirded out by Niamh, and I'm beginning to regret bringing you. What if you tell everyone at school my mother's a nutcase? I shudder when I think of the shame of it.

In the kitchen. The breakfast dishes are still on the table, leftovers of my morning Weetabix have hardened in the bowl. I clear them away and put them in the sink.

'You OK?' I ask. 'We can grab something and take it to the park.'

'What, and freeze our arses off out there?' You give me a little push. Maybe it will be all right after all.

I wash two glasses and fill them up with Vimto, which Niamh drinks by the gallon in the morning to quench the wine thirst from the night before.

'Stay here,' I tell you as I walk back into the living room. 'What's for tea?' I ask Niamh louder than necessary. I make it sound like an everyday question. She ignores me. 'I have a friend from school,' I say, quieter this time, 'is there anything to eat?'

She throws her cigarette butt in the ashtray and looks up. 'A friend? That's nice.'

'Is there anything we can have for tea, Niamh?'

She sighs and rubs her eyes. 'You're hardly going to starve, are you darling?'

I don't bite back but I don't move either and finally she lets out a long sigh like a deflating balloon. 'Oh for God's sake, there's a pizza menu on the fridge, ring for one, and order some extra for me. A plain margherita, I don't like any of that crap they put on them.' She doesn't look at me once.

We sit in the kitchen eating our Hawaiian and drinking Vimto. We listen to the Verve and Boyzone and All Saints on a tape I recorded from the top forty countdown which gets annoying when the DJ keeps interrupting the songs. We're about to go upstairs when Niamh comes into the room bringing a trail of smoke with her.

She opens the fridge and leans on the door for a moment.

'Aren't you going to introduce us, Rachel?' she says while peering in the fridge. It's empty save for a mushy cucumber, some yoghurts and milk. And wine, always wine. 'I appear to have brought this girl up without any manners.'

'I'm Clara, nice to meet you Mrs Walsh and thanks for the pizza,' you say in a voice that sounds so happy I wonder whether you're taking the piss. 'It was deeelicious.' And you smack your lips together.

'Clara,' she repeats, finally turning to look at you. She blinks as if to clear the fog in front of her eyes. '*C l a r a*.'

She rolls each letter over her tongue before releasing it into the room. 'I haven't come across many Claras.'

'Me neither,' you say, 'I'm the only one in my school.'

She takes another look at you, narrowing her gaze to focus. 'And you're in the same class?'

'Yes, though I'm older. I'm fifteen you see, I just had to repeat a year.'

'Well Clara,' Niamh says, 'I'm glad you liked the pizza. Make yourself at home.' She closes the fridge door quickly. Her empty wine glass is sitting on the counter. She looks at me briefly, then back to you, and walks out of the room, her kaftan floating behind her.

After tea we go upstairs to my room. I take a jug with me to water my plants, just as I do every evening. You watch, bemused, as I test the moisture in each pot with my finger, before giving them the correct amount of water. Then carefully I wipe the dust from their leaves. 'I keep them in here,' I tell you. 'So they're safe, away from Niamh because she's been known to use my flowerpots as ashtrays.'

'I guess that's one use for them,' you say with a laugh.

'They die if you don't look after them, you know.' But I can see from your face that you don't know, you don't understand anything about plants and flowers and how to nurture and care for them so I drop the subject and come and sit next to you on the bed.

'It's funny isn't it,' you say, turning to me, 'I don't live with my mum and you don't live with your dad.' I'd never really thought of it before but I smile when you bring it to my attention. I like the symmetry of it. As if we are two halves of the same orange.

I've asked you about your mum before but you have always been evasive. You say she's still alive and sometimes sends you letters which are secret from your dad but I'm not sure I believe you. I wonder whether she's dead and you just won't admit it. Maybe she exists in your head, where she's beautiful and smells of pancakes and syrup and flowers. I don't probe you though. I know that being the child of a parent missing in action is a sensitive subject.

Still, I'm happy to share what basic details I have about my dad and you seem happy to listen. I tell you his name is (was) Lawrence McDaid and he is from Scotland which is where I was born.

'So he's the one responsible for your red hair,' you laugh and I nod. I tell you he is tall, though for obvious reasons I can't specify the height, and has blue eyes (Niamh bitterly described them as deep blue ones that could make you believe anything).

According to my mother the last time she saw him was half an hour before she gave birth to me, writhing in pain as the contractions clawed at her stomach. You look up at this, surprised by the revelation.

'Apparently my father knew how to choose his moments,' I say, recalling what Niamh had told me. I was ten when she sat me down at the kitchen table, sticky with the residue of spilt drinks. I remember staring at a tomato ketchup stain which had turned a dark reddy-brown colour. Not that I cared. She'd given me a glass of apple juice and laid out a bag of salt and vinegar crisps for us to share. I ate them slowly, hoping that the longer they lasted, the longer we would stay there chatting.

'We were doing family trees at school,' I tell you. 'I had drawn branches and on one side I'd written all the names of Niamh, her sisters and her parents. Only my dad's side was bare.' I still remember looking at that bare branch, how it exposed a hole in me I never knew existed. A hole I wanted filled with information. 'So Niamh said she would tell me all about my dad.'

I picture my mother talking to me through rising clouds of cigarette smoke, particles separating in the light. I thought there was something magical about that moment, as if by speaking she was releasing the stories of my past, allowing them to float above our heads. I needed a wee so badly I had to cross my legs. There was no way I was going to the toilet; I didn't want to move in case I broke the spell.

'Lawrence told Niamh he was going out to get help. But he only got as far as Betty O'Driscoll's next door who was in the middle of watching *Take the High Road* and wasn't too pleased about being interrupted,' I say, happy in the knowledge I have your undivided attention.

'And then what?' you ask.

'He walked out into the night and Niamh never saw him again.'

After shouting expletives at Mrs O'Driscoll, Niamh gave two agonising pushes and I came out screaming into the world. She shouted for Lawrence to come and see his baby daughter, all slimy and new, and kept calling until Mrs

O'Driscoll went to look for him and finally broke the news to her that he was nowhere to be found. Fearing him stranded in the fierce Scottish night, Niamh reported him missing. For nine days the police searched for Mr McDaid until it transpired he was living with Mary Donaghue three miles away, and her three children. Who also happened to be his own.

'That's why we came back to England when I was two weeks old, on the Flying Scotsman in the middle of the night, just me and Niamh and a few essentials.'

'Got any photographs of him then, your ginger dad?' you ask.

'There's a shoebox somewhere with my baby photographs but I don't know where it is.' You look disappointed.

I think of the old box with the faded picture of ankle boots on the side (price twelve pounds ninety-nine) which must have been Niamh's once. 'I haven't seen it since the day she told me about my father,' I say. She'd brought the box down to the kitchen and carefully picked out the photographs of my father, and a few of me as a baby, leaving me to look at them as she busied herself in the kitchen cooking pasta and chopping onions and garlic for the sauce.

Lawrence had red hair down to his shoulders and the most striking blue eyes I've ever seen. In one photograph he had a hand on Niamh's pregnant belly, smiling as if he couldn't quite believe his luck. Her eyes were twinkling with happiness and I remembered wondering what my life would be like if my mother still had those happy eyes. Of course there were none of my father and me together, thanks to his untimely exit as I entered the world, just a few of me as a baby, tufts of red hair shooting up from my head, sitting in a bouncy chair or on Niamh's lap. Even by that time her eyes had lost their sparkle. She looked tired and drawn.

I had laid them out in front of me on the kitchen table and stared at each one, willing them to offer up their secrets. Those six faded photographs told me so little. There must be more, I reasoned. I wanted to see them all.

I looked around for the shoebox and saw it sitting on the sideboard, with its lid back on. Niamh had her back turned to me, stirring the sauce on the hob and humming to herself. The rich tomatoey smell was making my stomach growl.

I got up from the table and walked across to the sideboard. Taking the lid off, I saw there were indeed more pictures, some lying loose, and underneath those, a small album. I reached in and pulled one out. It was of Niamh leaning into a man with dark hair. It was a cosy embrace that suggested they were at ease in each other's company. Her hair was longer, her face rounder in these ones. I wondered if she'd been in love with this man before my dad came on the scene and snatched her from him. My hand reached into the box for more photographs and clues when I smelt her breath on me, wine-sweet. I looked up and saw her eyes dark with anger. I didn't know what I had done wrong, but whatever it was I had broken the magic spell.

'You always have to spoil things don't you, Rachel,' she said, ripping the shoebox from me and marching out of the room. I waited for her to return, kept praying she would, but when she didn't I sat and ate dinner on my own.

'Are you all right?' you ask me, snapping me out of my reverie. I give my head a little shake as if to empty it of troubling thoughts.

'Of course,' I say, smiling at your concern. 'Shall I tell you something?' I ask to change the subject.

'Be my guest.'

'Do you know why I love my flowers so much?' You grunt, disinterested.

'No, surprise me,' you say in your bored voice.

My mind pings back to the day I presented Mrs Rippon my teacher with my family tree project. I explained that the photograph of my dad in the flares was old, really old, but it was the only one I had of him. 'I've never met him, you see,' I explained to her. She fixed me with one of those smiles, where someone's lips are turned down instead of up but you know they're thinking kind thoughts.

Later that afternoon when we were coming in from the playground she called me over and pressed three little envelopes into my hand.

'You have to plant these and look after them carefully if you want them to grow,' she said.

I looked down at the envelope and saw pictures of pretty flowers.

Sunflowers, irises and violets.

'So you see,' I tell you, 'my plants remind me of my dad.'

I realise I have been talking for ages and you are unusually quiet. I think you might want to tell me a bit more about your mum now, after hearing so much from me, but you shake your head. 'Nah, let's try on some make-up,' you say, jumping up from the bed.

You open my drawer where I keep various bits of make-up I've bought with pocket money when Niamh remembers to give it to me. You find a purple eyeshadow and stand in front of the mirror using your little finger to rub it on. After that you take the liquid eyeliner and apply it in one perfect, steady sweep of your hand. Then you take a step back to study your work.

'How do I look?' you ask me.

Your eyes are enormous; the purple eyeshadow has turned the blue darker and stormier. I have to look away before they hypnotise me.

'Stunning,' I say, wishing I had your eyes.

You turn to me with your head tilted to one side.

'Purple's not your colour, Rach,' you say, rummaging for something else in the drawer. 'But this one is perfect.' You hold up a light green eyeshadow. I screw up my face. 'Trust me, it'll look amazing with your eyes.'

'Yeah right,' I laugh. But really I'm just playing along because I do trust you, implicitly. I marvel at how you know what looks good and what doesn't, how you always seem to make me look better than I could ever have imagined.

You sit me down on the edge of the bed and you start work on my eyes. 'Ten minutes,' you say, 'ten minutes is all I need for the full makeover.'

I nod my approval. I would happily stay there all evening just to be the centre of your attention. Sometimes I have to pinch myself that you chose me to be your friend when you could have chosen anyone. I've watched you in the playground, I've seen the way people gravitate towards you, eager for your approval. You're not even aware of the power you have, but I see it. You could turn your sunshine smile on any one of them and make them glow, but you don't, you save it for me and that makes it all the more beautiful. Maybe one day I'll be able to explain this to you properly; I'm like one of my sunflowers under your gaze, Clara. Your friendship makes me feel special and alive where before I was empty and grey.

Finally you've finished the makeover. Pulling me up from the bed, you shuffle me towards the mirror, your hands covering my eyes.

'Dah dah!' you say, finally moving your hands away. 'You can look now.'

The person looking back at me isn't me, it can't be. The eyes that have always been dull and pale seem to look green now, and big and wide. I catch them twinkling back at me. My whole face has been transformed. I can see my cheekbones and my lips glisten under a thin coating of gloss. I almost look pretty. I think I might cry.

'You see, Rach, I'm never wrong.'

'Thanks,' I say. It doesn't even begin to capture how I feel but it's all I can manage.

You come and stand next to me in front of the mirror,

pulling a model face, all sultry and pouting. It makes me laugh and I try to do the same. Then we fall back on the soft bed, gazing up at the Artex ceiling with its swirls and peaks. I feel like I'm floating through clouds with you next to me, just the two of us. I hope it's always like this.

'You know, Rach, I'm going to be an actress one day. I'm going to star in those big budget films in Hollywood. I want to be famous. My dad says I can start drama classes next term.' And then you laugh, 'Well that's my dream anyway.'

I think of you creating ripples of excitement wherever you go, swishing up the red carpet, wearing one of those dresses with slits up the thigh and the back all scooped out. I see your hair, snaking down your bum, and the paparazzi calling out your name, *Clara, Clara, Clara,* the flashbulbs going off in your face.

'I reckon you will be famous,' I say, rolling over on to my side to look at you. 'Just don't forget me when you are.'

'As if,' you give me a little kick, 'best friends . . .' and you hold out your pinkie so I can hook mine into yours.

'Forever,' I say, finishing your sentence, and we laugh together at how childish we're being.

When we unhook our fingers you jump up from the bed and put a CD in my ghetto blaster. 'Here,' you say, handing me a hairbrush. 'If we're going to be famous we need to practise. I have a dance routine all worked out.'

I hear the sound of 'Relight My Fire' and you try to teach me a dance you have choreographed. But when I outstretch my arms I see them wobbling and all I can hear is the sound of my graceless feet thumping as they hit the floor. I throw myself on to the bed and catch sight of my face, now red and sweaty, in the mirror.

'God, I'll settle for being your assistant when you're a film star. I can't dance or sing, there's not much hope for me,' I laugh.

'You can judge my performance then, marks out of ten.'

I sit back and watch as you spin around and move your arms in time to the music. Your limbs seem to go on forever, long and slender and smooth. There's a ball of energy around you and it is sparking, like electricity lighting the room. You are everything I am not. I can't take my eyes off you. When the track finishes, you take a bow.

I clap madly. 'Ten,' I shout, 'bravo.'

Five minutes later a knock on my bedroom door surprises me. Niamh never knocks. But this time she even waits until I open it. Her eyes look misty, bloodshot from the smoke, I think. 'Your dad is here for you,' she says, trying to focus on you. Her cheeks are burning. Too much wine and it's only six o'clock.

You grab your bag and together we go downstairs. I expect to see your dad waiting for you in the doorway.

'He's outside in the car,' Niamh says. I stick my head out to catch a glimpse of him, and see his shape sitting in a white Saab with a soft top, engine purring. He doesn't look my way.

'Thank you for having me, Mrs Walsh,' you say as if she's been the perfect hostess. There is a pause, an awkward moment, when she leans in towards you and I think she's actually going to kiss you. My heart lurches, then mercifully a horn beeps from the road and saves me the shame.

'See you tomorrow, Rachel,' you shout, running down the path.

Closing the door I see Niamh walking away. Her footsteps, small and shuffled, take her back to the kitchen. She grabs a bottle of wine from the fridge and pours herself a large glass. It shakes as she lifts it to her mouth and downs it as if it's her morning Vimto. She doesn't look around for me, she just stares ahead at nothing in particular.

Chapter Eight

How does someone slip through walls unnoticed? Through locked doors and windows and take what's not theirs and leave again without being seen? Those thoughts crept through my head, shivered through my body. I had no answers. One reality sat on top of another and another, like a weird chemical-induced hallucination.

Finding the photograph of me and Jonny would have helped. To see it with my own eyes. To know I hadn't dreamt it. I ran around the flat, pulling out the white labelled boxes and files with paperwork, the drawers. I wanted to tear down the white walls and rip up the floorboards just so whatever was being hidden from me could reveal itself. But it was hopeless. The picture had disappeared, sucked into the ether. Just like you.

I sat on the soft cream carpet in my bedroom and surveyed the mess. I had ransacked my own flat and now I couldn't look at the result. The chaos made my head spin and knot. I thought it was going to implode. I needed to hide somewhere, to be safe. I pulled the wardrobe open on Jonny's side and shuffled in amongst his shirts. One of them fell off the hanger and I wrapped it round me. It was night-time dark, silent dark. Closing my eyes I hoped and hoped and wished and wished that when I woke up in the morning the shirt would be filled with bones and muscles and ligaments, that the chest would heave with breath and the arms would fold around me and never let me go.

It was before dawn and a dirty light had settled on the room. I thought I might be the only one awake in the world. Everything silent and still as if the day was out there waiting for everyone else to realise it was ready.

I was in the wardrobe; I'd fallen asleep there, my limbs twisted and achy. My body wanted to move and stretch but I couldn't summon the energy.

Then – the sound of a phone ringing. My mobile. A noise normally so unwelcome early in the morning, had my whole body tense with possibility. I saw it on my bed, flashing. I leapt out of the wardrobe to grab it. And I answered. Searching for the right words and then I found them.

'Hello,' I said. 'Is that you?'

'Rachel?' A man's voice, a southern accent like Jonny's and deep too. For a moment I let myself think it.

'Jonny?' There was a pause and then I knew. I knew.

'Rachel, it's Nick.'

'Oh . . .' I said. I had no more words.

'Look, I'm sorry to be calling at this time but I need to speak to you.' There was a softness to him that filled me with dread. Nick didn't talk like that; he boomed and bellowed. Whenever I saw Nick I saw Jonny, the pair of them laughing like schoolkids who had never grown up.

My grip on the phone loosened, it slipped down away from my ear. But his voice, I could still hear it.

'I'm sure there's a good reason for it,' he said in a way which made me think he didn't believe it. 'But the fixer, we managed to contact the fixer overnight and Jonny isn't there, he didn't arrive on Monday.'

'He must have been delayed on the way,' I said, recalling his plans to fly into Kabul and down to Kandahar where he was to meet the fixer. 'You know what it's like over there, Nick,' I went on, but even that theory opened up another flurry of possibilities I didn't want to consider. I heard Nick's sharp intake of breath on the phone, enough to send me into meltdown. 'Oh my God, has something happened to him out there?' The nightmare, the homemade video, masked men surrounding Jonny, forcing him to talk to the camera, to beg for his life. 'Fucking hell,' I said, 'isn't there supposed to be fucking security?' I was saying all this and aware at the same time that the prospect of Jonny being kidnapped by al-Qaeda was somehow preferable to the alternative, the collusion with you. The betrayal.

'He hasn't been kidnapped Rachel.' Nick's voice was firm.

'How can you be sure?' There was no way of knowing; how could he dismiss it so quickly?

'Rachel . . . we called the police last night when we realised he wasn't there. They checked with the airline. Jonny didn't even make the flight.'

Dawn gave way to a fierce blue-sky day from which there was no hiding. The huge folding doors we'd had fitted in the kitchen at great expense let the light flood through. Outside, in the garden, the sun, brilliant and harsh, danced on the patches of frost; inside it reflected off the white gloss units and the stainless-steel worktops. How perfect it looked, how empty its promise. And the brilliance of it, I thought, was so inappropriate, like a brightly dressed guest showing off at a funeral.

There was a cloth in my hand, working its way over the surfaces, the table top, the worktop, the hob. Occasionally I stopped to spray more Dettol, the one that says it kills 100 per cent of all known germs, which was all very well but what about the unknown ones? I shuddered at the thought. Once, twice, three times I went over the surfaces. Then I stood back and surveyed my work. The shine. All clean. I turned to my plants.

There were ten of them, placed around the flat according to their need for sunlight or shade. The peace lilies in the living room were drooping, forlorn, the thin red-trimmed leaves of the marginara in the kitchen were brittle, brown-tinged at the ends. The African violet, my flamboyant, high-maintenance performer, looked like an actress whose hair and make-up needed retouching. Only the spider plant, a gift from a teacher years ago at school, showed no signs of neglect. I watered each one, watching the liquid seep through the cracks in the dry, parched soil. I imagined it soaking down to their roots, reviving them, bringing them back to life. The thought hovered as it always did: they needed me, it was down to me whether they lived or died. Somehow I found comfort in that.

Back in the kitchen the sound of coffee gurgling as it made its way through the Gaggia machine surprised me. I had no recollection of putting it on. For a moment I wondered if Jonny had done it. And then I remembered. *He isn't here.*

One, two, three, I counted back. Three days since Jonny was standing here, coffee in hand, kissing me goodbye.

'Do you have to go?' I had asked pointlessly. 'Can't you find a documentary to film in France instead of Afghanistan?' This was his second trip in three months for a Channel Four *Dispatches* on international-aid money ending up in the pockets of government officials.

'Darling . . .' He came up behind me and wrapped his arms round my waist. His words tickled as they landed on my neck. 'I came back last time didn't I?' he said as if that was a guarantee it would happen again. 'And I promise I won't talk to any masked men, you don't get rid of me that easily. I'll try to call midweek but don't panic if you don't hear, OK?'

'OK,' I said even though it wasn't. The lack of communication was the worst thing. Not knowing, imagining.

His kisses crept up my neck and on to my lips. I could still taste them as I ran out the door, late for work.

Friday. I hadn't seen Jonny since Friday. All this time I had imagined he was thousands of miles away, in a brutal Afghan winter, putting himself at risk. And yet he had been close by and I hadn't known. It was that single thought that tormented me the most.

Did I ever tell you about the first time I saw him, Clara? I'm at the bus stop on Ladbroke Grove. I've been at the Electric with friends from work and I'm drunk, but not so drunk I can't feel the cold because I can feel the cold and I feel the rain, hammering against the shelter. Number 138 is the one I want but it doesn't come. Not forever. I'm not aware of him at first, too busy shaking my head and swearing under my breath about the fucking rain and the bus and then finally I turn round and there he is, smiling as if to say, it's only a bus, it's only rain. It's the smile and the face and everything, just everything, that pulls me in. I think I could look at it forever and still want more. And I don't know how we started talking or who said what first because it felt like there had been so many words between us already.

After a while I don't want the bus to turn up any more; I want to stay there in the cold and rain and talk to the man with the smile and the face all night. My hair is like rats' tails and my mascara is smudged from the wet but none of it matters. It's just him and me and possibilities stretching out ahead of us. It was that quick, Clara, lightning-fast.

The newsroom was ripe with the smell of last night's microwaved dinners and overtired nightshifters. Empty crisp packets abandoned on desks and half-empty cups of tea left in open defiance of laminated signs that warned people to clean up after themselves. Stacks of newspapers strewn across the desks and on the floor, and the noise, the noise; the phones were ringing, never silent. People shouted about trucks and headlines and clips for packages and *fuckwits who don't do their jobs properly* and slammed down phones and answered them, dispensing – always – with hellos and goodbyes.

I waded through all this like treacle, moving at a different speed to everyone else. There had been no question of staying at home, the home I shared with Jonny, surrounded by his clothes and belongings, all taunting me in his absence. The constant churn of questions in my mind: *where was he? Where had he gone?* I needed to escape, to find some normality, but as I walked into the newsroom I realised it didn't matter where I was; my thoughts followed me everywhere.

I threw my bag down on the desk, startling Jake. He turned to see me.

'Jesus,' he said, and he looked at me through pinched eyes, 'hard night?'

I picked up an old letter on my desk and pretended to read it.

'Coffee?' I asked. He nodded.

'I'll come with you.'

Crossing the newsroom he talked about a court case that was happening later on in the week, about filming a back-grounder, about setting up interviews. The white noise of his chatter drilled into my brain. I nodded and looked at the wall of TV monitors to distract myself. Picture feeds coming in from different locations and countries; one showed soldiers in Iraq, another one had footage of last night's football game. And then, a square in Brighton. Where you lived, Clara. Your flat. The recognition hit me like a jolt. Even when I didn't see your face I couldn't forget.

On another screen I saw Jane Fenchurch, one of the new reporters, getting ready to go on air, doing her make-up in the camera lens, unaware that half the newsroom could see her. She looked like she was in a cave, bathed in an eerie orange light and dressed, alarmingly, in a leopard-print fur jacket.

'Fucking hell,' Jake said, looking at the same screen, 'Robbie's going to love that.'

The coffee bar was breakfast-busy, people toasting bread, stuffing croissants into their mouths, serving watery bacon and beans. I saw the girl from online who never washed her hair leaning into the vat of porridge, examining its consistency in the ladle and then shaking her head. Even she wouldn't eat it. All that food congealing under hot lamps, breathed on, coughed on, stirred and fingered, it made my stomach turn over. Still, couldn't remember the last time I had eaten so I grabbed a muffin in cellophane wrapping. Clean, sterile.

At the far end of the canteen there was a small TV with the sound down. Pictures of cars skidding on ice, kids sledging down snowy hills were being played under the strapline: BREAKING NEWS – FROZEN BRITAIN.

'Breaking news, my arse,' Jake said.

We sat down at a free table, me flicking the crumbs away with my napkin. My coffee was too hot to drink so I stirred it, clockwise, anticlockwise, making dark swirls in the foam, avoiding Jake's stare. I was buying time, thinking, rehearsing the words. '*Oh by the way, Jake, you know that girl who's gone missing, she's a friend and my boyfriend was the last person to see her, more sugar?* How was I to parcel up my bombshell and deliver it with coffee and croissants in the canteen?

But he met me halfway.

'Soooo . . .' he said, his mouth forming an O. 'Before that car pulled out, you were about to tell me something.'

'I was?' I asked, finally looking up. He was sitting back in the chair, hands clasped round his head, the short sleeves of his T-shirt showing his muscles stretching. The contrary nature of NNN's heating system meant you had to dress for summer when it was freezing outside and vice versa.

'Come on, Rachel, I don't bite,' he said, and then, 'Is it Jonny, are you two OK.'

I smiled at that – the way he thought we'd had a tiff, or split up. How innocent that would have been. So ordinary and fixable.

'Yes and no.' And then I closed my eyes and jumped in, like diving into a cold pool of water, 'I don't know where he is.'

His eyes narrowed into slits, his face a puzzle.

'I thought he was out in Afghanistan filming? You can never get hold of anyone there, you know that.' He was trying but he knew there must have been more. His lips settled into a half-smile.

'Nick, his friend, his colleague rang last night. Jonny didn't get on the flight.'

'Oh.' It was all people could think to say to me. 'I don't get it.'

'You're not supposed to, I'm not supposed to, it's all hidden and twisted and I can't see what's going on, I can't see anything.' My hand banged on the table, shaking the coffee cups. And then his hand was on mine, gripping it.

'It's OK, it's OK, he'll be fine, he's only been gone a day or two, he'll turn up,' he said as if Jonny was a cat who had strayed too far.

'It's three,' I said. 'It's been three days.' His grip loosened but his hand remained on mine. I glanced around, suddenly aware of how it might look. Jake's stare didn't leave me though, searching for the answers to his questions on my face. For a moment he said nothing and I thought I had said enough.

'What else, Rachel?'

And then I saw it from the corner of my eye, your face on the TV screen. Your timing, always impeccable. Clara.

'That,' I said, nodding to the screen. And somehow everything loosened and the words flowed, like I couldn't stop them even if I wanted to. 'Jonny was with her on the night she went missing.'

'Her?' Jake was incredulous, eyes saucer-wide. 'What the fuck . . . why? I mean how do you know?'

'I went to see the police in Brighton, they showed me the CCTV, Jonny and Clara walking along the promenade, then they're gone.' I laughed a jittery laugh. 'Just like that.'

'Why would he have been with her, Jesus Christ?' He was shaking his head in disbelief.

'He knows her,' I said as if that explained everything. I knew it explained nothing.

'Oh,' he said, his words eluding him. And I could hear the thought turning over in his head: *he knows her, he knows her*. It made everything darker, murkier.

'Clara,' I said, pausing to make sure I had his full attention, 'Clara O'Connor is my best friend.'

'I pay you all that fucking money and you turn up on air looking like you've escaped from a zoo?' I was standing at the news desk next to Robbie and watched as a bit of spittle flew from his mouth and landed on his computer screen. I heard a muffled voice on the other end. Jane must have been trying to explain. Always a mistake.

'Jane . . . Jane, listen to me, dear. I haven't got a fucking clue what you were saying about the champion potholers down the cave. It could have been a Bafta-winning fucking commentary but I did not hear a word of it. NOT A FUCKING WORD. And you want to know why?' He paused and I looked around to see the rest of the news desk smirking, waiting for Robbie to finish the assassination.

'Good. I'll tell you why, Jane. I couldn't take my eyes off the monstrosity you were wearing. I wouldn't let my gran go down the bingo with that on. And here's the thing I'm guessing Jane, just hazarding a wild fucking guess from the e-mails we're getting, is that ninety-nine per cent of our viewers felt the same.'

He slammed the receiver down, his fat hands shaking from excitement, and turned to me.

'Haven't you got any work to do?' His face was deep

red, chest heaving. I noticed a spot of yellow on his green polo shirt, a leftover from his fried-egg breakfast.

'I need to speak to you,' I said and it was there, a flash across his face. Anger, sympathy, I couldn't work it out.

'Let's go to the meeting room,' he said, hauling himself out of his chair.

The meeting room was a rectangle with no windows, a large white table, twelve chairs, a flip chart in the corner and too-bright lighting. Despite the name it was clearly designed to discourage long meetings, or meetings of any kind at all, because sitting there it was often possible to experience the physical sensation of your soul escaping you.

I pulled out a chair and looked up at the flip chart. Someone had written in red marker pen *BANNED WORDS* and underlined it three times as if to press the point home. Under the headline were the words:

STRIKE ACTION = STRIKES
FLORAL TRIBUTES – who the hell sends these?

And in capitals:

HOSPITALISED – POLICE SPEAK DO NOT USE.

Robbie wheezed as he sat down, wedging himself into the chair. He rested his arms across his beer belly.

'Jake tells me you know this missing woman.'

'She's a friend,' I said. He rolled his eyes to the ceiling and shook his head.

'The press conference was on Monday and it's . . .' He paused and in an overdramatic gesture lifted his wrist up to read the date on his watch. 'Today is Wednesday.'

'I did try. I mean I tried before I went on air but . . .' I stopped. My excuses sounded so hollow. 'I was in shock', such a clichéd phrase, such a get-out-of-jail card, I couldn't bring myself to say the words. Robbie wasn't listening anyway. He was looking out of the door, eyes fixed on something beyond the meeting room with a glassy concentration like an animal sizing up its prey. He shook his head and then turned back to me.

'See, I'm thinking, Rachel, that I've had a fucking correspondent talking about an investigation on the bloody news one moment then helping police the next. I'm thinking newspapers, stories, front pages. I'm thinking how much they'd love it,' he said, wiping a film of sweat from his brow.

I stifled a smile, pretending to yawn instead. With anyone else I would have been subjected to a lecture on professional ethics, on conflict of interest and not becoming the story. But Robbie was a creature of the gutter, an old-time hack who would do anything for a story if he thought he could get away with it. I knew what was coming next.

'You're off the story,' he said. 'I won't tell anyone why, it's none of their business.'

I knew there was no way round it. I couldn't front a story when I was one of the characters in it. But still, I hated the thought of Robbie wresting control from my hands, of another reporter talking as if they knew you and Jonny, telling the world about your character, your past. I wanted to make Robbie realise what he was losing. I wanted him to sweat his decision a bit more.

I sat back in my chair and nodded. 'You're right,' I said, 'especially now that the police are telling me things in confidence, I can't be seen to be close to the story, no matter how frustrating that is for me.' My face settled into a weak smile and I waited.

A beat, a flash in his eyes and then it was gone. He screwed up his face in an attempt at sympathy which made him look like he was trying to pass wind.

'Rachel, I want you to know I am really sorry to hear she's a friend. I hope they find her,' he said. I knew he hadn't finished. 'And uh . . . the police, they saying much to you?'

'A bit,' I said in a whisper and I leant so close to him I could smell the stale coffee on his breath, 'quite a bit.'

He smiled, salivating like a dog who'd eyed a treat.

'So . . .' the word whistled through his teeth, 'any leads?'

I paused to choose my words and nodded my head slowly. 'They've got a few really interesting ones,' I said and saw his mouth hanging open, waiting for me to hand it to him. I leant closer still. 'But like you say, Robbie, I need to keep my distance.'

Chapter Nine

NATIONAL NEWS NETWORK claimed to be 'first with the news' – a motto its team of journalists, to Robbie's fury, managed to prove wrong time and time again. But when it came to disseminating gossip my colleagues were unsurpassed. A rough calculation told me I had about five minutes from leaving Robbie in the meeting room until the place was buzzing with talk of me and you.

As a rule newsrooms don't do pity or sympathy particularly well – the last thing I wanted were awkward hugs from Jenny in accounts, or sympathy strokes from the lecherous Ian in charge of the early bulletin. But I knew they would be chewing me over along with their lunchtime chilli jackets and tuna wraps and making sly jokes about me in the Duke of Cambridge after work. The whispers, the stares, becoming the story; I couldn't sit around and wait for that. Instead I went back to my desk and pulled up my list of running stories on the computer, searching through it for something to do. That's when I came to Ann Carvello's name. She had said no to so many people. She had already said no to me but I'd never let that stop me before.

'If anyone asks,' I said to Jake as I grabbed my bag, 'tell them I'm meeting a contact. And I'm taking a crew.' I ran out of the newsroom before he could ask any questions.

The blue sky that promised so much earlier in the day had been consumed by clouds. They grew thicker and thicker as I drove out of London until there was nothing left but grey. By the time I reached the A10 gobstoppers of hail started to fall, shattering like pieces of glass on the windscreen. A trail of white spray fell off the car in front. I pinched my eyes in an effort to see the road, to find a way through.

I twisted my neck one way and the other and tried to loosen the tension that seemed to have calcified my bones. Tiredness was bleeding into my head.

What was I doing, out there, driving into the middle of nowhere (or Leigh-on-Sea, which was the same thing)? Ostensibly I was taking a punt on a story, but don't think I had forgotten about you and Jonny. You were the real reason, Clara. I'd run out of places to look for you. I was too close to the search, so tight up against it, I couldn't see a thing. I needed clarity and perspective and without space I knew I would never achieve them.

Entering Leigh-on-Sea the road opened up to reveal the water, thrashing and black and desolate. I didn't see a soul on the approach to the town, no figures out walking, wrapped up against the elements; the benches were empty, the trees bare of leaves. The place was bleak, abandoned; even the fish and chip shops were boarded up.

I'd approached Ann Carvello the week before, just after the verdict. I had been standing by our live point blown about by the wind which tunnels down the Old Bailey, when I caught a flash of her white hair out of the corner of my eye. Turning round I saw her scurrying away from the court, head bent down so far her scarf almost swallowed her up. She couldn't run, not at her age, and anyway it would have attracted too much attention. She wanted to slip by unnoticed and she very nearly did because no one else saw her except for me. I ripped out my earpiece and walked as fast as I could. By the end of the street I'd caught up with her.

'Mrs Carvello?' I said as if I wasn't sure it was her. I'd stopped right in front of her and she almost walked into me. She lifted her head and looked at me with her bloodshot eyes.

'I don't think so, love,' she said through her trademark red-lipsticked lips. 'There's nothing I can say.' She nodded and went on her way, a woman with nothing left in her life except a story that everyone wanted to hear.

I found her house a few streets back from the beach. A largish semi with a neatly tended garden. On either side of her painted green door empty hanging baskets swung in the wind. Appearances, I thought, must have mattered a lot to Ann Carvello.

I knocked and waited, pulling my cagoule around me to hide my workwear. Behind the door I could hear footsteps, padding through the hall, then a face mottled through the glass.

'Who is it?' she asked gently.

'It's Rachel, I hope you don't mind, I was passing by.' I imagined her thinking of a Rachel she knew – it helps having a common name – a niece, a friend, and not wanting to offend them by following up with a 'Rachel who?'

I heard her unhook the chain and open the door slowly, her white hair appearing through it first, then her face, red lipstick even at home. She was dressed in a pale blue cardigan and a tweed skirt. Immaculate.

She stared for a moment, sizing me up, and then I saw the recognition creep across her face. The door began to shut again. I moved my foot quickly to stop it.

'I thought you might like to talk to me,' I said.

'I have nothing to say.' She pushed the door harder against my foot.

'I don't think you knew anything about it, did you? All those interviews your so-called friends have given, your neighbour in the *Sun* today, your old schoolfriend in the *Mail on Sunday* at the weekend. They believe it but I don't.'

There were footsteps on the pavement, the sound of the gate opening. A man delivering a free newspaper was coming down her garden path. She shifted uncomfortably and shook her head in his direction and he went on his way. I raised my voice against the rain, loud enough for him to hear.

'They don't understand that you could live with someone for so long and not know. But I know people are good at hiding things when they really want to.'

'The rain,' she said, 'sometimes I think it's never going to stop.'

'I understand.' It was dripping down me now, running off my nose and soaking through my hair.

She peered out of the doorway and turned her head from side to side to see if anyone was looking. Then she said; 'Five minutes, that's it, and I won't be quoted, do you understand.'

'Of course.'

A woman pushing a pram walked past her gate craning her neck to see who Ann was talking to.

'Quickly,' she said, ushering me in, 'before I change my mind.'

The living room smelt of polish and Shake n' Vac and the trail lines of the Hoover on the carpet suggested it had been recently vacuumed. On the windowsill a neat arrangement of china, figures of a girl in a petticoat and hat with a lamb, another of a dog. A little basket of potpourri gave off a sickly sweet smell. School-uniformed children smiled out from photo frames on the mantelpiece, and couples kissed in wedding photographs. A young man in a graduation picture. A timeline of happy family events. Not one of Ann though. None of her husband.

She plumped a green velvet cushion unnecessarily and motioned for me to sit down. Then she left me and went into the kitchen; the sound of a kettle boiling and cups arranged, and a few moments later she reappeared carrying a tray with cups and saucers, a teapot and a plate of garibaldi biscuits. These little things mattered to her, perhaps even more so now.

She sat down in the chair opposite me and pulled her skirt down around her, flicking an imaginary crumb from her lap.

'You're probably wondering how I could have been so stupid?' Her voice was stretched and thin.

'That has never crossed my mind,' I said.

'My friends,' and she gave a weak laugh, 'those who still come near, they say they believe me but it's in their eyes. The doubt, it's there all the time. Not that I blame them, I wonder how I could have lived with him all that time and never suspected a thing.' She looked away from me and lifted the cup to her lips, her hands shaking, and took the smallest sip before placing it back on the saucer.

'He was your husband,' I said as softly as I could.

'I had five children to look after, he worked all hours, he'd come in at night and I'd have his tea on the table. That was the way it was then. There was none of this 'sharing roles'. He'd go out to the pub a few times a week like most men. I never questioned it. He always provided for us, never so much as raised a hand to me or the children. It was all so . . . so . . . ordinary.'

'When you're not looking it's hard to find something,' I said. I noticed how green her eyes were, watered down now through age but still striking.

Ann nodded and fixed me with a stare as if she was sizing me up. 'You seem sharper than the others,' she said. 'When you're too close to something everything is out of focus, it's only when you step back and see it through a different lens that it all begins to make sense.' She reached for her cup and saucer again and let her hand hover over them as if she was making a decision. 'When I look back now,' she said, 'I can see my whole life was a lie.'

Her confession startled me, the way it came so easily, how it was still so raw on her. Throughout the trial she'd been silent, supportive. She must have seen my surprise.

'Oh I never believed he did it, not for a moment,' she said. 'I didn't want it to be true, every ounce of me, everything, I wanted it to be shown as the awful, cruel lie that it was. He kept on saying that I had to believe him, that I was the only one left who did. And I did. I told him over and over again that I did.'

'Sometimes it's easier that way,' I said, reaching for a garibaldi.

She closed her eyes as if to summon up the memory. 'One day in court, I remember so clearly, I heard him telling the prosecutor why he went out driving late at night. He said he was an insomniac, he couldn't sleep so he'd take the car and go for a drive.' She paused and I saw her lips wobble, something catching in her voice. 'But the thing is, he fell asleep the moment his head hit the pillow. Always. Not once in all the years we were together had I known him to have trouble falling asleep.' She clicked her fingers. Snap. 'It was only a little lie but I knew then that he'd lied about everything. That's when it all came crashing down. All those years of marriage, the children, everything just imploded.' She pulled a handkerchief from the inside of her sleeve and wiped her eyes. 'It's the little things that give people away, that's how they can hide for so long because those things are so little we often miss them. But if you look carefully enough you'll find them.' She paused and in a whisper said: 'I was married to him for thirty-one years and I hope he rots in hell for what he did to those women.'

Those women.

Four women – mothers, wives, daughters – murdered by Charlie Carvello, whose crimes went undetected for decades until science finally caught up with him. He'd been sentenced to life at the Old Bailey the week before.

'I'm sorry,' I said, 'and I'm sorry no one believes you.'

'You asked me if I had something to say love, well it's this. You can be so close to someone for a lifetime and not know who they really are.'

I looked at Ann and tried to see beneath her immaculate make-up, the hair set into place. And all I could see was a hollow nothingness that told its own story. All the memories built up and treasured through the years, her children, her love, all the smiles and laughter and hard times, they'd all been stripped out of her by his lie.

'Now,' she said, 'looking back, I think there were signs. There are always signs and clues, it's a question of whether we want to see them. Most of the time we only see what we want to see.'

We talked for another hour until the tea went cold and she made another pot. We talked about her children, her treatment by journalists, 'most of them were awful, not like you', and by the time I suggested my cameraman came in and record a few minutes with her – *your story, how you want to tell it* – there was no resistance.

When we were finished I gave her a hug as I headed to my car, her body even more frail to touch than it looked. 'Thank you,' she said, 'for understanding.' I told her not to mention it and saw the relief in her face, her features softened. A weight lifted. I'd given her the chance to have her say. And then I waved her goodbye taking with me thirty minutes of the interview everyone wanted with Ann the wife of a serial killer. At work people always said I had a knack of getting people to talk, as if it was luck. But luck had nothing to do with it. I could just see what people needed, what they wanted, before they even knew themselves.

It was dark by the time I arrived in West London. Pulling up outside the aircraft hangar that was the NNN news factory I could see the harsh lights of a newsroom hard at work. Once parked, I ran from the car to the door, swiping my ID card to let myself in. I stopped for a moment to find my phone and check for missed calls – *has Jonny tried to reach me?* I felt the hard edges of the tape inside my bag and smiled, imagining Robbie's face when I told him the interview it contained. Finally I found my phone in the side pocket of my bag. Five missed calls: one from my Aunty Laura, two from Jake, two from Sandra, Jonny's mum. *The police have contacted her. I must call her.*

I marched on towards Robbie's desk and was within earshot of his ranting, 'You missed your slot, you idiot,' when I felt a hand on my arm pulling me in the opposite direction.

'You might want to give him a wide berth,' Jake said, nodding in Robbie's direction.

He said nothing else, but his arm was firm around me and I felt myself being swept from the newsroom. When I tried to protest he said he would explain, *outside.*

We'd almost made it back to the door when I saw it. The photograph on the big screen, towering above the newsroom. I didn't recognise the suit, the tie, and the face was younger, but unmistakable. The room slipped away from me; nothing else was left but the picture of him until he disappeared too, replaced by DCI Gunn talking to the camera. And even before I saw it flash up on the screen I knew what was coming next. The CCTV of you and Jonny together on the promenade. It was there in front of me, the shot zooming in, closer and closer still. So close, I thought I could reach out and touch you.

'Let's get out of here,' Jake said and I followed him without a word.

We went round the corner to Ozzie's, an old-style greasy spoon. Only the old hacks still went there at lunchtime for fried bread and sausages. Everyone else went to the new deli that sold carrot and ginger and spirulina juice and smoothies and weird combinations of soup. Ozzie himself was an old Greek guy who had eaten too much of his own food and insisted on combing the remaining strands of his dyed black hair over his bald head. The café was empty but he showed us to a table by the window, looking mildly pissed off when we insisted on sitting at the back, out of sight, next to a large mirror. We ordered two teas and pretended to look at the yellowing menus he'd given us.

'They announced it this afternoon and released the CCTV at the same time. I tried to call you.'

'It's all wrong. It's so wrong. Jonny wouldn't have touched her. He wouldn't, he couldn't.' I wanted to say it over and over again and scream it very loud until everyone understood: Jonny had nothing to do with your disappearance.

'You said you'd told Robbie everything, Rachel,' Jake said, shaking his head. He was wearing an olive-green 'boarding jacket which he unzipped and pushed over the back of the chair.

'I told him enough.' I didn't want to look at Jake, I didn't want to answer his questions.

'But you didn't tell him your boyfriend was the last person to see her,' he said, slamming the menu shut.

'I don't know that he was.' I was still staring at the words in the menu: omelette and chips, sausage and chips, pizza and chips, thinking of Ozzie's greasy hands touching the food.

'For fuck's sake, Rachel, I'm trying to look out for you here. You can see the headlines: "TV Reporter's Lover Prime Suspect in Friend's Disappearance."'

'You'd never have made it as a subeditor,' I said, watching Jake screw his face up in frustration as Ozzie make his way across the café with our teas.

'What can I get you to eat?' Ozzie asked.

Jake ordered egg and chips. I shook my head and handed Ozzie the menu, prompting him to mutter something about being too thin and needing to fatten up.

Jake sat studying my face and then after checking to see that Ozzie was out of earshot, he smiled weakly and said, 'You're not as good as you think you are. I know what you do, Rachel, I've seen you in action too many times. The way you operate. You tell people what you think they need to hear. You keep from them what you think they don't. It works, time and time again, the way you cast a spell on them. But don't make the mistake of thinking it works with everyone.' I could feel the heat of his eyes on me. He looked different somehow, serious, not to be messed with, unshakeable. I think it was the moment I decided I wanted him on my side.

'OK,' I said. 'Everything.'

I sat there in the dimming light of Ozzie's, with its once-white paint, yellowed by years of frying food, and the smell of chips sinking into my clothes, and I told him about you, Clara, my best friend in the world, the person who'd shot into my grey life like a burst of sunshine. I described the girl who'd laughed and partied with me and promised we'd be friends forever.

I told him that I had believed you, but somehow when you became ill our friendship was derailed and no matter how hard I tried to get us back on track I never quite succeeded.

And then I described how I'd found the photograph in my bedroom, the one of me and Jonny switched for one of you and my mother. I watched his face cloud over, his eyes grow wide and I listened to his questions: *Wasn't I mistaken? How could that happen if no one had broken in?* When I offered no answers I watched it grow darker still.

He asked about you and Jonny, about your relationship – a word that stung me, Clara – he talked about the pair of you in the same breath as if you were a unit now, bound together by the threads of the story. I told him what I knew, going back to the beginning. The first time you and Jonny met not even eighteen months before.

Chapter Ten

September 2005

EIGHT THIRTY P.M. – that's the time I told you the party was starting, which was half an hour later than Jonny and I had told everyone else. I thought it would be better that way, to have more people around when you met him for the first time. I thought it might make it less obvious that there were three people now where before there had only ever been the two of us.

But when we arrive at seven forty-five you are already lounging on one of the deep sofas in the section reserved for Jonny's party and cordoned off with rope. You sit, one leg curled under the other, sipping a mojito. Your dark hair is teased back, like you haven't bothered, and your face is glowing, the whites of your eyes are super-white, set off by black eyeliner which makes them seem unfeasibly big. You're in a purple dress which is low-cut front and back, and killer heels. You lift a long slender arm in the air and wave it in my direction. I see Jonny watching you, then he turns to me, asking with his eyes if it's you. I nod.

The bar is dark, still early-evening quiet, and we make

our way across to you. As we do you stand up, arms outstretched. Your teeth flash a white smile. 'Rach,' you say and kiss me on both cheeks so I get a waft of your perfume. Then you stand back and look at Jonny, taking in his dark hair, his almond eyes, his dress-down cool.

'You always did have good taste in friends, Rach,' and you wink at me before leaning in to kiss Jonny. 'I'm Clara,' you tell him unnecessarily.

'Finally, I get to meet you. I've heard a lot about you,' Jonny says.

'All good things, I hope,' you laugh, a little nervously. 'Did I hear you say you were going to the bar, Rach, mine's a mojito.'

You listen to me groan. 'Nice to see some things never change,' I say.

'Come on, I've only just met him, we have a lot to talk about.' I make a face and you say: 'I promise I'll get the next round in.'

You sink back down on to the sofa and pat the seat next to you. Jonny sits down. 'Rach never tells me a thing,' I hear you whisper as I walk away. 'I'm relying on you to fill in the blanks.'

From the bar I can hear your laughter. It's thick and intoxicating. I'm not in the mood for cocktails, I need something heavy and alcoholic so I buy a bottle of red wine. A couple of Jonny's friends arrive and I say hi to them. When I return to our little section it's filling up – Jonny's colleagues, his gang, the friends he's known for years. The people who have become part of my circle too.

I look over to the sofa and Jonny is smiling, laughing with you. He doesn't look around for me, for his drink even. He's in your thrall. I say hello to a few people on the way and make it over to you but it's awkward because the sofa is only big enough for two people which means I'm one too many. Jonny sees me and gets up to stand. 'Rach, you sit down, you two must be dying for a gossip.'

'Don't worry about us,' you say to Jonny, 'we've known each other so long we have nothing left to talk about. There's nothing we don't know about each other.' Finally you turn to me, fixing me with your smile.

It's a strange thing to say, Clara. You have been away for so long there's a lot you don't know about me. But I catch it, the electricity that sparks between us.

'I can still surprise you, Clara,' I say, chinking your glass as Jonny gets up and makes room for me.

We watch Jonny mingling with his friends, embracing each other in that bear-hug way that men do.

'I was wondering whether you'd turn up. I've been trying to call you all week,' I say, digging my elbow into you gently. 'A few phone calls or texts wouldn't go amiss.'

It's only been a few months since you returned and less since your dad died. I worry about you in Brighton, on your own. I want to make sure you're OK.

'I can see why you're smitten,' you say, eyes trained on him.

'I'm glad you came though.' I give your knee a squeeze. 'It was beginning to feel weird that you hadn't met him. I've told him everything about you.'

'Everything,' you repeat. Your voice is flat, distant. I don't know whether it's a question or a statement. And then you add: 'Not everything, I bet.'

I laugh but I hear it crackling with nerves.

Your hands are on mine, enveloping them, and you look so deep into me, the way you used to when we knew everything about each other, when we could think each other's thoughts, and I wonder if I'm wrong. Maybe you are pleased for me. You're just so hard to read these days.

'It's touching . . .' you say, eyes sparkling, dancing in the light.

'You can see why I love him.' I feel you loosen your grip. Then you lift your hand and use it to flick back a strand of my hair that has been falling into my face. 'He loves me too,' I say and you reach out to me and pull me into a tight embrace. A happiness fizzes through me and then I feel your breath in my ear and your words reach me.

'He doesn't even know you, Rachel,' you say in a whisper, 'he doesn't know who you are.'

It's twelve thirty a.m. and we're out on the street. The cool air is sobering me up after the warmth of the bar. Jonny's friend Dylan has his arm draped over you. I want to go home but I hear your voice, 'Jesus Rachel, you're twenty-five, not forty-five, for God's sake come on.' A cab with its orange light on approaches and you hail it.

I'm sure Jonny doesn't want to go either but Dylan insists. It seems you've rediscovered your old magic tonight and you're using it on him. He has that look in his eyes, fired up with a promise of what might happen, and he's not going to let go. We go to a nameless Soho club, the kind that makes you want to forget everything in the morning. We pay too much to get in and when we slip through the dark curtains that are draped over the door the music thumps through me. I turn to look at Jonny and I know he's feeling the same. You must catch it because next thing you're pulling on my arm, dragging me off to the toilets. Once we're in the cubicle together you produce a little rectangle of paper.

'You need a pick-me-up,' you say.

You cut two fat lines of cocaine on the toilet seat and don't listen to me when I say I'm not in the mood. You swing round and say: 'Come on, Rach, don't tell me you've gone all straight.' You hand me a rolled-up ten-pound note and say, 'It'll be like old times.'

'I don't think so,' I say and I slip out the door.

When I find Jonny I shout in his ear that he needs to take me home. He has a word with Dylan, telling him to make sure you're OK. Even if you don't make it back to my flat I know you'll have a bed for the night.

It seems like ages before we get a cab but for once I don't mind. I'm pleased to be alone with Jonny. It's September, a warm late-summer night. I've always loved London at this time, when most people are asleep, but the city is still alive, awake. It feels like it all belongs to me, the streets, the lights, the moon shining down.

'Looks like your friend is going to make Dylan a very happy man tonight,' he says.

'She was everything you expected, I guess,' I say and wait for you to agree.

We're holding hands but Jonny's grip gets firmer and he pulls me closer. 'Honestly? I thought she was a bit full-on.' I look at you, sensing there's more. 'Oh fuck it, she seemed a bit needy. I guess I wasn't expecting it, not from one of your friends. Does that make me a bad person?'

'Not at all,' I say. There's a smile escaping from the sides of my mouth, creeping across my face. He sees it and kisses me.

He knows me better than you do, Clara. You are wrong.

Chapter Eleven

THE POLICE HAD a search warrant. They were in my flat; I can't tell you how that felt, the violation of it. Knowing they were in there ripping through our belongings, dismantling piece by piece the life I had so carefully, painstakingly constructed. They would be reading the letters, the cards, the e-mails that Jonny and I had sent each other, sharing our moments of intimacy between themselves like a top-shelf magazine to salivate over. And all the time they would be looking for something, the something that would connect Jonny to you. To your disappearance. The something that didn't exist.

I'd filmed those scenes so many times for my TV reports, the men and women in white suits, *forensic experts*, combing through houses and gardens; going about their business under tents erected to shield bodies from prying media eyes. Now I had become a character in the pages of my own storybook.

I wanted to believe that maybe you had just taken flight, Clara, left without trace. That there was no one to blame and that all this was an innocent misunderstanding. But at the back of my mind a thought lurked, a sliver of recognition, like I had known this would happen all along. I'd just been waiting, waiting.

I hadn't returned Jonny's mum's calls. I'm not afraid to admit I was putting it off, like a piece of work you know you've got to tackle but that seems so huge you don't know where to start. And I'd been so absorbed with my own emotions I couldn't face confronting someone else's. But when I saw her number flash up for a third time I knew I couldn't ignore her any longer.

'Sandra,' I said. 'I'm so sorry, I was just about to call you.'

I listened to her echo my own thoughts – *It doesn't make sense Rachel, it doesn't make sense,* and waited patiently while she cried, trying to make comforting sounds. But as she fired her barrage of questions – none of which I could answer – I was aware I was about to lose patience. Didn't she realise I was going out of my mind too? And then the guilt got to me and I offered to drive out to St Albans that evening, 'so you're not alone, Sandra,' I said, 'I don't like the thought of you being alone.'

She agreed, qualifying it with a weak, 'Only if it's not too much trouble.' I thought of the hour's drive to St Albans in traffic at the end of a heavy day.

'Not at all,' I told her. Besides, I had nowhere else to go.

Jonny always joked that if St Albans was a sport it would be golf: prim and proper and ever so middle class. When I confessed to admiring its neat order he teased me that I was turning into his mother: 'Secretly you want that life, don't you? – the detached house with a garden and hanging baskets swinging from the door. If I catch you buying a Nissan Micra I'm going to get very worried,' he joked.

I noticed as I pulled into the driveway Sandra's pristine ten-year-Micra had now been replaced by a shiny silver VW Golf.

The wind whipped at my face as I rang the door and waited, listening to Sandra make her way through the hall. When she appeared from behind it she welcomed me as if I had just popped in for a cup of tea. I gave her a kiss and a hug because I thought the circumstances demanded more than a peck on the cheek but feeling her tense in my arms, I realised my gesture was unwelcome. 'Come in,' she said, taking my coat, 'I'll put the kettle on.'

Once in the kitchen, she sat me down at the heavy oak table and busied herself opening and closing the fridge, the cupboards and drawers, extracting from them teaspoons, plates, milk and mugs, a cake (lemon drizzle) that looked freshly baked, and laid them neatly and precisely on the table, as if they were the framework on which our chat would hinge. Jonny's name, still unspoken between us, hung oppressively in the room. I studied the floral patterns on the oil-cloth table cover to distract myself from her manic whistling and resisted the urge to throw the china milk jug across the room and watch it drip down her perfect duck-egg blue walls – anything just to grab her attention and force her to sit down and talk about the real reason I was here. Jonny. Instead I took a deep breath and focused on the sound of the rain drumming against the window.

Sandra has always struck me as a model of composure, a little schoolmarmish perhaps and prone to saying things like 'nonsense on stilts', but solid and firm in a stiff-upper-lip kind of way. When Jonny's dad died two and a half years earlier he told me how she threw herself into life at the golf club and entering baking competitions, filling her time instead of sitting around and moping.

And don't get me wrong, I could see the lemon drizzle and perfectly laid table was just her way of trying to cope, but that was the problem. She wasn't coping, it was obvious she was falling apart. Her flashing eyes, her sunken face and bed-messy hair told me a truth she would never have admitted to. She was being eaten up by anxiety. Her son was the only family she had left and now he was slipping away too. It was painful to see.

Finally she sat down and fixed me with her searching, pleading eyes. I felt myself reeling under the pressure. She needed me to offer her theories which would explain away *the situation*, when I was still searching for them myself. God knows I wanted to help her; I just wished she could have looked at my face for more than a second and seen it etched with pain. I was floundering too, sinking deep, deep into despair. Jonny was her son, but he was also my boyfriend, my future.

She poured and strained the tea and I heard her say, 'Just a splash for you, I always remember these things.' I knew she was waiting for me to begin the conversation so I reached for the jug to add a little more milk to my tea and took a sip of it just to play for time, to allow my brain to turn over and come up with a form of words that hit the right note, both soothing and comforting.

'They're talking about him like he's responsible,' she said finally. 'He's the headline every hour. I can't listen to it.' She turned to stare at the radio on the counter as if she didn't trust it to be silent and took a slurp of her tea. 'And your news station too, Rachel, I would have expected more from them. Can't you make it stop?' Her eyes flashed at me for a second before darting back to the table. 'Cake?' she said, pushing the lemon drizzle towards me.

The inflection in her voice was unmistakable. *Can't you make it stop?* I began to wish I hadn't come.

'They'll carry on running those stories until he's found, Sandra, and as much as I wish I had the power to stop them, you know I can't. He was the last known person with Clara, that's why he's a suspect,' I told her as gently as I could.

'I know how the law works, Rachel, I've watched police dramas too,' she said dismissively. She began tapping her teaspoon on the side of her mug. 'What I don't understand is why he was with Clara. He didn't even like the girl.' She spat the last words out, as if they were dirt in her mouth. 'He said she always acted like you owed her something. I thought that was a strange thing to say, Rachel, very strange indeed.'

My reserves of patience were almost exhausted. I knew Sandra was hurting, I knew she was tormented not knowing where Jonny was, but all this, it really wasn't fair. *Don't make me your punchbag*, I wanted to shout. I found it hard to believe Jonny had confided in her, and even if it was true he certainly wouldn't have wanted her to use the information as ammunition against me.

Reaching over to the lemon drizzle I cut a slice of cake and put it on my plate. My hands were sticky with the icing so I licked it off. She waited, expecting an answer, but I wasn't in any hurry to give her one. So I looked around as I pulled the cake apart with my fingers. Next to the wooden dresser was pinned her calendar. Today's date was circled and BOOK CLUB, written in capitals.Tomorrow was GOLF/MARJORIE. Further down into the following week was BRIDGE. All the events that punctuated her middle-class existence. They would happen without her now, though I suspected the chat would make her ears burn.

'I don't imagine Jonny told you everything,' I said finally and without waiting for a response I told her that you'd had some tough times – my exact words were *'Clara struggled with mental health issues,'* which I thought couched your illness in suitably formal terms for her consumption.

I sat back picking at the cake, hoping the explanation would suffice.

'I still don't understand why she would take that out on you as if it was your fault she had a breakdown,' she said, staring at me for longer than necessary. I let out a long, frustrated sigh. That wasn't what I had meant. She was twisting my words.

A pain sliced through my head. I thought it might be

hunger so I took another bite of cake; the sugar and citrus immediately made my mouth water. Seeing that I couldn't talk with my mouth full Sandra carried on. 'When was the last time you saw her, Rachel?' she asked. It was the obvious question, one I would be asked again and again until I could tell it so word-perfectly I would be accused of reading it like a script.

At that stage I'd only recounted it for DCI Gunn, carefully picking my way through the details, making a mental note of what I'd said and how.

'Two and a half weeks ago,' I told her, 'at the flat. It was a bit awkward really. Jonny and I were meeting friends in town for dinner but she insisted on coming beforehand.' I watched Sandra's eyes narrowing, her clouded mind trying to glean something from my words.

'She'd called me a few days earlier to tell me she was coming, said she was going to a gallery in Bethnal Green and would call by on the way back. I told her I would be pushed for time because I had to be in Soho for nine p.m. but she wouldn't let it drop.'

What I didn't tell Sandra or DCI Gunn was why you came, Clara. That the date, January the seventh, seemed to matter to you more than it should. It was my mother's birthday. A day I'd never celebrated with her when she was alive and one I let pass by unnoticed until you returned eighteen months before. I was surprised how you'd insisted on seeing me to mark it. I didn't understand why you'd want to rake over the past but I humoured you that first year. Now you were coming back for seconds.

'I can't let you mark such a big anniversary on your own,' you said like it wasn't an offer but a demand. 'We can have a few glasses of wine, toast Niamh and then you and Jonny can go out. I don't mind. I'll be quite happy to chill at home.'

By 'home' you meant my home.

'I won't be back from work until after seven,' I said, feeling pushed into a corner.

'Fine, I'll let myself in,' you told me and I made a mental note to get my key back from you.

That evening when I opened the door to my flat a heavy garlicky smell wafted out from the kitchen.

'Rach,' you said, emerging from the kitchen wearing my apron, 'have this, I know you'll need it.' You handed me a glass of cold white wine. You were wearing jeans and an angora sweatshirt in dusty pink; your hair was down, shining as the light caught it.

'I told you. I'm eating out,' I said as I watched you dish up two bowls of risotto and put them on the table.

'An hour, Rachel, tell me you can spare an hour?' You pulled out a chair for me and sat down in yours. I watched the steam rising from the risotto and you blowing it before you put it in your mouth.

'How was the gallery? I asked. I noticed you had used the Skandium dishes I kept for good.

'The gallery?' you said, and stopped blowing on your fork.

'The one you were visiting in London today.' I saw your eyes flash, a blush warmed your cheeks.

'Oh, that one. Disappointing really, overhyped in my

opinion.' You weren't looking at me, just down at the bowl in front of you. And then you said; 'Would you bring her back, you know, if you could?' I sighed and pushed my chair back from the table. I didn't understand the fixation. Why you wanted to revive an old ghost.

'You have no idea what it was like,' I said, 'what she was like. To live with a mother whose eyes are full of disappointment and every day you see that. And as if you needed to be told she explains to you time and time again that you are a reminder of where her life went wrong. And she drinks to block everything out, she gets so drunk that nothing else matters and that's what you come home to every day from school.'

You hadn't even looked up; your head was still peering over your bowl, blowing, blowing, softly. *You ask a question and you don't even fucking listen to my answer.* I didn't want to talk about my mother; I didn't want to be with you at that moment. All the times when I'd called and invited you out over the last few weeks and you hadn't responded, and there you were when I least wanted you. It wasn't about comfort or remembering. It was something else buried deep, something I didn't want to touch.

'So that's a no then?' you said.

'My life got better when she died, I think that is obvious.'

'And you always knew that it would,' you said, fixing me with a smile that made me shiver. 'You always knew.'

I got up to leave the table and walk away from the conversation you kept dragging up. I thought you would have got the message by then that I didn't want to talk about it. You'd tried once before, hadn't you? Only a few weeks before on our skiing holiday. On one of those endless chair lifts when there was only me and you and we imagined we were being taken up and up through the clouds to the top of the world. You'd breathed it then along with the sharp Alpine air, dancing around the subject before spelling it out. Judging by your face that day I could tell my answer was unsatisfactory but we didn't bring it up again because shortly afterwards you had fallen badly on a black run and we'd been too preoccupied with getting you to a doctor to revive an old conversation.

'We both know what happened, Clara,' I said firmly and watched you shrink a little under my stare.

'We both know the truth,' you said, and taking my bowl you walked into the kitchen and threw the risotto in the bin.

I left those conversational details out when I recounted my story to Sandra and DCI Gunn. I think most people in my situation would have done the same. We all know words uttered in the heat of the moment could in hindsight be taken out of context, imbued with meaning that was never intended. You can't blame me for sticking to the sanitised version.

A little while later when Sandra and I had run out of conversation we called it a night. Once upstairs she walked me past Jonny's old room with the double bed where we normally slept to the spare room with a few sheets and blankets laid out on a camp bed. It was clear there were some privileges I was only entitled to in Jonny's presence. I slept fitfully, the springs of the mattress digging into my back, and each time I woke the same thought fluttered through my head, moving, teasing me, offering me glimpses of something I couldn't catch. Fragments of our story I needed to piece together one by one by one.

Chapter Twelve

I LEFT SANDRA'S house early the next morning, driving down the M1 as the dark of the night faded out to a milky, dusty light. It was too early to see the sun proper but occasionally little promises of it hit my windscreen, causing me to blink. There were few cars around, nothing to stop or stall my journey; I felt like I was floating through the air towards something brighter in the distance ahead.

By the time I reached Westminster the sun was glinting off the river. The outlines of Big Ben, the Houses of Parliament and the surrounding buildings slicing up the cobalt-blue sky. I crossed Westminster Bridge and parked close to the South Bank, pulled my sunglasses from my bag and my winter coat around me and started walking along the banks of the Thames amongst the early-morning joggers and suits heading for breakfast meetings.

From the moment I had seen your face in the police station, Clara, a thick fog had filled my mind. I had been blinded, incapable of working out what I needed to do. Now in the chill of the morning it began to lift. My thoughts had a sharpness to them, a clarity that had been lacking. I realised I had found myself locked out, kept in the dark, the flow of information about your disappearance siphoned off before it reached me. DCI Gunn had publicly named Jonny as a suspect without so much as even a phone call to warn me. And since I was officially off the story I was no longer privy to the private police briefings. I couldn't even rely on Sarah Pitts with her schoolgirl grudges to keep me up to date. So many pieces of your puzzle were missing, Clara, and I knew that before I found you and Jonny, I had to find them first.

There was only one person who might be able to help.

I sat in one of the riverside cafés and ordered a soya latte, smoked salmon and scrambled eggs, watching the waitress move out of sight before I called the landline in your flat. It rang, once, twice, three times and then a whisper of a voice answered it as if she was unsure how to speak into a phone.

'Amber?' I asked, knowing it was her.

'Who is this?' she said, suspiciously.

'It's Rachel, Clara's friend, we don't know each other but I need your help, I—'

'I can't talk to you,' she said. Another moment and I knew she would hang up.

'Wait, please Amber, just hear me out, for Clara. It's important. That is all I ask,' I said. And I explained softly that we both wanted the same thing, how you would want your friends to work together. Would it do any harm to meet?

⊸o⊷

In Brighton hours later, I waited on the beach with a coffee which cooled in seconds under the bracing sea winds. The sea air was sharper than in London, the blue sky endless. Would she come? Amber: your friend, not mine.

It was then I saw her descending the steps from the promenade, her slight figure crouched against the wind. She looked over to the café where I was sitting and when she saw me she gave a wave and a smile which she seemed to regret as soon as it left her lips. She didn't look up again until she was next to me.

She was different to how I remembered her at the press conference. Looser, by which I mean less stiff and tense. Her blond hair was tied back casually and she was wearing trainers and wide trousers that billowed and fluttered in the wind. I noticed a blue yoga mat sticking out from her bag.

I stood up and pushing my sunglasses up on to my head, reached out to hug her. She recoiled, offering her hand for me to shake instead. When I did, it was cold and limp in mine.

'I've told the police everything I know. I'm sure you have too,' she said as she sat down opposite me with a weak smile. She fished a thick mustard scarf out of her bag and wound it round and round her neck, dipping her chin into it so I could only see her top lip move as she spoke. 'I don't really know how we can help each other.' I pushed my sunglasses back over my eyes and followed her gaze out to the horizon. Then she said; 'The reporters have been calling nonstop. I don't want to talk to the papers or do television interviews, I've already done what I can to help. I can't do any more.' She turned to look at me, 'You are here as Clara's friend, aren't you?'

Her voice was cold and flat but there was a sting in her words that surprised me. I had imagined we might exchange a few conversational pleasantries before I manoeuvred the conversation round to what I had come for – information that might lead me to you.

'Clara is my oldest friend, this has nothing to do with my job,' I said and watched her raise her eyebrows. 'Oh my God,' I shouted, throwing myself back in the chair, 'it wasn't like THAT. I got sent on a story – the first time I knew it was Clara was when I walked into the press conference and then it all started and before I knew it I was on air talking about her. It wasn't planned. I told my bosses I couldn't do the story as soon as I got back to the office. You can't think I would have chosen to report on my best friend's disappearance.' I let my head sink into my hands. 'The last few days have been the worst of my life. I'm here because I don't know where to turn. I don't know what to do next.'

She moved her head up out of her scarf and let my words sink in. But still she stared, unsmiling. There was something else, something she was holding against me. I picked my words carefully.

'I think Clara found me a bit suffocating lately,' I told her. 'I never meant to be like that, it's just . . .' I paused and waited for my admission to disarm her. 'It's just that she is so fragile at times I felt like if I didn't look out for her nobody would.'

'You're not her only friend, Rachel,' she said defensively. And then; 'Look, I shouldn't have come.' I saw her finger her bag as if she was getting ready to leave. 'I don't know what happened between you but I know something wasn't right.'

'I always tried to look out for her, I never meant it—'

'When I saw her after Christmas she was different, like she was shrinking into herself. '

'She'd had a bad fall when we were skiing,' I said. 'She'd bruised her ribs. It shook her up. I think it would have shaken anyone up.'

Through my sunglasses I could see Amber tilt her head to one side and narrow her gaze as if she was trying to see something she couldn't quite make out.

'Why did you bother with her? I mean, she hardly made an effort. If someone treated me like that I would drop them.'

I winced. Amber was painting me as this desperate, needy person who wouldn't let you go. You must have planted those seeds in her mind, Clara. It made me worry about your mental state even more because nothing could have been further from the truth.

'I guess you don't understand her like I do,' I said quietly.

'Really? All I could see were the calls and the texts and the invitations she turned down. She wanted some space.'

I saw Amber's cheeks colour a little, flushed with rage on your behalf. But how could she understand our friendship, how could anyone? You can't just let something so special shrink and die. You have to do everything within your power to save it. Shaking my head I looked over to the old pier where we used to go and sit as teenagers, now burnt and charred, the metal framework twisted and bare.

I took my sunglasses off and laid them on the table.

'I'm sorry you've got such a bad impression of me. It's hard to explain. Clara was like a sister to me.' I waited for a moment as if struggling to find the words. 'I really don't want to sound patronising here, Amber, because I know Clara has other friends and I'm really happy for her. But I'm not sure they all understand where she's come from.' I watched Amber's face cloud over. *You hadn't told her, Clara, you hadn't told her.* 'Have you any idea where she spent some of the last seven years?' I asked.

Amber shook her head slowly. 'I guessed as much.' I leant in to be closer to her. 'I would never normally tell anyone this, but in the circumstances it's important we're honest and open. You need to understand that Clara's grip on reality was not always as firm as it should be.'

Finally I had her attention. She sat, mouth open wide, and listened, occasionally making sympathetic noises as I told her the story of you, Clara. 'I understand,' I said as a final flourish, 'that you might not want to believe me. But the police know everything. I'm sure they'd tell you.' Amber shook her head as if to say no need. And I could feel her resistance ebb away.

We started with Friday night. I laid out my version of events first, signposting to Amber my blind spots, suggesting where she might be able to shed some light. I knew she would have gone through her story with the police once already. I hoped I would be able to glean from Amber the information the police had withheld from me.

She said you had planned to meet me, at least that was her understanding. 'But I knew there was someone coming to the flat first, maybe he was delayed and that was why she was late.'

You'd never mentioned anyone coming to the flat. You were supposed to be ill.

'He?' I asked.

'It was a guy, that's as much as I knew.'

Jonny.

I saw it again, the image of both of you together, his body leaning into yours on the promenade. Had you invited Jonny to your flat, Clara? What did you talk about? The thought made my mouth go dry. I rummaged in my bag and retrieved a bottle of water. Then I found my phone and shuffled through the old texts to show Amber yours.

Rach, so sorry, feeling terrible, think I might have flu, in bed still but will heave myself out to make it. Will call later Clarax

'Oh,' she said. 'Maybe she forgot to mention him.' But her voice told me she thought it was as weak a theory as I did.

'Did she tell you his name?'

'No, but she said it wasn't her fella.'

'Her fella?' I wondered how many more secrets you had kept from me, Clara.

'He was called Jim or something, I never met him. I think it was someone she knew from years ago. Anyway,' she said, refusing to be sidetracked, 'it wasn't him. She seemed preoccupied, a bit hyper, you know how she is sometimes,' and she looked towards me for my agreement. I nodded. I thought back to the previous week. The daily phone calls to check I was coming to Brighton, so out of character, Clara. And me happy that you were finally making an effort.

'I asked her a couple of times if she was OK,' Amber continued, her gaze fixed on the horizon, 'because she seemed hyper but jumpy too. Like she was scared of something. She said she had a few things on her mind but she would have dealt with them after that night. I didn't pry any more, it was almost like she wanted to cultivate this air of mystery. It could be a bit infuriating at times. Now I wish I'd asked more. I wish I knew who she was meeting. Though the police think it might have been that guy in the CCTV.'

'Jonny?

'That's the one,' she agreed.

'He's my boyfriend,' I said and watched Amber twitch.

She muttered something about being sorry and how she was sure it was a mistake and then started sprinkling her story with extraneous details so we wouldn't have to talk about Jonny.

'I warned you I wouldn't be much help,' she said, putting her coffee cup to her lips and grimacing when she realised how cold it was. I smiled and reached out to put my hand over hers.

'You've been more help than you know.'

She gathered her things together, her phone from the table,

her bag, and apologised but she had a yoga class she couldn't miss. 'It's the only thing that relaxes me at the moment,' she said. I stood up and thanked her, holding out my hand to shake hers. This time she leant into me and we embraced. She scribbled her mobile number for me and then she was gone, her trousers flapping in the wind.

I sat there for a while longer watching the flock of seagulls span out above me, climbing high, so high into the white of the sun they almost vanished.

We both know the truth, Rachel.

Those were your last words to me and suddenly the thought was there again, fluttering into view. I saw glimpses, flickers of it. But when I tried to hold it down it disappeared into the sun.

Chapter Thirteen

YOU SLIPPED AWAY from view over the weekend. Your name unspoken on the radio, your face absent from newspapers and television, Jonny's too. You have to offer a new twist, an unexpected turn, to stay in the headlines and you had gone silent.

In my flat there was silence too. No laughter, no chat over breakfast or Saturday night TV or Sunday papers, no Jonny. Only one-out-of-the-blue phone call from Sarah Pitts to break the quiet, surprising me with its apologetic tone.

'Look, Rachel, I'm sorry for the other day, I'd had no sleep. I was going crazy thinking I could have done something to keep her safe but I shouldn't have taken it out on you.'

I thought back to our frosty exchange in the café, how I had so desperately wanted us to understand and help each other, how I saw all too clearly the shadows of our past still lurked between us.

'Apology accepted,' I said slowly, allowing Sarah to pick up the conversation. She told me she'd been interviewed by the police but hadn't heard anything about you since. She asked me what I had been up to.

Drowning.

Slowly drowning.

'Oh, you know, nothing much, can't seem to concentrate on anything at the moment,' I said.

'I know what you mean. Listen Rachel, you don't mind if I call you now and then do you,' she asked. 'It's just that you'll probably get more information than me.'

I hesitated, and then relented.

'No problem,' I said, fully expecting never to hear from her again. ''Bye for now.'

I hung up and sank back into a big black hole of nothingness.

The irony was that Jonny and I wouldn't have been together that weekend anyway. He should have been in Afghanistan, which was always going to be hard, but missing someone and knowing their absence has a purpose was a whole world away from this, this torture. A huge fault-line had opened up in my world and swallowed up the two people I cared for most. Yet somehow, somehow, I hadn't felt the slightest tremor until it was too late. All I could see now was the damage it had left behind.

I remember that weekend in shivers and coughs and aches. My throat was raw, my body felt as if it had been stretched to the point of snapping. I wore layers of clothes, jumpers, socks, slippers, turned the heating up full blast, but still the cold wouldn't shift from my bones. I ate without restraint in a way I hadn't done for years: takeaway pizza, Thai, curry, biscuits from the cupboard, whatever I could lay my hands on, anything to fill the huge void inside me. In the end I was sick, which only made me feel even more wretched.

My thoughts were chaotic, my emotions swung like a pendulum between raw fury and utter desolation. I didn't know what to think, whether to feel devastated, grief or betrayal. In the end I experienced all three.

In the rare moments of calm I held imaginary conversations with Jonny, where (after walking through the door, arms open wide) he'd scoop me up and kiss me all over and put me out of my misery with an innocent explanation and an apology for not being in touch. But when I couldn't think of any such innocent explanation and I began to scratch my own skin in frustration, the confusion set in again. For my sanity I forced myself to focus on something else. My thoughts turned to you, Clara.

It was the song that came to me first; I found myself humming it before I even realised what it was and then the name flashed in my head like a neon sign and I had to laugh at the beautiful grotesque fucking irony of it. The song of our summer 1995, Everything But the Girl, 'Missing'.

Can you remember it, Clara, that weird slice of time when we weren't quite adults but we were definitely no longer children? We'd ditched Take That in favour of DJs and dance compilations and promised ourselves that this was the summer we'd make it (underage) to the Zap Club.

We'd been talking about it for months but hadn't worked up the courage to go on our own and be turned away for being too young in front of a queue of cool people. Then Matt, the sixth-form guy you were seeing, said he knew someone on the door, Paul Oakenfold was going to be playing, did we want to go?

It was the summer holidays and all week long we'd hung out on the beach, or on the old pier eating Fab ice lollies quickly before they melted in the sun. The smell of coconuts from your tanning spray followed us everywhere as did my factor twenty-five lotion and the wide-brimmed sunhat I wore in the hope of stopping the march of freckles across my face.

As the days passed and your skin turned a deep brown colour we talked of nothing else but Saturday night; what outfits we were going to wear, what we would tell your dad to convince him to let you stay out late; no need to persuade Niamh – a rare perk of having a neglectful mother.

When Saturday came I arrived at your house early, two bottles of Diamond White and Castaway hidden in my bag. We drank Blastaways and danced to Everything But the Girl's 'Missing', 'Dreamer' by Livin' Joy and 'Rhythm is a Mystery' by K Klass which we played repeatedly, not just because we loved the tunes; our musical tastes had developed faster than our CD collection, which still groaned with Take That hits.

'Well?' you said when you were dressed. 'What do you think?' You did a little turn which made your hair swirl around your face, catching the light. Moments passed and

I couldn't take my eyes off you, this vision in front of me: your dark skin glowing under a white dress, those impossibly blue eyes dancing with excitement, thick black eyelashes, deep red lips. I wondered whether or not you were real.

'You look . . . stunning,' I said.

You reached over to kiss me. 'Good, that makes two of us then. Come on Rach, let's go and party.'

On the way out we promised your dad we'd get a cab home, the only way we could stop him coming to collect us himself. 'One o'clock, Clara, that's the absolute latest. If you're not back by then I'm sending out the search party,' he said. 'And girls, enjoy the concert, you both look beautiful.' We smiled and left quickly so he wouldn't see the flush of a lie creep across our faces. We'd told him we were going to see Blur at the Paradox, knowing he'd never have let you go clubbing at the Zap.

Down by the arches on Kings Road, the home of the Zap, dance music pumped out on to the street. A snake of people waited, dressed up, dressed down, shuffling from one foot to the other, chatting, laughing. To me, they were older, hipper, they acted like they belonged here. Looking down at myself, my plain black trousers, the green halterneck top I'd bought in Oasis last week, I realised how plain and ordinary I was in comparison. You, on the other hand, outshone everyone there, just like you always did, Clara.

We went to stand at the back of the queue but as soon as we met up with Matt and his mate Scott they swept us to the front. I kept my head down, anticipating the embarrassment of being turned away by the woman with the long blond ponytail and clipboard. But to my surprise she nodded, opened the door and ushered us inside.

It was still filling up, dark and dank; the smell of stale alcohol and smoke hung in the air. Matt wouldn't leave your side, whispering into your ear, nodding his head in agreement with everything you said. I'd watched his reaction when he caught sight of you in the queue, and I think he must have known that you were out of his league but still, he was determined to cling on to you for tonight at least. I was left with Scott, who had started waving his arms out in the air and dancing too close to me. After all the anticipation, the huge week-long build-up, I wanted to turn round and run away. I was still thinking of what excuses to give you when you came over, hooked arms with me and said, 'Come on, I need a wee,' and suddenly we were heading towards the toilets.

In the cubicle together I realised you didn't need a wee; we were there for another reason entirely. You opened your hand to reveal two little white circles, smaller than paracetamols and embossed with little doves. 'Shall we?' you whispered, eyes flashing with mischief. 'Matt says they're really good ones.'

I didn't know what to say. In all the hours we'd spent talking about tonight we'd never discussed taking Ecstasy. It hadn't even been on my radar. You must have seen me wavering. 'Come on,' you said, handing me one, 'everyone else will be doing them,' and I thought about how I was going to leave because I felt so out of place and then I saw you put the little round circle into your mouth, throwing your head back and sloshing it down with a swig from a bottle of water. All the time smiling, daring me to do the same. 'No going back now,' you said. And I grabbed the water from you and placed the pill on my tongue, wincing as the bitter, chemical taste hit me, and then I washed it away with a drink. Two minutes later we were out of the toilets, emerging into the club again, no idea what would happen next.

The answer was nothing, not for ages. The club had filled up, hot and sweaty bodies too close to each other, dancing to thumping music. Matt's face was red, glistening from the heat, staying close to you, wondering no doubt when the pill would work and you would melt into him. We kept on looking at each other: *Is anything happening?* Shaking our heads because we both felt totally normal. I began to wonder what all the fuss was about.

Then a song I didn't recognise came on and slowly I felt the beats of it playing through me as a fuzzy warmth took hold in my head, like liquid velvet, smoothing and soothing me, melting away every worry I'd ever had. Before long I couldn't tell where the music stopped and I began because it had become part of me, and all I could do was let it take hold.

I turned to you and saw your pupils big and wide, our smiles connecting. Then you were next to me, your hand on my back sending tingles all the way up my spine and into my head. My whole body had come alive, so wonderfully, deliciously sensitive to even the gentlest touch.

That's when we heard the first bars of 'Missing'. Our song. And we couldn't stop grinning because it was all too good to be fucking true, as if someone had made a drug just for us and planned the whole evening with the most perfect cosmic timing.

I felt your hand take mine and in our own little bubble we were pulled by the music right down into the noisy heart of the club where the song pumped through our hearts and the strobing lights danced on our eyelids.

You leant close to me and shouted in my ear so your words vibrated through me, 'Let's never lose this, Rach.'

You weren't talking about the drugs and the music, however beautiful it all was. You were talking about us and the clearest, sharpest thought ran through my head. *If I ever lost you, I would lose myself.*

'We won't, I promise you,' I said, 'I'll never let you go.'

We stayed there, dancing together because we couldn't stop until finally we moved away to a quieter, darker spot, sinking to the floor our backs against the wall, just drinking it all in. We'd lost Matt and Scott long ago in the throng but when I mentioned it you just shrugged and closed your eyes.

'Never mind,' you said and took my hand in yours, leaning your head on to my shoulder. One moment stretched out for hours until finally the heat faded from our bodies. Your eyes were open again and you looked at your watch as if you had just remembered something. 'Shit,' you said dreamily, 'think we're about to turn into pumpkins. We need to go.'

Outside the cold air tickled our skin. We crossed the road and were drawn by the noise and the dark shadows of the waves down on to the beach. 'Stop,' you said, as we stumbled over the pebbles. 'Look at them.' Your hand was pointing upwards to the sky. 'Can you see how big they are tonight?'

I sat down and looked up towards the stars. They seemed enormous, so close to us I thought they might drop out of the sky.

You sank down on the beach next to me, the lights dancing above us. And together we lay back reaching our arms high above our heads into the black sky, stretching them out further than we ever thought possible. That was when we felt it, the electric heat sparking on the tips of our fingers and charging through our bodies. The waves lapped on the shore close by and we swore to each other that we had both just touched a star.

Chapter Fourteen

MONDAY MORNING, BACK at work and your name was in the air again, hovering out of my reach. I felt a twinge in my stomach knowing that I would be left on the sidelines while someone else reported on it.

Swiping myself through the doors to the newsroom, I walked straight into Richard Goldman, another correspondent, who tipped his coffee all over my cream wool coat.

'Fuck's sake,' I muttered under my breath, trying to move past him, but he blocked my way.

'Shit, sorry,' he said in his public-school drawl before he looked up and saw it was me. 'You're the last person I expected to see in work.' His eyes wandered up and down me searching for signs of emotional collapse.

'Best to keep busy,' I said.

'Well, whatever works for you. But I wanted you to know you have my sympathy.' I studied his face, trying to work out whether he was being genuine or simply enjoying seeing everything fall apart for me. I'd always had the feeling he'd never forgiven me for beating him to the crime correspondent job. I remembered the words of a colleague when I first started at NNN: *the more you know him the less you like him*.

'Anyway,' he continued, 'it might make you feel better knowing that the story is in good hands.' He rubbed his own together. 'I'm just off there now.' And with that he swiped himself through the door and disappeared into the car park.

I'm not a vengeful person but there are times when natural justice needs a helping hand and this was one of them. I didn't want Richard's grubby fat hands pawing you and Jonny, and yes, if I couldn't be on the story, at the very least I wanted to be kept updated of any off-the-record briefings from the police. Richard would rather die than give me any privileged information. I had to do something. Though what, I couldn't think.

Then lunchtime arrived and an opportunity so tantalising landed in my lap, it was impossible to ignore.

Richard was in Brighton, on the promenade doing a live headline for the one o'clock bulletin. All he had to say was *I'm Richard Goldman in Brighton where police spent the weekend questioning motorists and revellers in the area where Clara O'Connor disappeared more than a week ago,* and then the shot would cut away from him to the next headline.

It's not the kind of thing you can fuck up because

you have ten seconds, no more, and that's not enough time to recover if you fluff it. But Richard stumbled as soon as he opened his mouth. And then – so quick I almost missed it – at the bottom of the shot I saw his hand move down to his crotch where he gave himself a small but noticeable tug. Remarkably he recovered his composure as if his dick was hotwired to his brain. The gift, the gift of it. I looked across at Jake but his face was fixed on the bulletin with a look of concentration. I played it back, wondering if I had imagined it. But no, it was still there.

Instinctively I pulled out one of my old notepads where I had written the password for a false e-mail account I'd set up a few months ago. I'd been posing as an elderly woman during an investigation into a company that was pressurising pensioners to have useless security systems fitted. The account was in the name of Jean Beattie, a name I borrowed from an old neighbour in Dover Road who used to pass me custard creams through the fence and talk to me about my plants.

I typed in the password and clicked on the compose button.

In the address field I wrote: newsdesk@nnn.co.uk

And then:

Dear Sir,

At 67 my eyesight is certainly not what it was. However I am convinced I have just seen your reporter Richard Goldman fiddle with his penis during his report on the one o'clock news. I'm hoping this kind of behaviour is not encouraged at NNN. I have always enjoyed watching your news programmes but I'm not beyond defecting to the other side.

Yours,

Jean Beattie

I read it once over before hitting the send button.

Thirty-two minutes later a response dropped into Jean's inbox.

Dear Mrs Beattie,

Thank you for your e-mail. I have looked at the report in question and although his hand does quite clearly appear to sit in that general area I doubt it was for the purpose you mentioned. Please accept my apologies if this offended you in any way. Rest assured I will be talking to the reporter in question to make sure this doesn't happen again.

I hope you continue to enjoy our news coverage.

Regards,

Robbie Fenton

News Editor

I gave it ten minutes before I sauntered up to Robbie's desk, the taste of freshly applied lip gloss in my mouth, ready to execute the next part of my plan to get Richard off the story.

I saw him look up.

'Nice package from Richard at lunchtime,' I said without a trace of irony.

He mumbled something under his breath. 'Everyone else was busy.' I took a step to move away and then turned as if I had just remembered something.

'I met Amber Corrigan the other day,' I said. His features screwed up as he struggled to put a face to the name. 'The girl from the press conference,' I reminded him.

'Ah . . . her,' he said. 'Will she talk?'

'I doubt it,' I said, 'she was only speaking to me as Clara's friend. She's told everyone else to get lost.'

'I see,' Robbie said, stroking the stubble on his chin, 'I see.'

And I knew he did.

The idea formed in my head a little later in the afternoon. At first I thought it was too cruel but I told myself he'd only fall for it if he was as ego driven as he'd led me to believe. And, I reasoned, if that was the case, *he* would be the author of his own downfall, not me. Besides there were more important things at stake than Richard Goldman's career, such as finding you, Clara. The more information I could glean, the better chance I would have of tracking you and Jonny down.

I checked the running order of the bulletin. Richard was the second story. A report from Brighton then a live DTL – or down the line with him immediately afterwards. I knew he'd be thinking of something wise to say, some analysis to offer or, even better, a piece of exclusive information. I also knew it was unlikely he'd have any to give.

I waited until five fifty-one to make the call. I imagined Richard pacing up and down the promenade rehearsing his lines for the live, the adrenalin pumping through him. To be honest I thought I might have left it too late. He could have switched his phone to silent, but I had no choice. I didn't want to give him enough time to make any check calls.

It rang four times before his plummy voice answered.

'It's Rachel,' I said. 'Look, I've just had a call from one of my contacts in Sussex to say they have found Clara's car abandoned up near Devil's Dyke. They haven't released it officially yet, but thought we should be the first to break it.'

'You're giving it to me?' he asked incredulously, just as I had expected.

'Call it professional generosity,' I said, knowing my explanation wouldn't convince him. 'Look, if you want the truth, it pains me to give it to you, but since I can't do anything with it myself, I'd rather you get it first than the competition. The lesser of two evils so to speak,' I finished with a laugh.

'And he's a good contact?'

'One of my best. I can't tell you to go with it, it's your call. And you can't tell anyone it came from me. Maybe you should wait, I think they'll announce it to everyone later. You better go, you're on in five minutes,' I said and I hung up.

I wasn't at all convinced he had the balls to do it. My only hope was he would find the prospect of a scoop too delicious to resist.

Five minutes later Richard Goldman announced on national television, in a voice an octave higher than usual, that he could *reveal exclusively* how Clara O'Connor's car had been found abandoned in a ditch near Devil's Dyke.

It only took another three minutes to bring him back to earth when Sussex police rang the news desk to complain that they had made no such discovery. Ten minutes later my BlackBerry vibrated with an e-mail from Robbie. 'I need your help with the Clara O'Connor story. Talk tomorrow.'

I was buoyed. A door that had been shut in my face had swung open again. I took it as a sign that finally events were shifting in my favour and when Jake suggested we go for a drink I surprised him by taking him up on the offer.

We stayed in the pub until they threw us out, two bottles of Bordeaux to the good. My head was warm and fuzzy and mellow; I even laughed at his jokes, blocking out for a few blissful hours everything else that was happening around me.

Out on the street Jake flagged down a taxi and said I couldn't go home alone 'not after the break-in'. It was the first time he actually referred to it as if he believed it. But when we pulled up outside my flat, we realised I wouldn't have been alone anyway.

A police car was sitting directly opposite with its lights off. As we paid the fare I heard the door of the police car slam and, heart lurching, I watched two officers make their way towards us. Jake turned to me for reassurance, information, whatever. I wasn't able to give him any. When they reached us, one of them introduced himself as PC Simon Ramilles, 'Can we come in?' he asked in a solemn voice which told me it wasn't a question.

The WPC followed him up the path and gave me a pitying smile as I let her in. Once in the living room I sat down and tried to focus to stop the room spinning. From the kitchen I could hear the sound of the kettle boiling and Jake crashing about, opening cupboards to find mugs and tea bags and sugar.

The moment before PC Ramilles spoke stretched out for so long I thought it would never end. A suffocating silence bore down on all of us. Finally, perched on the edge of the sofa, with his hands clasped together, he took a deep breath and told me that they had found a body.

Brighton's mortuary looked like a seventies chalet bungalow with a carport fixed on to the side as an afterthought. Inside a synthetic blue carpet lined the floors of the waiting room. Cheap paintings of the sea and the beach hung on the wall. They looked like they'd been picked up at a car boot sale.

An elderly woman offered me a cup of tea as if tea had the power to make everything better. But tea can't prepare you for being taken into a side room with red velvet curtains and flowers and being cold, so cold you think you might never ever feel heat in your bones again. It doesn't prepare you for what you are supposed to say when they remove the cover and you see a person that you once knew but who is now grey and waxy and still. So still it's like they've never been alive. Like you only imagined the life they led. I looked at the toes first, which were yellow but blue underneath the nails, and then slowly up the legs, which were thick and strong and lifeless, and to the groin, a source of pleasure once, now flaccid, limp. The chest where I'd lain, where a loud heart once thumped out. And then the face, that beautiful face I first saw almost two years ago. It wasn't you, was it, Clara. It was Jonny. Cold and dead and gone forever.

They'd asked me to identify him at Sandra's request. She couldn't bring herself to do it. To see her baby, her boy, lying there like that. His hopes and future cut short on a slab in the mortuary. She was waiting outside, with a cold cup of tea. And when I came out she looked, a begging look that will haunt me all my life, pleading with me to tell her something I couldn't. That it was a mistake. That it was some other unfortunate soul in there. I have never wished that I could do something so much. Instead I shook my head and held her as she crumbled in my arms.

Chapter Fifteen

IN MY NOTEPAD I still have the words I wrote down when I was told how Jonny died. My handwriting is unsteady and would be illegible to anyone but me. I think I can see the words without actually reading them. Their imprint will stay in my mind for the rest of my life.

I remember the WPC, our family liaison officer, relaying the details softly softly with her head cocked in sympathy, looking at Sandra, then turning to me and saying a million times over, 'I understand, I understand.'

She told us that Jonny's body was found not far from Preston Park in a wooded area which ran off a path. It had been covered for days, they presumed by heavy snowfall, until Monday when it melted and a dog walker came across it.

'When we found his body, he wasn't wearing a coat, just jeans and a T-shirt. It was minus six over the weekend.'

He was out there alone and needing me and now he was gone.

I told them Jonny would never be that stupid, he wouldn't have just got drunk and fallen asleep. He was supposed to be flying out to Afghanistan the next day.'

Sandra was sobbing next to me. The WPC took her hand and gave me a look that said, *This isn't helping.*

'I understand it's a traumatic time,' she said again, as if she had just seen the person she loved most, cold and blue on a mortuary slab.

On the train back to London I sat alone, staring out of the window as the empty, frozen countryside zipped past. Daylight was falling; a dark gloom settled over the carriage. I wondered: what if the sun never rose again; if the world stopped turning on its axis and we were forever trapped in this grey half-light. Would the trees and plants be the first to shrink and die? Then we would surely follow.

Because we all need to feel the warmth of the sun to survive, don't we? Just as we need to be loved and wanted, to be the focus of someone's attention and adoration. If we don't have that, how do we know we even exist?

I had basked in the heat of your attention once, Clara. I'd sprung to life like a flower under your gaze, and then you let it drift elsewhere and I was left to shiver in the cold. I remembered the pain of it so clearly, like a knife slicing through me, hollowing me out. Oh, I'd recovered, Clara, I'd found a way through it, but it wasn't until Jonny came along and made me the centre of his universe that I realised how cold I had been, how much I had missed the warmth. Now he was gone I could feel the freeze gripping my bones again and a suffocating blackness rolling in like sea mist. I was sinking into it, disappearing once more.

The invisible woman.

I heard the sound of the drinks trolley trundling through the aisles and looked up just in time to see it pass me without so much as a word from the steward. Had I vanished already? Only when I ran my fingers through my hair, pulling hard, did the strands of red in my hand convince me I was still there.

I didn't want to be alone again. I didn't want to go home, slip through my front door and disappear. I needed someone to see me and talk to me and reassure me I was still living and breathing.

Jake.

He was the only one I could turn to.

I arrived at his flat early or late, I can't remember which. The concept of time had evaporated. I was caught in a drift. Minutes and hours belonged to another world. The one I was stuck in had no beginnings and no ends.

His flat was on the ground floor and when I buzzed he came out to meet me. I remember falling into him, as if the effort of holding myself up became too much at that precise moment. He held me for what seemed like a long time, still and silent, before leading me inside.

I took my shoes off and curled my legs beneath me on the sofa as he went to the kitchen, emerging with a bottle of wine and two glasses.

'Here,' he said, handing me one of them.

I glugged at it and waited for the heat of the alcohol to warm my throat. But my body had been cold for so many days now it had forgotten how to absorb heat.

We didn't say anything for a while, just listened to the music playing and a man singing with a deep velvet voice, a soothing sink-into-yourself kind of song. I let it wash over me, taking sips of wine.

It was then it occurred to me.

'I haven't cried since I saw his body, not one tear. I feel like everything has dried up, like I have nothing left.'

'Everyone reacts differently,' Jake said. He put his wine glass on the table and got up to change the CD. I watched him scan his collection, fingering the cases, pulling one out only to put it back again until he found what he was looking for. There was a Banksy hanging on the wall, a picture of people in a bowling club playing with bombs instead of bowls, along with a faded *Star Wars* cinema poster. The walls were a dark neutral and the light was low, inviting, a kind of effortless cool that would have impressed me normally, but not that evening when my senses were numb.

I heard the music playing softly again and then he was sitting next to me, his arm round me. 'Go easy on yourself, Rachel,'

'Everything's disappearing; sometimes I think I might have imagined it all,' I said, my voice flat, emotionless. His hand touched my chin, lifting my face up to his, surprising me with the heat of his touch.

'You will get through it. I promise. You are the strongest person I know,' he said, pulling me towards him in an embrace. Against my chest his heartbeat vibrated, thud, thud, thud. I wanted to stay there long enough so its beat could jump-start my own heart, so the heat from his body could thaw mine. So the cold in my bones and the numbness in my head would ease. Finally he pulled away, his dark eyes shining into mine. I think I must have closed mine at that point because I didn't see him lean into me again. All I felt was the touch of warm lips on my cheek. When I looked again his lips were all I could see, red and warm and full, and I was drawn to them, pulled in by a desire to touch something that wasn't cold and blue and dead. And for a second I didn't think about how wrong it was, all I thought about was that kissing his lips might be the only thing that would keep me alive that night.

When I snapped back to my senses I flinched, the shame hitting me like cold water in my face.

'I'm sorry,' I said, 'I didn't mean . . .'

'Don't apologise, Rachel,' he said and he got up to fill our wine glasses.

I awoke the next morning in his bed. The duvet pulled over me, still fully clothed. Jake must have carried me there when I passed out on the sofa. I got up and looked in the mirror. My hair was a wild mass of red. I pulled it back from my face into a ponytail. My eyes were bloodshot and smudged with mascara, if only from crying I thought. My mouth was dry, in desperate need of water.

'What time is it?' I said, emerging from the bedroom.

Jake was sitting at the island in the kitchen, coffee and papers laid out on the wooden worktop. 'Shouldn't you be at work?' I asked, seeing the clock on the wall. Half-past nine.

'Rachel . . . I . . . you need to see this,' he said. He pointed to the newspaper and then with one hand rubbed his eyes as if something was causing him pain.

Three steps across the open-plan living room and I was leaning over his shoulder, reading the same newspaper he was reading. I scrunched my eyes, not wanting to believe what was in front of me. The darkness, the doorway. Jake and I embracing. An image stolen from us the night before, now shared with the world. The front-page picture in the *Daily Mail* and underneath the strapline:

TV girl seeks comfort with colleague after discovery of boyfriend's body.

'I'm sorry, Rachel,' he said, 'I'm so so sorry,' and I saw his mouth open to say something else but I didn't hear any more because I was running out of his flat into the icy morning.

Running, running through the streets. Thc cold cutting into my face. Cars and buses and horns and people. People everywhere. I wanted to click my fingers and make them disappear. To make space for me, to leave me alone to think and breathe. The cold burnt into my lungs but still I kept going, I couldn't stop; if I stopped it might catch me, this avalanche roaring in my ears. It might scoop me up and bury me alive.

Ahead, an expanse of green. Queen's Park. Through the gates still running. Mercifully free of kids. Too cold for kids today. The space became mine. I was free to fill it with my breath and thoughts. A bench, over there, I saw it and sat down. My knees pulled tight into me, then tighter again so I was small enough to disappear. For a moment, stillness. The traffic and the people and the workmen, everyone quiet all around. A window of silence. Then a searing pain in my stomach as if I was being ripped in two. They came, then, the tears, warm on my freezing face, slipping down to my lips with their salty taste. So many I thought they might never stop. And the images flickered like the old cine films Niamh used to play, of Jonny, of his body, lost to me forever. I had loved him in a way I never thought possible. My tears were for him, but mostly they were for me. For the future I had lost. Jonny had been healing something that was broken inside me. He had offered me a way out. And now he was gone there was no one left to fix me.

Chapter Sixteen

The incessant drilling was loud and reassuring. For days I had worried that behind every noise and shadow lurked someone uninvited. Now the locksmith was here and the click-click of every lock and bolt being replaced told me I could be safe once more, that my flat was being sealed up, watertight, so no one without a face or a name could slip through doors and windows unnoticed again.

The air smelled of bleach from the hours I'd spent cleaning and hoovering and washing when the police finished their search a few days earlier. I had scrubbed until I wore holes in my Marigolds and my arms ached, stopping only when I was convinced every fingerprint, crumb, every germ and scent of the people who had trampled through my home had been removed. With a certain satisfaction I looked around, coffee in hand, and saw my reflection in the shining surfaces. Nothing out of place, only a pile of mail to deal with.

I can keep this at bay, I can hold it back.

The flash of a message on the answerphone caught my

attention. I wanted to block everything out but I knew it would flash at me all day long and give me no peace so I pressed play.

'Rachel, it's Laura here,' said the voice so like my mother's. 'I'm so so sorry for everything. I've been trying to reach you since Clara went missing and then I heard the news about Jonny. Please call me and let me know you're OK.'

I pressed the stop button. She wanted me to reassure her I was OK.

I am not OK. My boyfriend has died, my friend is missing. Nothing will ever be OK again.

My call to Aunty Laura could wait.

On autopilot I moved over to the kitchen table, eyeing the pile of post that had grown little by little over the past ten days. Mentally, I needed to tackle it, if only to wrest back control of the little things in life that were slipping away from me. I'd opened one letter, an invitation to join an exclusive health club, when my mobile phone rang, Sarah's name flashing up on the screen.

'Hi babe.' (No one had ever called me *babe* before or since thankfully.) 'It's me,' she said like she was the only person who ever called.

'Hi.'

'I didn't know whether to phone, I mean I just wanted to let you know I'm thinking of you.' She stumbled over her words. 'It's so awful, I can't imagine how you must be feeling.'

'Thanks,' I said, barely able to hear her above sound of the drill.

'Fucking hell, what's that? Sarah asked.

'Oh,' I said, 'Just a locksmith doing a few jobs.' I didn't have the energy to go into detail.

'I understand,' she said though I wondered how she could. 'Listen, I've got to go, there's a gang of us going around town today putting posters up of Clara. You never know, it could make a difference.'

I doubt it.

'Good luck,' I said and hung up.

I got back to the pile of letters, starting with the official-looking ones, the bills, my credit-card statement, which I put to one side – most of it I would claim back on expenses. A tasteless card with butterflies on it from my Aunty Laura, obviously sent before Jonny's body was found. Inside, in her scrawly handwriting, a note:

> Darling Rachel,
>
> I'm so sorry to hear about Clara, I know you must be going out of your mind. I've called your flat several times but I can't seem to reach you. Do get in touch.
>
> Love as always,
>
> Laura x

I threw it on the pile along with the predictable letters from estate agents promising us (me) they had hordes of imaginary buyers waiting to snap up our flat. Then I came to a large brown envelope with my name typed in capitals and my address underneath. It was hand-delivered, no stamp, but it was so light I wondered if it contained anything at all. I waited for a moment, listening to the locksmith's drill growing louder and louder as he worked his way around the flat to the kitchen windows, before I took a knife to it and sliced it open. I tipped it upside down and watched two pieces of paper float slowly to the floor. The drilling tunnelled into my brain. I wanted it to stop. I bent down to retrieve the contents of the envelope and saw a newspaper clipping with a typeface I recognised instantly as the *Daily Mail*'s. I shook my head to stop the pain. The front page was facing down; all I could see was the day's weather forecast and a nib about Gordon Brown. But I knew that wasn't what I was meant to read. Slowly I turned it over and saw myself and Jake embracing in the dark of his doorway. And when I looked at the sheet of A4 that had fallen from the envelope I saw it was blank, save for the words:

DON'T YOU FEEL ANYTHING, RACHEL WALSH?

The drilling stopped but the pain in my head was fierce, red-hot. Next to me I felt a presence, a breath on me that made me jump. I turned to see the locksmith who, noticing my surprise, took a step back. His lips were moving but I couldn't hear the words, so he repeated them, this time louder.

'Didn't mean to give you a fright love, but I'm done now,' he said. 'How many keys do you want?' I watched him pull his saggy jeans up over his waist only for them to fall back down again. His name was Mickey, he owned the locksmith's round the corner. That was as much as I knew.

It could be him, it could be anyone.

I looked at the letter in front of me, my name written in angry capitals.

DON'T YOU FEEL ANYTHING?

I slid it under the pile. 'You sure you're OK?' he asked.

'Fine,' I said, hoping he couldn't hear the thud of my heart.

'How many sets of keys you after? Just you here is it?' He had a friendly face, a ruddy complexion. But that didn't count for anything.

'No,' I said. I didn't want anyone to think I lived alone. 'I'll need three. Two for me, one for my boyfriend.'

'Right you are.'

I reached for a cheque, wrote his name and the amount and handed it to him, breathing with relief as I watched his bulky figure fade through the door into the afternoon.

The curtains were closed to shut out the day and I was wrapped cocoon-like in my cream cashmere blanket. With the remote I flicked through the TV channels until a programme about Great White Sharks on Discovery caught my attention. I let myself drift with it, imagining I was cutting through the deep waters with the sharks, as graceful and powerful with nothing to fear.

The voiceover was deep and gravelly and suggestive of danger. It told me Great Whites could smell a drop of blood from over a mile away. 'There is no hiding from the Great White Shark, they can detect and home in on small electrical charges from hearts and gills.

'They plan their attacks and choose their prey long before their victims see them.

'It's what makes them so deadly.'

The credits were playing when the phone rang, startling me with its noise. I wasn't expecting a call. I didn't want to deal with the unexpected so I let it ring out. But the caller was persistent – no sooner had it stopped than my mobile started to vibrate. It was Sandra's number. I hadn't spoken to her since we parted in Brighton a few days before, the image of Jonny's body fresh in our minds. Initially I had harboured the illusion we could support each other in grief but when I looked at her that day I knew we would drown each other with the weight of it.

'Rachel.'

'I was just on my way out,' I said, turning the volume down on the television.

'It's the postmortem . . .' I heard an intake of breath, as if she was trying to deliver her news with control but failing, failing miserably.

'They say he might have tried to commit suicide,' she said and then she stopped, no more words, just the sound of her breaking into a million little pieces.

I glanced at the television; the picture was fuzzy with interference and the walls moved in and out as if they were breathing. My vision had switched to black and white, the colour had dropped out.

'Sandra,' I asked finally, 'how did he die?'

'Hypothermia in the end,' she said. I wondered what that meant, *in the end*. 'But they said . . .' She paused, struggling with the words. 'They said he took an overdose of sleeping pills first. He would never have done that, not Jonny.'

The telephone slipped from my hand. A sliver of sunlight poked through the curtains and fell on the room.

By degrees, my vision was restored and suddenly it was so clear, so very very clear, everything turning in on itself.

Sleeping pills. Such an obvious clue.

You did this.

And the photograph in my room, the texts and letters too.

You wanted revenge.

I trusted you and you betrayed me.

I waited, not drawing a breath, the stillness of the room like the dead calm of the sea before a tsunami strikes. I slumped to the ground, curled into myself, my hands gripping my head for protection.

Through the phone a muffled voice: 'Rachel . . . Rachel, are you there . . .' and then the voice disappeared, drowned out by the deafening roar in my ears. My body started to shake, I could feel the wave of white-hot rage thundering towards me.

Then it hit, sucking the breath from me, my lungs on fire. Everything around vanished, eaten up by the anger that was now consuming me.

The pressure built up in my head, ready to explode. I couldn't do anything, just sit and wait for this to pass; my whole body was pinned down by a force greater than me.

I don't know how long I stayed like that, but finally there was silence. Quiet settled on me again. The pain in my head dulled to a warm fuzz.

My hands fell to down to my lap, my fingertips tinged with blood where my nails had dug deep into my scalp. I looked around the room; the tidiness and perfection of it gave no clues as to what had just happened. Everything was the same. But inside, inside me, everything had changed.

I listened as words echoed in my head, searching to put a face to them.

We don't see the signs because we choose not to. We see what we want to see. We're all guilty of that.

Ann Carvello.

At that moment I felt her words resonate through every fibre of my being.

I should have known, Clara, that what we had was lost, eaten away by years apart, by the unspoken doubts and misunderstandings we had allowed to fester and rot.

Most of all I should have realised that when you betrayed me once you would do it again.

Clara, my best friend: not dead, just haunting me like a ghost.

Chapter Seventeen

June 2005

It's the imprint of you but it's not you. Your mannerisms are different, the way you flick your hair, more abrupt, less elegant; the way you throw your head back when you laugh, even your laugh itself; deeper, throatier, the result of too many Marlboro Reds, I think. The smoking shows in your face, your skin looks tired, I can see the red spots of burst veins; the glow has gone. And your speech is peppered with words you never used to use, like *totally* as in *totally amazing*. Then there's the slight inflection at the end of your sentences that makes them sound like questions. But it's your eyes where I see the biggest change. They're still blue, deep blue, but duller, as if the light that made them dance and sparkle has been extinguished. It's you, but it's not you.

It's been seven years since we've seen each other, Clara, and now we're together once more I realise there's a gulf between us. I don't know how to reach you, to find you underneath the layers of suspicion and years of conversations we rehearsed in our heads but never actually spoke.

Maybe I was expecting too much, to be flooded with your warmth. Give it time, I think.

But the way you pinch your eyes and look me up and down unnerves me. 'There is nothing left of you,' you say as if my weight loss is unwelcome and threatening. It's clear to me you were expecting to see my eighteen-year-old self and that makes me bristle with anger. Did you think I would have stayed the same? Did you think so little of me? That girl doesn't exist any more. She disappeared shortly after you left, taking her pounds of fat and baggy clothes with her. When I think of her it's as if I'm thinking of another person. I try to regain my composure and make a joke about how funny it was to be thin at first. 'The smaller I got, the more people noticed me,' I say, and I wait for your reaction but I can't read the look on your face. I no longer know what you're thinking. We are distant. I wonder if we will ever get the connection back.

Later, I sit on your squashy sofa blowing into my peppermint tea to cool it, admiring your new flat. It's housed in one of the imposing whitewashed Georgian mansion blocks that border the sea. From your front window I can see the pier and a jet ski bobbing about, buffeted by the wind. Inside it's pretty bare, apart from a red sofa which you've covered in a beige wool throw and a few wooden carvings picked up on your travels. 'It needs some work,' you say and tell me how your dad bought it especially for you.

'Lucky you,' I remark without thinking and immediately regret it. Your dad died two weeks ago. I wanted to come to the funeral but you told me firmly that it was just for his close family and friends. I didn't ask where that left me.

'He spent the last seven years trying to make it up to me,' you say, waving your arm around the room, 'this, all this, and everything else, it was his way of saying sorry.'

You leave that thought hanging heavy, weighing us down. I move uncomfortably in my chair and take a sip of tea.

I ask to see the pictures from your travels, seven years in photos, so I can see where you've been. I'd kept in contact with your dad ostensibly to find out how you were doing but sometimes we'd just chat about life or work, adult to adult, and he'd tell me how he'd watched me on TV. I always felt proud when he said that. He'd tell me how he still missed the days when we filled his house with terrible music and singing. I'd tell him I missed his sweetcorn fritters and bad dancing. He just wanted everyone to be happy, didn't he? It was one of his greatest strengths but it was also his weakness. He couldn't cope with confrontation.

You whizz me through the albums: in Granada teaching English and you outside the Alhambra. 'Feels like an age ago,' you say, pinching your stomach which used to be so flat. 'All the free tapas gave me this and I've never been able to lose it.' Then we're in Madrid and you, tanned and smiling with a Spanish boyfriend, Francesco, his arm wrapped round you possessively. After that the landscape changes. We move to India, you wearing sarongs, squinting with sun-strained eyes into the camera. You're in Jaipur, the skies are whiter, hotter, the signposts more exotic; Agra, the Taj Majal, Palolem Beach in Goa, an ashram in Kerala. You tell me you learnt some *totally amazing poses* and you stretch into one right in front of me. You extend one leg behind you and stretch your arms out front and you stay like that, statue-still, for minutes. The veins in your head pulse and the muscles in your arms bulge from underneath your tanned skin. And I see them, still visible, the criss-cross lines of the razors up and down your arms. The scars of your past.

'This is "warrior three" pose,' you tell me through deep breaths. 'It's all about control, Rachel, you fix your eyes on one thing and you don't move.'

The show of strength over, you sit back on the sofa, your forehead glistening from the exertion, and you turn to me triumphantly, as if you have shown me a window into a different world. 'There's life beyond Brighton, you know.'

I tell you I've been living in London for five years but you shake your head as if it doesn't count. And suddenly I'm taken back seven years. We're eighteen again, you are in control, out front, shining for both of us, and I am in your wake. I realise you expect me to assume my old role. But I won't, I won't let that happen.

'I'm glad it all worked out for you,' I say and see the flash of steel in your eyes. I am treading on dangerous territory but I know I have to walk here if I'm to regain ground. Uncertain of how you will react, I carry on. 'It was the hardest thing I ever did,' I say, my heart beating through my words. 'I only wanted to help you, we both did, your dad and I. I hope you understand that.'

You flick through the pages of the photo albums faster and faster, without looking at the pictures, finally pausing at a photograph of your dad outside the Sydney Opera House.

'It was the guilt that killed him in the end.'

'He died of cancer,' I say.

'It ate away at him. He saw what it was like for me in there. It made me worse, not better. He realised he should never have put me there. He should never have listened to you.'

The anger is frothing up inside me. You aren't allowed to rewrite the past, to pick your own cast of villains and heroes. This might be your truth but it's not mine.

'Do you really think I did it all myself? A doctor had to sign the form along with your dad. He was the one who took you to hospital. He left you there and he did it because he could see you were ill. What about the times he found you cutting yourself, bleeding? He was terrified that one day he would come in and find you dead. So yes, I supported him, I'm not afraid to admit it. Yes we talked about it, he needed someone, but I didn't put you in that unit. He could see you were broken; he wanted someone to put you back together.'

I think of the weeks running up to that day when he told you he was taking you out shopping and drove you to hospital instead. Our secretive chats when we shared our concerns over you. Slowly, your dad had taken me into his confidence; he began to court my opinion as he deliberated on how best to help you. He came to me as if I had all the answers, and it made me feel special in a strange way, to have his undivided attention.

The day he returned, red-eyed after leaving you, I comforted him all afternoon. He said he could still hear your pleas ringing in his ears.

'*Sometimes you have to be cruel to be kind,*' I told him.

For a while we are quiet; only the noise of the seagulls squawking breaks the silence as it drifts in through your window.

Then you close the photo album and walk across the room to the mantelpiece. Someone has sent you a postcard from Melbourne. You pick it up and turn it over absentmindedly.

'Did you miss me,' you ask softly, your question easing the pressure in the room.

I think of how it was towards the end, you and my mother, colluding and dragging me down. I remember how I felt when you'd both gone, the sense of weightlessness. I was energised, as if whatever had been sucking the life out of you had fed it directly into me.

I don't tell you this. I don't want you to think I benefitted from your absence.

'Every day,' I say. 'I missed you every day.' You walk back to the sofa and I stand up, my arms outstretched. 'Can we put it all behind us?' I ask and I pull you close. 'Friends?'

'Friends,' you lie.

Chapter Eighteen

OH THE TIME I wasted on you, Clara: the hours of phone calls, e-mails, the invitations, the laboured arrangements, the holiday (a whole week's skiing), they all came rushing back to me in snapshots, flickering through my mind. This huge, monumental effort on my part to rediscover the indefinable magic that brought us together and made us feel we were always meant to be. All for nothing.

Why didn't I see the magic had evaporated long ago?

You'd been playing a game with me, Clara, a cruel sport.

And I'd been playing your fool.

Because the results of the postmortem were no coincidence. You must have planned it all, imagining the moment that they were read out to me, the moment when the truth, sick and twisted, announced itself so clearly and loudly there was no room left for doubt.

You wanted to hurt me.

And you'd chosen the person, the only person after you, who could ever fill the huge void, the aching hole inside me.

You had almost destroyed me once before when you shut

me out without warning. I had recovered, built a life for myself, and then Jonny came along, and we were so perfect. He was everything. You must have looked at us and thought we were too perfect. You must have watched us together and thought you wanted to destroy us.

To do that you must have hated me.

The thought of you hating me and me loving you hit me with such force it winded me. The thought knotted and spun around in my mind, making me dizzy. And all the time as if on a giant screen the image of Jonny's body filled my head, those blue, dead lips, and the waste, the terrible, awful, needless fucking waste of a life.

A scream travelled from my stomach into my throat and out to fill the room but the room was too small for it so it travelled down the hallway and into the kitchen before it burst out on to the street. The whole of London must have heard my scream that night, powered by the furnace that was burning inside me.

Anything that happened now was down to you, Clara. You had driven me to this.

You had set the rules and forced me to play you at your own game.

I couldn't shake the thought of Jonny, I couldn't begin to accept he had gone, was never coming back. His loss didn't follow me around like a shadow; it became part of me, lodging itself deep within my being. I was possessed by it.

Yet the madness of grief also spurred me on, like an engine whirring inside me, never running out of steam. Some people are crushed under the weight of it, others are driven to do more, to be more than they ever thought possible. I don't need to tell you what category I fell into, Clara.

Initially, when you disappeared, I'd wanted to stay close to your story to gather as much information as I could to find you. That was when I still believed you were lost. But now there were other more pressing reasons for me to be pulling the strings of our coverage. If it was going to be me pitted against you, I needed people to see what you were really like.

So far, in common with most dead people (or those *presumed dead)*, the Clara O'Connor the newspapers wrote about was a carefree, beautiful, *everything-to-live-for* young woman, the heroine in her own tragedy. Even the police had glossed over the murkier elements of your past, desperate to keep your story at the top of the news agenda and help their faltering investigation.

I needed to recast your image and let you know I was on your trail. I needed, somehow, to persuade Robbie to put me back on your story.

My reappearance in the newsroom, just days after Jonny's body was found, caused its own problems however. Walking towards the news desk I was aware that my presence, my made-up face, my dressed-for-business attire, silenced the chatter. It dropped to a hush, a whisper. Heads lifted, eyes opened wide in surprise. If you carry on as normal when you're supposed to be locked away, crying and howling and succumbing to your grief, you arouse suspicion. I wanted to shout for everyone to hear: *Just because I can walk and talk and breathe doesn't mean I'm not dying inside.*

But what use would that have been?

Besides, I realised I too had made those judgements; questioning the motives of the father who was too composed at the death of his child or the husband who remembered too clearly the timeline of events leading up to his wife's disappearance. The bereaved have to act out the roles we cast them in, otherwise they will be the villains.

In the end I just put one foot in front of the other and walked until I reached the news desk. And then Robbie caught sight of me. 'I'll buy you a coffee,' he said uncharacteristically and swept me out of the door.

The *Daily Telegraph* was on the table in the canteen, your picture next to Jonny's and mine on the front page. Robbie sat down, bacon sandwich in one hand, the other twitching over the newspaper, fighting the urge to turn it over, deny it was happening.

Two Weeks on and Police Draw a Blank, the headline claimed, and the column inches below were devoted to criticism of the investigation. Robbie's eyes pinned me down. He expected at the very least a tear, some evidence of emotion, because Jonny was gone and you were still out there, because all the papers carried the story and there was no escaping from it. But the truth was I had found ways to cope, reserves of strength. That's what people do, isn't it?

We sat silent amongst the chatter and the sound of the

coffee machine, the snatched glances in my direction, people saving their gossip for the walk back to the newsroom. I watched Robbie eat his bacon roll and pretended to read a feature on women having babies in their forties. Instead I rehearsed the argument I was about to present to him.

Finally he licked each finger with a smack of his lips, wiped his mouth with a ketchup-stained serviette and sat back in his chair.

'Amber Corrigan will do an interview with us,' I told him. Of course it wasn't entirely true. At that point she hadn't agreed to anything but a lie isn't a lie if you can make it happen. And I knew I could make it happen.

Robbie sat up, the initial flash of excitement giving way to a look of fear.

'You can't do it,' he said.

'No, but someone else could,' I said, adding softly, 'I would just be in the background.' He squirmed in his chair. He knew it was all wrong allowing me anywhere near the story, especially now that Jonny had died, but I could see him making the calculation in his head. 'Officially, of course, you would know nothing about my involvement.'

'This Amber girl, she won't do it with anyone else?' he asked, scrunching the serviette up in his fat hands. I shook my head.

'I wouldn't be asking you otherwise. Look,' I said, dropping my voice to a whisper, 'it's far from ideal, I know that. But Amber was one of the last people to see Clara. An interview with her might jog a few memories. Clara's my friend after all and I'll do anything I can to help find her, because so far the police don't seem to be doing such a good job.' I tapped my finger on the newspaper.

'Who do you suggest?' He was warming to the idea, his hunger for the exclusive stronger than any notion of ethics. I paused for a moment before I told him.

'Jane Fenchurch,' I said, 'she's perfect.'

'You've got to be joking.'

'Look, she's not exactly Kate fucking Adie, I know, but with the right support and help I think she could do a good job. I'm offering you an interview with Amber Corrigan. Jane is unthreatening. I think Amber will warm to her. There is no one else. You can hardly send Richard after his almighty fuck-up the other day. I can guide Jane, feed her the right questions. Trust me,' I said and saw him twitch at the sight of his phone flashing. 'We could have it in the can this afternoon if we leave now.' I took the newspaper from the table and folded it away in my bag.

Robbie wiped his greasy brow and picked up the phone, 'Hold,' he barked. And then he nodded his agreement. 'For God's sake though,' he said, resting his hand on the phone's receiver to block out our chat, 'don't leave her to her own devices.'

I found her at the furthest corner of the newsroom, her shoulders hunched, disappearing into the newspaper she was reading. I felt a stab of sympathy. To most of the editors she was already invisible, the latest casualty of a system which chewed up and spat out young reporters for the slightest transgression. Often it wasn't even clear what they had done wrong, if anything at all. Careers were simply made or ended on the whim of an editor.

I knew Jane Fenchurch probably thought it was her animal-print coat that did it for her but that was simply a convenient excuse. She was just another mousy blonde who had failed to make her mark.

'Jane,' I said, making her jump from behind the newspaper. She looked and me and then looked behind to see if I was talking to someone else. 'I'm Rachel,' I said with a smile. 'Grab your things, we're going out on a story.'

We were in the car, heading out of London on the A40, when I explained to Jane the purpose of our trip. She was already familiar with your story and my connection to it and looked slightly embarrassed by it all, in the way you would if a stranger had asked you to observe an intimate moment. 'It's delicate,' I told her, 'let's just say my involvement today is a little under the radar.' We were sitting at the lights and I turned and saw her pale washed-out face now flushed with excitement. 'I'm sure you won't tell anyone I was with you.' She shook her head vigorously. 'Not a word,' she said, her eyes sparkling in collusion. As I predicted, Jane Fenchurch couldn't afford the privilege of asking too many questions.

'Just let me do the talking when we get there,' I said.

I pressed on number twenty-five. It was your flat, Clara, and Amber's too. I began to worry she wouldn't answer, that I had promised too much to Robbie, dragged Jane down here for nothing. I remembered you saying she worked from home writing magazine features and thought of the yoga mat sticking out of her bag, the hint of free time on her hands that came with a freelance life.

No answer. I buzzed again. And then her voice, a muffled hello?

'It's me,' I said. 'It's Rachel, Clara's friend.'

'Rachel?' was all she said.

In the square a traffic warden was patrolling, seeking out his next victim. A seagull swooped down to peck at a bag of rubbish left in the street, flying off with a chicken leg in its mouth.

Finally I heard the zzzz of the intercom and we were inside. In the lobby a handful of letters lay uncollected on the floor. I glanced quickly but none were addressed to you. We moved across the hallway to the stairs, Jane slipping in behind me. I could sense her nerves, the reluctance. 'Maybe it's best if you hang back for a while, let me do the talking,' I watched the relief wash over her.

Amber's pale face was waiting for us in the doorway when we reached your flat. It was only a week since we'd last met but I was struck by how tired she looked, purple shadows circled her eyes. She was wearing tight jeans which grazed her bony hips and a red woollen jumper which showed off a slice of her sunken stomach. Her blond hair was shower-wet. Poor Amber, I thought, living in the flat with the ghost of you. A spasm of guilt twisted in my stomach over what I was about to do. And then it passed. There are times when the end justifies the means.

'Amber,' I said, out of breath from climbing three flights of stairs. I kissed her on both cheeks and felt her wet hair against my face. 'You look surprised to see us.'

'I wasn't expecting you,' she said. She looked like a frightened animal caught in a trap.

'Oh God,' I said, 'Don't tell me Hilary hasn't called you.'

'Hilary?'

'The police press officer. She was supposed to call and ask you.' I took a step back from the door and raised my hand to cover my mouth. 'Oh fuck, this is really embarrassing.'

'Why would she call me?' Amber said defensively. 'I've told them everything I know.'

I sighed and shook my head. 'Maybe we should go and come back . . .' I said, taking a step away from the door. 'I knew it was a bad idea, it's just that . . .' I paused.

'Just tell me what she wanted.'

'I told them it would be too much to ask, it's just that you were one of the last people to see her and the police . . .' I pulled the folded-up *Daily Telegraph* from my bag and handed it to her. 'They need all the help they can get.'

I watched as she scanned the headline in the newspaper, shuffling on her feet. And then it clicked. 'I can't do it again. I told them I wouldn't do anything else. I'm sorry Rachel, I just can't.' She wiped her eyes with her sleeve. 'This is like living in a nightmare.'

'You don't have to apologise,' I said. 'If anyone understands it's me. She's in here all the time.' I tapped my finger at the side of my head. 'I see her everywhere: in the supermarket, sitting in traffic. I see her when I wake up and last thing at night. I can't stop thinking of her out there, cold and alone. She hated being alone.' My voice was unsteady and to my surprise the tears came sliding down my cheeks. 'I'm sorry,' I said, wiping them away with my index finger. 'I wish I could do this myself, it's not fair to ask you. I just want to help her. I don't know what else to do.'

Those tears that I once found so hard to cry kept coming and I did nothing to stop them. I was aware of Amber watching me, her hand reaching out to me then pulling back, searching for words or gestures to console me.

And then above my sobs I heard her say: 'Come inside.'

My tears were real, Clara. They were tears of anger and frustration. But Amber only saw her own grief reflected in them.

In the eighteen months since our first meeting there your flat had been transformed from the stark, empty space it once was. Black-and-white photographs of street children and wizened old ladies that you took on your travels hung from the wall alongside your own paintings; abstract flashes of colour on dark canvases. An old sunburst mirror you'd picked up on eBay, a coffee table groaning with photography books and unopened post. It was the same as always; only the bookshelves I hadn't seen before and they made me laugh. You with your principles, the kind only the wealthy can afford, had finally succumbed to the lure of Ikea.

I could still smell you in the living room. Or maybe it was just the smell of your flat. Every home has one, don't they, and yours was a sickly vanilla that made my nose itch. Amber handed me a box of tissues, 'I have no idea what to say,' she said which was ironic since my own head was bubbling with words and sentences and accusations I wanted to throw at you.

'I'll help. But I can't tell you what to say,' I told her.

'Thanks,' she said, with a weak smile. 'I guess this all comes easy to you.'

I started to unpack the small self-shoot camera I'd brought from work, anticipating the presence of a cameraman would unnerve Amber even more. Besides, the fewer people who knew I was there the better.

I let her talk about you as Jane skipped around us, opening and closing the curtains, checking the exposure on the camera. Mostly, Amber just repeated what she'd told me the week before, little revolutions of the same story which would have irritated me normally. But not today. She told me again about your mood in the weeks leading up to your disappearance, how you seemed anxious on the Friday she last saw you, flitting between excited and worried. I let my head fall into my hands.

'Sorry,' she said, pausing mid-sentence. 'I don't want to upset you.'

'It's not your fault. It's just that the more I hear the more

I think she was getting ill again. Those highs and lows, that's exactly how she was in the lead-up to the breakdown. I'm so angry with myself for not picking up on it. I should have done more to help her.'

I watched Amber turn the thought over in her head. 'You think she's done something to herself, don't you?' she said.

'I don't know what to think any more,' I told her.

By the time the camera started rolling all those little seeds I'd planted must have flowered in Amber's mind. Jane asked her one question and she delivered the soundbite I desperately wanted. I doubt I could have said it better myself. It was as if by osmosis my own thoughts had become hers.

'Was that OK?' she asked, secretly pleased with her performance.

'Perfect,' I said. Because it was, Clara.

From the kitchen, the sound of the kettle boiling. Amber and Jane's voices drifted out, chat about the comparable merits of yoga and Pilates. I packed the radio mic into the kitbag and marked the interview tape carefully. Then I sloped off down the corridor.

Do you remember how I moaned about your bathroom with its noisy flush being next to your bedroom? Well, that day I was glad of it. The proximity of the two rooms would have been a good cover if Amber had seen me; thankfully she didn't.

The door to your room was slightly ajar. I pushed it softly, mindful of potentially creaky hinges. On the wall, a huge painting I recognised as your abstract interpretation of the old pier. 'My best work' you told me once and I had to agree. There was something hypnotic about it: the red and purple and orange of a summer sky on fire, the flames licking at the charred and twisted frame of the old pier. Underneath the painting, a pair of jeans and a jacket had been discarded on a chair, pink Converse on the floor, the scent of vanilla stronger here. And on the battered chest of drawers next to the wardrobe were photo frames, one of you with your dad on a beach, though which beach I couldn't say. He was standing behind you, his arms on your shoulders. Fleeces and weather-beaten faces and sun-wrinkled eyes. The next one was of your dad alone, wearing the same fleece, sitting over a camping stove outside a yellow beach hut. The last photograph was an old one of a toddler I hadn't seen before. It looked like it was taken in the eighties. The eyes were unmistakably yours.

In the background I heard the reassuring sound of Amber and Jane talking, teaspoons tapping against mugs. Quickly I reached into my bag and pulled out the photograph I'd brought with me, placing it amongst the others. Then I slipped out as quietly as I'd come in.

'It would be great,' I said as we nursed our mugs of tea, 'if we could get a few shots of Clara's paintings. It just gives people a sense of who she is, you know, rather than just this missing woman.'

Amber beamed. 'That's a lovely idea, there are two in here,' she said, picking them out on the wall.

'Her favourite was the one of the West Pier. Actually it's my favourite too,' I said. 'Shame she never got round to putting it up.'

'It's in her room,' Amber said hesitantly and looked at me first, then Jane. 'I'm not sure we should be going in there.'

'We don't have to be in the room, we could just zoom in on it from the doorway.' It was Jane, surprising me with her unsolicited contribution. 'Great idea,' I said and saw Jane standing up to grab the camera, looking pleased with herself.

'You finish your tea,' I told her, my hand on her shoulder. 'I'll knock the shots off myself.'

I went back to the doorway of your room and fixed the camera on to the small tripod. I took one shot of the painting, zooming in on it slowly, and then another which started on the West Pier and panned down to the photographs below. And then when I was finished I slipped the picture I had placed there back in my bag.

On the way back to London I gave Jane DCI Gunn's direct number. 'Pin him down on the specific points Amber made,' I said, 'and check on the postmortem results while you're on to him.' They hadn't been made public yet but I assumed they would be later that day.

I sensed Jane stiffen, stuttering her words. 'You don't know how Jonny died yet?' We were in the car, sitting at a set of traffic lights on Lewes Road heading out of Brighton. I turned to her but she avoided eye contact, doodling little flowers in her notepad instead.

'I do,' I said. 'But you need to find out through an official channel.' She looked up, her pen resting on the petal of a flower she had drawn.

'This must be so hard for you. I can't imagine what you're going through.' There was softness to her words, velvet and smooth. Her concern touched me, interrupting my train of thought.

'Thank you for not judging me,' I said and I meant it. 'I know me being here, helping you, might seem weird, but it's my way of coping. If I don't do something I'll lose my mind.' The lights turned green and we started moving again, past the pound shops and takeaways. By the time we hit the A23 Jane was dialling DCI Gunn's number, on speakerphone at my request. I heard it ring four times until the familiar West Country voice said hello.

His tone was more abrupt, his answers shorter than normal, put off no doubt at being called on a mobile by a reporter he didn't know.

He said they would release the postmortem results in the next hour and no, he wouldn't tell Jane anything in advance. He refused to say whether Jonny was still a suspect. He was about to hang up when Jane announced we had an interview with Amber and explained in detail what she had said. A long silence followed.

'I'm not prepared to speculate,' he said finally, police-speak for fuck off. I waited in dread for Jane to thank him and hang up and kiss our chances of a lead story goodbye.

'You are aware that she had a history of mental health problems aren't you?' she said instead, scribbling furiously as she spoke.

'We are aware of that, yes,' DCI Gunn said defensively.

'But what you're saying is that you have categorically ruled out any link between that and her disappearance.'

'No, that's not what I said. We are considering all possibilities.' I could hear Jane's breaths through her words. The nerves and adrenalin that came with knowing you were closing in on a good story.

'So it's one of several possibilities?' she asked. And I smiled; she's not going to give up, I thought, I was wrong to underestimate her.

'Yes,' he conceded, wearily, 'that would appear to be what I'm saying.'

'Thank you,' said Jane, her pen finally stopping on the page. And when she hung up I didn't have to look at her to know there was a smile of satisfaction on her face. Jane Fenchurch had finally got her big break.

In what was left of the journey we discussed how to structure the package, what shots to use, which clips of Amber to include, and when we reached the studios I dropped her at the door, handed her the tape and drove off. A little bit further up the road I called Robbie to brief him on the news lines and suggested it was a lead story. 'Jane was amazing,' I told him and listened to him snort. 'You should give her another chance.'

I headed over to Jake's where he had offered to cook me dinner, sensing, I think, that I was keen to spend as little time alone in my flat as possible.

At six o'clock, with a glass of wine and the smell of lemon and saffron and lamb cooking in the oven, we settled down to watch the evening news. From the headlines I knew it was the lead story and I sat back and waited to see if Jane had executed my carefully laid plan.

Amber's anguished face filled the screen behind the presenter as he read the cue to the story:

'Police searching for the missing artist Clara O'Connor say they are now considering the possibility she may have committed suicide. Miss O'Connor, who had a history of depression, has been missing for almost two weeks as Jane Fenchurch reports.'

It was you again, the smiling photograph so infamous, but this time it zoomed in slowly until your deep blue eyes filled the shot. Jane's words ran over it: . . .'troubled artist . . . who friends fear may have taken her own life'.

It cut to Amber, sitting in your living room, so obviously your living room because in the wide shots you could see your photos, your furniture, your mug sitting on the coffee table.

'On the day she disappeared,' Amber told the camera, 'she was all over the place, up and down. Her mood was so unpredictable. Looking back now I can see it was something that had been brewing for weeks, months even. She wasn't stable. She kept on saying that she would feel better about everything after Friday evening but she wouldn't say why. Now I'm just so worried she had planned something, you know, she's done something to herself and I could have stopped it.'

This was what you had driven me to, Clara. I had to paint you as a creature on the edge, someone who was unstable, with a history of depression. I had to demolish the holier-than-thou image of you because you had gone too far, you had killed a man, I was certain of that. And not just any man. You had killed Jonny and you were hunting me. I needed people to see what you were like.

Were you watching? I hope so because right at the very end of the report was a message for you.

The best shot, saved until last.

The painting of the charred pier from your bedroom slowly panned down to the photographs displayed on the chest of drawers beneath. You and your dad, one of him alone. And the one I had added. The smiling shot of you with my mother, the very same one you switched in my bedroom.

You could torment me with your messages, but I could send you a few of my own.

Two could play that game.

'Who would have thought it? Jane Fenchurch has talent after all . . .' Jake said, kicking me playfully with his foot. 'Or did you direct her more than you're letting on.'

'She did it all on her own,' I said, kicking him back. We were lounging on his sofa, full of wine and tagine, our empty plates discarded on the coffee table in front of us. There was something about Jake's company that was so easy. He didn't drown me in sympathy. He didn't question my behaviour, or demand to see my grief, he just talked and laughed and jibed and allowed me to just be. He was strangely addictive.

He swirled the wine in his glass, and ran his fingers through the thick flop of hair. A thought hovered and then I tried to hide it at the back of my mind. He caught me watching him but instead of looking away he held my stare.

'What is it about you, Rachel?' he asked, his brown eyes flashing. 'You're a mass of contradictions. I can't pin you down. You create this tough image for work and then go and shatter it by sticking your neck out for a rookie reporter.'

The idea of me having a tough image tickled and irritated me in equal measure. It certainly wasn't something I'd set out to cultivate but at the same time I realised it was probably a widely held opinion amongst my colleagues in the newsroom. And it wasn't because I was good at my job or ambitious. I was most definitely both of those things but so were plenty of others. It was simply because I happened to be a woman; everyone knows you can't be ambitious and female without being cold and heartless too.

'So you're telling me everyone you know is either soft or tough or good or evil. Where have you been living, Disneyland?' I laughed and poured myself another glass of wine. Jake raised his hands in surrender.

'You just surprise me, that's all,' he said. 'I like being surprised.' I caught his look and for a moment it locked with mine, and it was there, a charge between us, and then we turned away.

Not now, so wrong.

'Tell me about Jonny,' he said. And so I did, honestly and openly.

'I loved him, I don't know what more to say, the thought of never seeing him again . . . I don't know, it could destroy me if I let it. But I can't,' I said, 'I have to keep going.'

He smiled. 'Couldn't have said it better myself.'

I was helping Jake clear up when Sarah called on my mobile, her inappropriately chirpy voice intruding into the evening. I could never ignore her, you see, still clinging on to the vain hope she might actually ring with some useful information one day.

'How you doing, Rach?' she asked.

'Oh, you know, coping,' I said in a weak voice, moving away from Jake and the clatter of dishes.

'I was going to ask you if you'd heard anything through work but I guess you'll have taken a bit of time off, have you? To give yourself a break.'

'I'm still at work. It takes my mind off everything,' I said.

'Bloody hell, you should go easy on yourself,' and then she paused, 'I take it you would have known about Amber whatsherbloodyface giving an interview then? Making out like she thought Clara had topped herself, like she would know. Some people'll do anything to get their face on TV.'

'I think she was just trying to help.'

'Yeah right, didn't see her rushing out to put posters of Clara up with the rest of us, did I?'

I was thinking about how Sarah's voice had gone from breezy hi-babe chirpiness to vitriolic in a matter of moments when Jake dropped a saucepan on the floor. 'You at home, babe?' she said, her breezy tone restored.

'At a friend's,' I said, 'being looked after.'

'You should have said you were with someone instead of listening to me bang on about Amber. Anyway, I won't keep you from your evening.'

'It's no problem,' I said, 'we've finished dinner.'

'Well, I'll call in a few days. Take care, babe,' and she rang off.

By the time the late-night news came on Jake and I were relaxing in the warm glow of wine. Your story had dropped down the running order, bumped from the lead by the first case of bird flu in the UK. There was to be a mass culling of birds at a Bernard Matthews factory-farm in Norfolk. I imagined them weighing it up at the evening news meeting. A hundred and sixty thousand dead birds or one suspected dead woman? 'But this is the first outbreak of bird flu in the UK,' someone would have said. 'It affects more of our viewers than one woman who might just have taken her own life.'

The birds won out in the end Clara. Dead turkeys over you.

The bulletin was almost over – the And Finally, a story about a record-breaking week for art sales, with works by Degas and Renoir and Warhol all going on sale – when my phone vibrated in my pocket.

The message simply read:

Coming to get you, ready or not.

Chapter Nineteen

YOU WERE GOING to be box office, Clara. You were going to be on *Crimewatch.* Remember when we used to watch it and Nick Ross would say: *Don't have nightmares, do sleep well,* which was pointless because they'd just shown a masked intruder kill an old couple in their home and all you thought was 'if it could happen to them, why not me?' But we would rather die than admit we were scared shitless and sometimes, if we were having a sleepover, you'd say you could hear footsteps on the stairs to spook me, or worse, you'd tell one of your ghost stories. You'd spin them so well I swore I could see ghosts floating amongst us.

I'd learnt of the reconstruction after spending the morning in Harrow Road police station reporting the break-in with no obvious signs of forced entry, which generated a wry smile from the PC taking notes, and the malicious texts, which drew a less humiliating response.

It was Jake's idea to go to the police and make it official, part of his drive to force me to take the 'threat' seriously.

I was resistant at first until it occurred to me there were advantages to be gained. I needed the police to have a record of my complaints. If not for now, then for later.

Out on the street, amongst the shops selling life-size ornamental tigers and halal meats and the fried chicken joints, I checked my phone to find Hilary Benson had left a message asking me to call her urgently. My immediate reaction was that Amber had rumbled us for stretching the truth a little to persuade her to do the interview. Instead, it was my help that Hilary wanted and I was only too happy to oblige.

I arrived at the *Crimewatch* studios in White City, a white cube of a building perched on the edge of Shepherd's Bush, with plenty of time to spare. If you closed your eyes you could almost pretend the sound of the traffic roaring in and out of London on the A40 was the sea crashing around you. I looked up at the sky, so brilliantly, optimistically blue, and thanked the angel looking out for me for dropping such an opportunity into my lap.

Not that I was without nerves. As I approached the huge BBC sign hanging over the entrance I realised I was apprehensive. Yes, I had plenty of experience facing the cameras, talking live, so much experience that little fazed me. I asked the questions, extracted soundbites from reluctant interviewees. I wrote my scripts, structured my reports. But that was the problem. Now the roles would be reversed. And I was about to relinquish control to someone I'd never met.

From my telephone conversations with Sally McDonald I had assumed she was in her mid twenties. Her chirpy Scottish voice, the way she sang, '*HEL LO*,' seemed to suggest a youthful enthusiasm unknown amongst more seasoned producers. So I was surprised to see a rather rotund woman in her late forties greet me at reception. '*HEL LO* Rachel,' she said a little too loudly as she approached. 'We'll sign you in and then we can go upstairs and get cracking.' She must have realised her tone was too jovial because she added with a look of pity, 'They're filming the reconstruction in Brighton today, let's hope it produces some results.'

On the way up in the lift she told me they had found someone who looked just like you to retrace your footsteps. They always ask a family member or friend if they can, but you didn't have any sisters to choose from and we didn't look alike, did we? Different hair, different heights. And of course I was now slimmer than you.

I followed Sally into a room where the crew, a cameraman and a sound recordist were assembled. The lighting was intentionally low, lit only by a special standard lamp covered with foil. It was the kind of moody atmosphere we often tried to achieve at work, though the time constraints of news meant we rarely pulled it off. Sally asked me if I wanted to put some make-up on and seemed surprised when I declined. I wanted to look the part, Clara, the shattered friend desperate to find you.

'Let's start if we can,' I said. 'I've got to be back at work shortly.'

Sally threw a few obvious questions at me but after the third one it was clear I wasn't giving her the soundbite she wanted.

'Forgive me,' she said, 'I'll ask you the same question a few times over so I can choose the best answer.' She must have forgotten who she was talking to, I used that kind of line every day when an interviewee wasn't delivering the clip I needed.

Not that I minded. Sally could have asked me the same question 100 times over and I would have given her the same answer. It was a trick I learnt from interviewing politicians. Acknowledge the question, then say what you want. If you don't offer an alternative answer they'll have no choice but to use the one you want them to.

Sally persevered for a good thirty minutes and of course I mixed up the words a little so it didn't seem like I was reading from a script but the message was still the same.

Sally: 'Can you think of anyone who would want to hurt Clara?'

Me: 'No one would have hurt Clara, she was someone who needed talking care of, made you want to look after her. And I can't bring myself to think that she is gone. And if she is out there and listening, and I hope she is, I want her to know, I will never give up looking, never. I will find her if it's the last thing I do.'

I paused and played with my hands, as if I was nervous, and then I looked up again at Sally, my voice bigger, stronger this time.

'We've been friends for so long, I know her inside out. I know what she's thinking, I know what she wants. So I can't give up on her, she knows I never will.'

Thursday night was *Crimewatch* night and Jake was with me at my flat. We were rarely apart in those days, sharing the same space but somehow allowing each other to breathe. Looking back I can see he was my link to normality, a life raft that stopped me from drowning in Jonny's loss. He was also separate from you, not yet contaminated by our story which would eventually spill like oil into his life.

Nine o'clock; my heart thudded in time with the beats of the *Crimewatch* theme music. No surprise, Clara, you were the top story. Your now universally recognised face so easy on the eye, and your middle-class credentials meant your story had caught everyone's imagination, while others of missing women and children were given a few lines in the 'news in brief' column or ignored completely.

We waited for the music to finish then Fiona Bruce popped up and, eyebrows knitted in concern, she read the cue to the reconstruction sitting perched on the desk.

'Tonight we want your help in finding this young woman' (*points to picture of you*). 'It's been more than two weeks since Clara O'Connor, a young artist from Brighton with a bright future ahead of her, was last seen meeting friends in the city on a chilly Friday night. Despite extensive media coverage and numerous appeals the police are still looking for that crucial bit of information that will bring them closer to finding her.

'So if you think you might have seen Clara, please get in touch. Your call could be the one that matters.'

And then the VT rolled.

In all honesty I wasn't convinced your double looked anything like you. Yes, she had long brown hair but it didn't bounce the way yours did when she moved, and although she was wearing the same mossy green coat you wore on the night you disappeared her gait was all wrong. Jake told me to shut up and watch the film, 'No one else would notice that,' he said. The cameras followed your double into Cantina Latina where she laughed with someone I presumed was Sarah Pitts. Then she was outside again on the promenade, saying hello to a man who wore Jonny's clothes but looked nothing like him. For a sickening moment I thought they might show you embracing, kissing even, a little nod to the police's narrative of events, but to my relief they just showed you walking along in step with each other.

That's where it ended. The pair of you on the promenade, heading into the black night, blown away by a gust of wind from the sea.

After the reconstruction it was my turn. I wondered if you were watching somewhere, Clara. I hoped you were. Me, sitting in the dim lights of the studio, my ashen face free of make-up, chewing my lips, fiddling nervously with my fingers. Playing the part of the tormented friend. What was your reaction when you heard my words?

'I know what she's thinking, I know what she wants. I can't give up on her, she knows I never will.'

'Remind me never to let you on air without make-up,' Jake said when it was finished. We were sprawled on the sofa. He prodded me in the stomach with his foot.

'Fuck off,' I said. There was a cushion between us. I picked it up and went to throw it in his direction but he saw me and grabbed my hand to stop me. It was there again, the flash between us. A look that lasted too long. He let my hand fall.

'Do you think it'll work?' he asked. He wasn't joking now, his voice heavy, reluctant to say the words that were forming on his lips. He breathed them, so quietly they floated out from him into the air. 'After all this time, it doesn't look good.'

I took the cushion and pushed it into my stomach, leaning forward. Everyone thought you had gone, swallowed up by a January night, sucked into the ether. No one would believe me, would they? But they had to; if I only convinced one person that would be enough and I decided there and then that I wanted that person to be Jake.

'Have you ever just known something?' I asked. 'I mean felt it in your bones, had that unshakeable conviction? Sometimes it doesn't make sense. But you just know. Well, I know Clara is alive.'

I waited for a pat on my arm, a touch to say *there there*. A pitying look – *poor Rachel can't face up to the truth*. Instead his eyes didn't leave me, as if what I was telling him had him gripped, as if he had never been as interested in anyone or anything as he was at that moment. Then I took a breath to steel myself.

'She's out there somewhere,' I said and I knew from the look on his face he was wondering why that conviction brought me no comfort, why my face clouded with fear. 'I think she's out to get me.'

He listened in silence, for so long, Clara, it broke my heart. He believed me. There was no sliver of doubt, no attempt to convince me otherwise. I told him our secret, I told him what you had done and how it sent you mad. I told him how you blamed me and how I had tried to make things better since you'd got back but how nothing had been right. And I explained how I realised you'd been storing your resentment, bottling it in the deep pit of your stomach, ready for the day when you unleashed it and took your revenge.

Of course there were 300 police officers out there searching for you Clara; your face was so well known it would be hard for you to move around without being noticed. But Jake didn't question my theory, he didn't ask how it was possible you could slip through the shadows like a ghost. Like me, he knew anything was possible.

I was so warm with relief I wanted to cry. It was like one of those secrets you guard and dread sharing, only when you do, you wonder why you thought it was so difficult, because the sharing can be beautiful really. Suddenly you are not alone.

I wiped my eyes and Jake's arm slipped round me. 'I'm scared,' I told him. And it was true. You had already destroyed so much, Clara, but you could do much more damage. His arm was pulling me in, little by little, and in his arms I couldn't be scared because they were strong and I was protected, sheltered. And his breath was hot on my face and I was tingling from that and from his hair which brushed my cheek. We looked at each other and it was there between us, so obvious we couldn't ignore it, and then I felt his lips, warm, like velvet on mine, and I didn't pull away. Not when his kisses trailed down my neck, not when his fingers were undoing my shirt, tracing the outline of my chest, not when his hand moved across my breasts. I didn't pull away. I was warm and alive and melted into him as if we were fusing together. And much later, when he was inside me, I wanted him to stay there forever because we seemed to fit so well but mostly because lying there with him made everything else go away.

I know what you are thinking, Clara: that it was all so wrong, so utterly wrong, such a betrayal of Jonny. But it wasn't a betrayal of him, not really. It was because I loved Jonny so much, because of the huge gaping hole he left inside me that I had to fill it with something otherwise I would have died. So don't judge me, not until you've walked in my shoes.

Our legs were locked round each other's, and the duvet, which Jake had brought from the bedroom, was wrapped round them, cold and refreshing next to the heat of our bodies. We were eating crisps and drinking gin because it was the only thing left in the cupboard. Jake snatched a look at his watch. 'The update is coming on any minute,' he told me. I didn't want you to come crashing into my living room and intrude upon us. I didn't want our little bubble of togetherness to be popped. But still, I was curious.

It was Nick Ross this time. He walked over to the makeshift Sussex police incident room where DCI Gunn and the petite woman detective I recognised from the day he showed me the CCTV were sitting. DCI Gunn's hair had been stuck down and I could make out a faint line of orange on his collar, his frown lines smoothed over with the make-up girl's brush. He looked stiff, sweating under the studio lights.

> Nick Ross: 'Now on to the disappearance of the Brighton artist Clara O'Connor. Police have had a very encouraging response. Three calls in particular you are especially interested in, is that right?'
> DCI Gunn: 'Yes Nick that's correct. We've had over fifty calls from members of the public who think they may have seen Clara in the early hours of Saturday morning. But in particular we have had three callers who mentioned the same name in connection with her disappearance. Two of those people have given their name, but one called anonymously. I want to appeal to that caller to get in touch again. Your call will be treated in the strictest confidence.'

DCI Gunn was just getting into his stride when Nick Ross said: 'Well good luck with that, now over to Fiona with news on that armed robbery in Sheffield.'

Three callers. One name.

'Maybe the net is closing in,' Jake said but I couldn't focus. If the police didn't believe Jonny killed you now, what trail were they about to follow? Whose name had been mentioned?

I voiced some of these questions to Jake who told me he had a contact, *an old mate who owed him a favour.* He would ask him to find out.

In the end though we found out who it was much quicker than either of us anticipated: announced by two police officers knocking on my door at six in the morning.

Chapter Twenty

CONGRATULATIONS, CLARA, I was the woman suspected of killing you. How did that sound? Did you roll it round your mouth, try it out for size? Did it feel as good as you'd hoped?

I kept thinking things couldn't get any worse and then bingo, this happened. Well, ten out of ten for imagination, for pure evil cunning. There I was getting my head round the fact you'd faked your own disappearance, you'd killed Jonny, not realising for one terrible moment that there was more to come. The icing on the fucking cake. I was it. Bound up so tightly in your lies it seemed no one would believe me.

I guess you must have loved me a lot to hate me this much.

As soon I was dressed I had been driven from London to Brighton police station where I was handed over to the custody sergeant. He was old and wheezing, bound to a desk because it was the only job he could do. Breathing his coffee fumes over me he explained that I was to be processed, like a slab of meat. I noticed him looking at me curiously. 'You're that woman off the telly aren't you? Don't you report on crime? Least you'll know what you're in for,' he said, smirking, as if the thought tickled him.

My face coloured with shame. *This can't be happening.* This happened to other people who took drugs and robbed and killed. It didn't happen to young women, with successful careers and property and money. I started to cry, hot tears of anger and frustration. 'There's been an awful mistake, this has nothing to do with me,' and the sergeant nodded as if he'd heard it all before.

After half an hour there was nothing left of me. The person with tasteful, expensive clothes and jewellery, the person I had taken years to construct, had vanished. My diamond earrings – a present from Jonny, my Tiffany chain, were all removed. My Mulberry bag, my BlackBerry, my wallet, the belt on my jeans, everything I had brought with me was recorded, bagged and labelled to be handed back to me when (if) I was released.

Next, I was marched to a room to have my photograph taken. The mug shot. My eyes were red from tiredness, puffy with tears. I imagined the photo finding its way into the pages of the newspapers, arranged next to a shot of me as I appeared on TV to show how far I'd fallen. *Crime reporter accused of murder.* How they would love that story. As Robbie would say, *It has all the elements.*

After they had taken a swab of DNA I was finally shown to the interview room where the fun was ready to begin.

⤚o⤙

The room was grey and fridge-cold. I sat at the table with my solicitor, a woman a little older than me whose name was Kirstin Taylor. I say she was older than me on account of her clothes, which were middle-aged (Boden chic), and the strands of grey that threaded through her dark hair. I remember being strangely relieved to see she wasn't a man. God knows why, I think I'd harboured some vain hope she would know instinctively that my arrest was an affront to justice. Perhaps I thought she would understand the mechanics of a close female friendship in a way a man never would. But if she did she kept it well hidden, nodding her head, taking notes and saying 'hmmm' with her finger over her mouth as if she was discussing a staff issue at work and not an accusation of murder.

I shifted in the chair, and pulled my winter coat around me to calm my chattering teeth. Underneath I was wearing only jeans and a thin cotton top, the first things I'd found to pull on when the police arrived. To make matters worse Jake had answered the door in his TV shirt and boxers. Such a cosy scene: girlfriend and boyfriend waking up together in their flat. Only it wasn't Jake's flat and my boyfriend had died less than two weeks before. It didn't look good.

DCI Gunn came into the room with a woman and sat in the chair opposite. He didn't acknowledge me, no simple hello, no smile thrown my way. He just sat down and looked through his notes. We were adversaries now, three years of lunches, banter and trust-building sucked out of the room along with the warm air. You see, being accused of murder is a great equaliser, no matter who you are in your outside life; in the interview room with the camera rolling and the eyes staring, you become the lowest common denominator.

'The time of the interview is ten twenty a.m. Officers present are DCI Roger Gunn, and DS Susan Tomey,' he said, still leafing through the notes in front of him, underlining a few sentences, scoring a few others out. I couldn't read them; the print was too small, the table between us too big. It's a file on me, I thought, all about me, and whatever was written inside it had led them to believe I killed you.

I hadn't seen DS Tomey before and her face was something of a welcome diversion from DCI Gunn's in so much as it transfixed me with its ugliness. The front teeth that jutted out, her freckle-covered face, the way her mouth twitched. Rodentesque, I thought. Her hair, tied back severely in a ponytail, was only a shade or two from mine. But I couldn't detect any evidence of ginger solidarity in the room.

'Can you tell us where you were on the night of Friday January the nineteenth 2007, Rachel?' she said. Her voice was soft and southern. I guessed she was local.

'I was in Brighton,' I tried to say, but my words stuck to my mouth; no moisture in my throat for them to form properly. I took a sip from the cup of water in front of me. It didn't help, a glue coated my tongue. 'I went to Cantina Latina with friends, for a small school reunion, Clara was supposed to meet me there, but you already know that.' I aimed that sentence in DCI Gunn's direction, hoping it might spark a reaction, but I got nothing back. 'I left about eleven and walked on to the pier.'

'Why would you do that?' she asked. DCI Gunn still hadn't said a word. He wasn't looking at me either. His nose twitched as he stared down at his pad.

'I went to buy some chips. It's what we always did.'

'We?'

'Clara and I.' Your name caused a ripple in the room, as if we'd all somehow forgotten why I was there.

'But you had just been out for dinner.'

'Well, dinner is stretching the description of the food served in Cantina Latina a little far. We'd shared a few bowls of soggy nachos early in the evening. I was hungry,' I said, remembering how I had refused to share the nachos, claiming I'd already eaten. Everyone touching, fingering, spitting over the plates as they talked.

'And how long were you there?' DS Tomey was beginning to remind me of a terrier with a bit between her teeth. Still DCI Gunn was looking down at the notepad.

It is a strategy; soon he will make his presence felt.

'I can't tell you that exactly, I mean ten, fifteen minutes. Long enough to buy chips, eat them and lose the feeling in my fingers from the cold.' DS Tomey raised her eyebrows, which infuriated me. 'Obviously if I had known you were going to accuse me of murdering Clara, I would have made a note of the exact timings, but you know, I didn't go out to bump off my friend that night. I was actually looking forward to seeing her, pretty pissed off in fact when she didn't turn up and switched off her phone. But not so pissed off I was ready to kill her. I like to think my anger management skills are better than that.'

Kirstin gently rested her hand on my lap. Enough, it said, you are not helping.

I watched, breathing deep, trying to recover my composure as DS Tomey retied her ponytail, tighter this time, so you could see it pull on her scalp, the way Niamh used to do mine when she was trying to be a Good Mum and all day long at school I'd have a headache.

'I walked to The Old Ship hotel and booked myself a room.'

'Along the promenade?' she asked, sounding too pleased with herself for stating what was the obvious.

'That is the general route you take from the pier to the Old Ship hotel.' Anger bubbled on my skin, my stomach clenched. *Keep calm, keep calm.*

'But you didn't mention you were on the promenade before.' She sang the words, as if she'd scored a point against me, as if there was a direct correlation between such an omission and my guilt. It felt like something was creeping up on me, a net closing in. My shoulders stiffened; I rolled my neck to loosen the tension.

'I have been very clear about what I did on the night Clara disappeared. If you are trying to suggest I deliberately kept something from you then I would say you are clutching at straws. It's a fairly obvious route, in fact the only one – to get from the pier you HAVE to walk on the promenade, unless you can fly. And I can't. But I left the bar before Clara. I didn't see her or Jonny on my way to the hotel. If I had seen her and Jonny I think that's the kind of thing I would have remembered.'

'Unless you were trying to cover something up,' she said. I looked to DCI Gunn with eyes that said *you have to do better than this*, and he looked back this time but there was nothing, no glimpse of emotion, no smile to say, 'I'm just humouring her, she *is* having a laugh.' And part of me was expecting someone to jump out with TV cameras and tell me it was all a joke. A joke in very poor taste. DS Tomey's line of questioning was a potent combination; totally ridiculous and utterly terrifying. I felt myself being spirited into some nightmarish parallel universe where innocent actions are twisted into something sinister and words become heavy with a meaning they were never meant to carry. I thought about all the days I had spent at court covering cases, listening to defendants protest their innocence and barristers telling them they had sounded too calm in a 999 call, acted too rationally when they found a body. How the truth is not an absolute, but subjective. How all our truths are different. And now it was happening to me. I wanted to stop talking. To end the nonsense. And my eyes glazed over because I was trying to block her out but my mind turned to you, Clara. My oldest friend, so clever, so conniving, who would have thought it? Not me. The frustration of knowing you had strung me up was one thing, but knowing no one would believe my version of events, *the truth,* floored me.

So you are saying, Miss Walsh, that your friend has faked her own disappearance to set you up? And what evidence do you have for this?

The humiliation of not being able to prove a thing would have been too much.

It came at me with force once more, the fire in my head and in my stomach a tightening fury. It had been bottled and buried deep inside me long ago but you had released it again.

When DS Tomey finally fell silent my gaze snapped back to DCI Gunn, pulling a piece of A4 paper from his file. He handed it to DS Tomey who laid the paper flat on the table so I could see it. It was another image, a CCTV image which I presumed was the one of you and Jonny. Then I heard her say:

'You say you didn't see Clara that night. But she obviously saw you.'

She pushed the photograph across the table. 'This was taken on the promenade,' she said, smiling in triumph. I looked at the image. Your hand raised in the air as if you were waving. Ahead of you, at the edge of the frame, was another figure but I struggled to absorb the information my brain was sending me. DS Tomey placed another picture on top of the one I was looking at. It was grainier, a close-up of the person at the edge of the frame, about 150 metres ahead of you. 'Just in case you're in any doubt,' DS Tomey said.

It was me.

So close to you, so very close.

Goose bumps crept over my body. My teeth chattered uncontrollably. I felt my blood freezing and winced, ice pumped through my veins. I heard Kirstin say something but I couldn't catch it. My eyes were fixed on the tape recorder right in front of me, the red record button on. And up above the camera, recording my every move and gesture from a twitch in my eye to the flush on my face. These were the interview pictures the police released to the press at the end of trials, guilty verdict secured. I'd seen so many before; murderers being questioned, saying no comment too many times, sweating to give away their guilt or just too blasé. There was no way to win. A wave of nausea hit me; bile rose up in my throat. And ahead, stretching out in front of me in terrifying, high-definition colour, was an image of what would happen if my words didn't matter, if my version of events was not accepted. It wasn't a life, Clara, it was a sentence, that extended from here far into the future.

I've said it before. Truth is subjective. It is not an absolute. My truth and theirs. Two against one.

His voice cut into the silence, distorted, booming. This time he didn't avoid my eyes; I couldn't escape his stare.

'You were that close to her, Rachel, and yet you never saw her. And she is waving. Who would she be waving at? Her best friend, who has just seen her with her boyfriend. Is that why she looks so worried? She's calling you back, to explain. And you heard her, didn't you? You saw them together. The man you loved and the best friend who was taking it all away from you. How did that make you feel, Rachel? What did you do, Rachel? What did you do to her?'

Have you ever dreamt, Clara, that you're speaking but nothing comes out? And then you try screaming but still there is nothing. You are in danger. You need your voice, you need your cry to be heard and you're straining every vocal cord, but all you produce is silence. Terrifying, isolating silence. You might be surrounded by people but really you are alone, you are drowning, sinking, disappearing. You're being attacked and no one comes to your rescue. You might as well not exist. That's how it was. The same questions asked over and over again. What did I do to you? Where had we gone after seeing each other on the promenade? Why did I kill you?

'I told you I walked to The Old Ship hotel. I didn't see Clara. I didn't see Jonny. I didn't see anyone,' I said in a stranger's voice. The pitch, the tone, not mine. But I knew once I'd started talking I couldn't stop; if I paused they would take control again and the barrage of questions would resume. 'The CCTV doesn't show me waving. I don't acknowledge them, do I? Have you thought that maybe that's because I didn't know they were there? Isn't that the most logical explanation?

'You really expect us to believe your best friend is fifty metres from you, waving to you, and you don't see her, you just carry on walking?'

Kirstin Taylor, who hadn't said anything useful up until this point, suddenly found her voice: 'Presumably we can see the CCTV from the other cameras, so we can see Rachel before she appears here?' She was cool, to the point.

She gave nothing away on her face. I waited, heart jumping, and then I caught something on DCI Gunn's that gave me a chink of hope. He turned to DS Tomey and it was barely noticeable but I saw it, the slightest shake of her head.

'We don't have it,' she said, this time without the accompanying sing-song in her voice. A moment before her chest had been puffed out, so pleased with herself, now it was deflating. I sat motionless, concentrating on the rhythm of my breath, not as quick now.

'The camera was out of order.'

'Hmmm,' said Kirstin Taylor. 'So this,' she tapped on the paper with her Parker pen, 'this is the only image you have of Rachel and Clara?'

'That's correct.'

'And it doesn't show anything apart from them being in the same vicinity.'

'Being within fifty metres of each other,' DCI Gunn said. 'What time did you arrive at The Old Ship hotel?'

He won't give up, I thought, he'll find a way of pinning this on me.

'About half one though I can't be sure.'

'One seventeen according to the hotel's records.' I flinched. I had been the focus of their attention for days without knowing it. 'The time also coincides with you appearing on their security camera in the lobby. So if you left Cantina Latina at, say, eleven o'clock and then bought chips on the pier and walked along the promenade, the camera picking you up at eleven forty-one, are you telling us it took almost two hours to check to see if Clara was at home and get back to the hotel? Or were you doing something else in that time?'

I looked at DCI Gunn's face. His square jaw jutting out at a right angle, the line of his nose, so sharp it could spear a fish, his grey skin, starved of sunlight, and those brown eyes, cold and seeking. Gone was the Poacher's Choice Roger with the flushed face and the sparkle of gossip in his eyes. All the connections we build, the relationships we foster, they count for nothing in the end. Everyone is a stranger.

The questions kept coming at me, whirling around in the room. One after another, no pause to allow me to answer, no answers to give. I had enough time to kill you, they repeated over and over, I almost began to believe it myself. And did Jonny see what I did to you? Was that why he killed himself?

I was in the scenes of a detective drama, praying to hear the snap of a clapperboard announcing the end of the take. But it never came. It went on and on. Every minute longer in that room was torture, the grey walls closing in on me, the fear shrinking me.

I have no idea what time it was when the questions finally stopped. But I remember believing I might die if I didn't sleep; shards of tiredness pierced deep into my brain, pain radiated from behind my eyeballs.

And the dirt crawled like lice on my skin. My mouth was dry, my breath rancid from fear and from talking too much, a layer of filth coated me, the kind of feeling that comes from spending too much time in airports, all canned air and body heat, only much much worse. I wanted to step out of the police station and run away and not stop until there were skies and oceans and land between me and you and them.

Finally DCI Gunn and DS Tomey left Kirstin and me in the room alone. She explained to me as if I was a child that the only evidence they had was circumstantial. 'It doesn't look good for them,' she said in a way which made me think she believed I had done it but it was likely I would get away with it. *Fuck you with your circumstantial evidence.* I'd seen juries convict on circumstantial evidence; it all boils down to who is the most convincing: the prosecution or the defendant.

I let out a groan of frustration and let my head slump in my hands. I stayed like that until I heard the door open again and looked up to see DCI Gunn and DS Tomey returning.

'We're releasing you on bail,' DS Tomey said, spitting the words out, as if she resented saying them which undoubtedly she did.

'What?' I asked. I shook my head to clear it of any other thoughts so I could savour her words. But the smile was creeping over my face. I couldn't contain it. I wanted to cry with relief.

'You are being bailed, that's all,' she said, her frown cut through her make-up.

'Thank you.' I smiled at her.

The custody sergeant explained the conditions of my bail; I was to return to Brighton police station for questioning in four weeks' time; if not a warrant would be issued for my arrest, and I was to stay at my flat every evening, which meant no escaping to Jake's. Then with a smile on his face he handed me back my belongings. I thought he was being kind until he raised his arm and pointed beyond me to the car park.

'Your audience awaits you,' he said.

About fifteen metres from the automatic doors of the police station was a wall of photographers, reporters and camera crews. And when they saw me they raised their cameras like a salute, standing to attention, ready to snap their shot. Gathering my things, I patted my hair down (old habits die hard) and caught my reflection in the window. Some kind of ghoulish Halloween version of myself peered back at me. A youngish female producer in a blue fleece who I recognised from Global was lurking by the doors and when she saw me ready to make my move she shouted, 'Here we go,' to the crowd as if I was the entertainment, which I suppose I was.

No one was allowed to film or take photographs on police premises so I had about twenty metres of clear pathway and then there was nowhere to go, just a sea of cameramen (and women) and photographs and reporters shouting my name.

'RACHEL, RACHEL, RACHEL!'

Click, click, click, the sound of flashbulbs in my face and the TV cameras jostling for space. I held my arm up to my face, not to hide, but to protect myself from being hit by a piece of equipment, from the flashes that were blinding me. I felt my feet being lifted off the ground as I was shoved and pushed in the middle of the scrum.

'Rachel, Rachel,' they shouted, 'have you got anything to say? Why were you arrested?' Different voices and accents competing against each other until they merged together into a cloud of white noise.

Somehow I picked out one voice that was closer to me, right up against me. 'Rachel, did you kill your friend?' I recognised the vowels, the haughtiness that ran through them. I looked up and saw his face. Richard Goldman. He was holding a microphone but it wasn't pointed at me. Legally he wouldn't be able to use that question on air. But that wasn't the point. My own newsroom was now hounding me and Richard wanted me to know it. Sweet revenge.

I felt someone take my arm and pull me through the crowd. I didn't look up to see who it was. I was familiar with the grip, I could smell his smell. Jake shepherded me towards a waiting car and it was only when we were far away, away from the vultures and the questions, well on the road to London, that I finally looked at him and said: 'Thank you.'

For an hour and a half on the motorway reality was suspended. The traffic jams on the M25 had never been so welcome, delaying my re-entry into the outside world. I knew the camera crews and reporters would be camped outside my flat, for a shot very similar to the one they had just got of me at the police station, all to feed the rolling news machine.

When we pulled into my street my chest tightened at the sight of them. I thought about telling Jake to turn round and take me away from here, but where? I had to face them sometime. So we parked up outside my house and sat, frozen in horror, as the whole circus awoke from its slumber. Lights snapped on, reporters emerged from cars, cameras ran towards us. The whole thing was fucking ridiculous really, almost comic. *You'll get your fucking shot, you vultures.* Not that I was immune to the irony here. A taste of my own medicine, the hounder being hounded, but, you know, my conscience was clear. *I* went after people who were murderers and rapists and paedophiles, not some woman who'd just lost her boyfriend and had been wrongly accused of murdering her friend.

But still, I was in trial-by-media territory now and whatever I thought of them I knew I had to play their game. Every word, expression, every move would be watched and analysed. I had to appear emotional but not look guilty, composed but not aloof. I needed people to be on my side and that's not the easiest thing to achieve when you're boiling with anger. In the end I just pursed my lips, kept my head down, and felt my way through the crowd to my flat.

Once inside I headed for the shower. I let the scalding hot water thrash against my skin. So hot it hurt, just the way I like it. I lost myself in the steam and the heat, washing my hair three times over in Ren rosehip oil shampoo, scrubbing my body until I was sure every particle of dirt from the cells had been removed. I didn't want to leave the shower, I felt so alive under it, so clean. Eventually through the fizz of the water I heard Jake shout that he'd made me something to eat and I emerged dizzy from the heat to steady myself on the towel rail.

We sat on the sofa eating bacon sandwiches with warm crusty bread he'd found half-baked in the freezer and mugs of tea. I don't think I have ever tasted a lovelier bacon sandwich or a cup of tea brewed so perfectly before or since. When we were finished we sat back on the sofa and he pulled me close, kissed my head with warm lips and said; 'You don't ever have to ask because I do.'

I sank into him and felt his warmth. With him I was safe; without him there was no one left. But still I had to offer him a get-out.

'I'd understand if you wanted to—' I started but I felt him place his finger gently over my lips to silence me.

'Sshhh,' he said and kissed me all the way down my neck sending little shocks right through me. Despite everything else falling down on me I realised I was very lucky to have him.

He left early evening, reluctantly, finally accepting my assurances that I would be fine on my own. Most of the camera crews and reporters had gone. Jake and I even allowed ourselves a wry laugh at the conversations we overheard outside the living-room window. 'She's not going anywhere, and there's no bulletin until the morning.' Or, 'We've got two shots of her already, isn't that enough,' all code for: I'm fucking freezing out here, it's edging close to eleven o'clock and I'd really like to go home. Still, we knew a few hardcore snappers might be out in the street and in the PR battle it wouldn't look good for Jake to stay overnight. I kissed him goodnight and headed to bed, my tired, aching limbs sinking into the duvet, my head desperate for sleep to find me and lift me out of the day.

You were in my dream, the Clara of old. The Clara who was my friend. We were at a party, drinking fizzy wine, in a house I didn't recognise, people our age in the background like film extras. But the camera was on us, drinking and dancing and having fun. You were pretending to dance like your dad, who we agreed had the worst dad dance ever. And your laugh filled the room like it had extra bass and was reverberating through my body. I was laughing too. You were so funny sometimes, split-my-sides hilarious, you did that to me. And when you saw me laughing it set you off again. The tears were running down your cheeks; you were hysterical, I didn't think you could stop. But it went on for so long that after a while I think I wanted you to stop because we had moved from the party now and your laugh was out of place, jarring. Cutting through the silence in the streets. *Stop it Clara, enough.* It was hurting my head but you still didn't stop and your face had grown distorted and weird, like a squashed-up version of you.

I opened my eyes. I was awake but there was no silence. You were still laughing. I couldn't be dreaming any more, could I? Not unless it was possible to be asleep with my eyes open and sitting up in bed. I began to think I was going mad, that someone inside my brain was laughing. Hesitantly I moved from my bed, flicking the light switch on. Nothing. But the noise hadn't stopped. My breath was coming too fast, my throat grew tighter. I thought I might choke. Still I moved forward, creeping through the flat. Your laughter louder and louder, bouncing off the walls, thumping through my bones. Then I reached the kitchen and flicked the light switch. For a moment my eyes remained closed; the fear of what I might find had immobilised me. But the laughter was still beating through me, louder than before. I knew I was close and then my eyelids clicked open. An empty room illuminated. You were hiding, you must be hiding somewhere. But I caught sight of a light in the corner, the stereo button on green. I never, ever leave anything switched on. I didn't understand. Your laughter was coming from the stereo. I shuffled closer to it, unsure, as if it was a dangerous dog to be approached with care. And as I moved closer I realised it was playing on a loop. *Someone is here, someone has been here in my flat again. Someone has come in and placed a recording of your laughter in my stereo.* My mouth tasted metallic, pure terror. Oh Clara, I wanted to scream, what depths would you stoop to? Where would this sick little game end? My hand hung over the power button, shaking too much to find its target immediately. Then finally I hit it and silenced you.

I was scared to sleep. I wondered if I would ever sleep again. There was no sanctuary any more, not here in my flat, not in my dreams. In the living room I curled into myself, a bottle of wine and a blanket to warm me. Every light in the flat burning bright. Every door and window checked and checked and checked again. I needed to change tactics. It was no good trying to fend you off, you kept finding a way in. And now you were laughing at me. And then the thought hit me like a slap in the face. Had you been laughing at me all along?

Chapter Twenty-one

August 31st 1996

THE AIR IS heavy with a heat that pricks your skin and dries your throat. It has been for days, maybe weeks now. No one runs any more, they walk, slowly, but no matter, the sweat gathers between your legs, under your arms, a film of city grime melts into your face. The grass is thirsty, luscious green has given way to brown. The streets carry a smell of melting tarmac and rotting food. On the news they're saying it's a heatwave and the tabloids say 'Phew'. We're hotter than Egypt and Madrid and Istanbul. I long for rain, to smell the moisture in the air, the release. I close my eyes and dream of a summer shower, the kind that falls without warning and soaks you in seconds. But it doesn't come, not today, the day before your eighteenth birthday.

Tomorrow is your party proper, organised by your dad for your friends. I've been trying to tease information out of him for weeks. 'Wait and see, Rach,' he always says with that mischievous glint in his eye which makes me want to ask him all the more. The other day I crept up behind him in your garage and saw him rummaging through of boxes of fairy lights and lanterns. I made him jump, 'Jesus, Rachel,' he said and then he laughed. 'You have to promise you won't say a thing.' I nodded and swore on my mother's life. 'It can be our secret,' I said.

'These are going outside,' he told me, pointing to your huge garden with its trees and bushes. Tomorrow, when night falls and the lights twinkle in the darkness, it will look like an enchanted forest. Your dad wants to create a fairy tale for you. He's just a big kid himself; he still believes in happy endings.

But before the big party we have the small matter of a second-rate barbecue Niamh is holding in your honour today. I had hoped you would say no when she offered (or insisted to be more precise). *Thanks but no thanks*. But you said the opposite. 'That would be great, Niamh.' And you gave her a hug, like she is the most generous, kind-hearted person which we know she is not. Anyhow, there's no going back now, it's a done deal.

This is what I don't understand. The way you get on with my mum better than I do. Or rather, that she likes you more than she likes me. The attention she gives you, the way she lights up when you're around. She talks *to* you, Clara, not *at* you.

It's been going on for weeks now. At first I told myself not to be ridiculous, *Don't be so fucking needy, Rach*, but it keeps happening. I've started to take notes, like a detective gathering evidence. Because one instance alone wouldn't stand up to scrutiny but add them all together and the cumulative effect is damning.

For example: last Saturday night when we'd planned to watch *Dirty Dancing* together (for the tenth time), I went to the corner shop to buy two cans of Tango and a big bag of Maltesers, only when I returned I found you and Niamh dancing and singing and throwing your heads back like rockers to Chrissie Hynde. *Chrissie fucking Hynde.* And when you saw me come in you just looked up, smiled like an idiot and carried on. You hate that music, Clara. *We* hate it, but somehow you seemed to have forgotten. I went upstairs and ate the whole bag of Maltesers myself. We never got to watch *Dirty Dancing*. I don't think you even noticed.

It's always just been the two of us, Clara. Can't you see Niamh is encroaching on my territory, taking away what is mine? 'She's just being thoughtful,' you said when I asked you (subtly) why she would hold a celebration for you. Niamh is never thoughtful.

But by far the most astonishing thing is that Niamh stays sober when you're around. She does that for no one. She uses it to block everyone else out, so that must mean she wants to let you in, and you alone. And it stings because every time you are there you hold a little mirror up, show me the woman who should have been my mother, the one who fusses around you, asks you questions about school, your boyfriends.

⊸o⟜

I want to let you know how it's making me feel, Clara, but I'm having difficulty working it out myself. Maybe if I told you that despite the heat, the fierce, unrelenting sunshine, I go cold when I see you and Niamh together you'd begin to understand. I'm being frozen out and I can't stand feeling like this; like I'm dead again.

The first thing I notice about Niamh today is that she *is* drinking. Not to the detriment of everything else, but she is most definitely drinking. She is getting the sausages out, making pasta salad with bacon and walnuts and grapes – an unsettling combination she insists on – a potato salad and a tomato salad too.

Three salads for three people. 'I'm not sure there are enough salads,' I say.

She glances up from the chopping board and narrows her eyes as she looks at me. Her gaze stays there for a moment longer than usual and then with the slightest shake of her head, she continues chopping.

I notice she is humming Bob Marley, 'Don't Worry', which I don't think was ever meant to be hummed and she is doing it too fast anyway. Slicing cucumber and strawberries for Pimm's and humming too quickly. 'Fuck!' she shouts as she cuts her finger. There is red on the knife and it's not from the strawberries but she just sucks her finger and carries on. I make a mental note not to drink any Pimm's. She reaches for the jug and I hear the glug, glug, glug of the liquid, three-quarters Pimm's, the rest lemonade. She sees me looking. 'Hardly any alcohol in it, and she will be eighteen after all.' She pours herself a glass and then tops it up with vodka. I hear the sound of it sloshing in her throat. I hate that sound. She goes to take another mouthful and I'm staring because her hands are shaking more than normal and normally her hands shake a lot. 'Is there something you want?' she snarls. I don't answer because I know it's not a question. 'What are you anyway, Rachel, the fun police? Why don't you do something useful. It's a party for your friend after all. Put the chairs out in the garden, so it looks nice when she arrives.' I look at her face and think she should have taken more care of it, stayed out of the sun. It has begun to shrivel around her bones.

Outside a car horn beeps impatiently at ten-second intervals. The next-door neighbour's kids are fighting in the garden. I hear her shout: 'Do it, Rachel. NOW.'

Leaving the kitchen to go outside, I pick up the watering can, fill it with the hose and take it to my patch of the garden. There are sunflowers and peonies and irises, my lovely irises. The flowers provide the only flash of colour in an otherwise barren space. And they are mine, I think with pride. They exist and stand tall because of the care and attention I give them every day. Niamh must be watching me admiring them because I hear her bellow, so loud the neighbours must hear too, 'The chairs, Rachel, leave the bloody flowers alone for once and do something useful.'

I ignore her, concentrating instead on the flow of the water to the plants. There's a certain rhythm to be found in it. You do it slowly and methodically, letting the water sink in a little before giving them some more, watching as the light-brown soil turns dark and moist. I'm almost finished when I hear footsteps on the dry grass and then the watering can is being yanked out of my hand.

'What is it with you?' she asks too close to my face. 'Why are you doing this?'

'They're thirsty, you of all people should understand that.'

Her hands are still holding the watering can but so are mine. There's something in the air today, in the heat of the sun, that emboldens me. That's when it occurs to me the easiest way to win is to do the unexpected. So I pull hard and wait for her to use all her force to pull it off me. When she does I let go of it completely and she's sent flying back on to the grass. The water from the can sloshes over her new teal-blue sundress.

'You little bitch.'

I leave her lying on the ground, swearing and shouting to herself, the adrenalin pulsing through me. Once inside I head to my room and switch on the radio. It's the Spice Girls, 'Who Do You Think You Are?' I'm not a fan but I turn the volume up to drown out Niamh's voice and the whirring in my head. I grab my *More!* magazine from the floor. Leonardo DiCaprio is on the front, a snatched photograph of him walking on a beach with a girl with honey hair and model-long legs. I'm looking at my own legs, white and mottled, comparing them with the model's, when the door swings open and Niamh comes charging towards me. She rips the magazine from my hands, grabs hold of my arm and wrenches it so hard I feel it tug on the socket.

'I asked you to do one fucking thing . . . one thing and you couldn't even do that. All morning I've been working to get everything ready and you . . . you go out and water the fucking plants. She's not even here and you've spoilt it all, totally spoilt it, just like you spoil everything.' Our noses are almost touching we're so close. I reel back but my head hits the wall, there's nowhere to go, I can't create space between us. The vodka fumes from her breath are turning my stomach. 'What's the matter, lost for words are you?' she says.

There's a fly buzzing close to me. Half of the window is open but it keeps flinging itself at the glass making tiny little *dunk* sounds on impact before flying round the room again to gear up for another shot at freedom. Zzzzzz, the noise vibrates through my head. ZZZZZZ.

It's easy to escape, so easy.

All it has to do is go through the open window. But it keeps being fooled by the glass, by the trick of it.

Stupid, stupid fly.

'Well,' she says, shouting now, 'Say something for fuck's sake.'

I hear myself sigh. My head is turned away from her so I am looking out of the window when finally I speak.

'I'll do the chairs when I'm ready. Right now I'm not ready.' My voice surprises me, so even and measured. I'm like a swan, pumped up and frantic below the surface but calm on top. But I'm troubled that I haven't found the guts to look into her eyes and say it.

I need to face up to her. The adrenalin is making my

shoulders tight, there is a heartbeat in my throat, my breaths are shallow. I have to look her in the eye, I can't keep running away, avoiding confrontation forever.

Today is different.

It takes sheer force of will to turn and square up to her. But when I do, when my eyes finally meet hers, I am surprised by what I find. It's been so long since I saw her properly and studied her face. All this time I have been avoiding her, scared of confronting her, but the woman who is sitting before me is pitiful. All the disgust and bitterness she's directed at me over the years, the withering looks and hard, empty stares seem to have set in her face. And she's let her frustration with life eat away at her to the point where there's little left. She's only a shell. For a moment I think what it would have been like if she had smiled more, opened up, let me in. It could have been different. But not now. It's too late. It's all set in stone.

I watch as her eyes grow glassy. I think it's anger and rage that are welling up inside her.

Then I see it. It's such a surprising thing that everything freezes for a moment. A single tear slides down her face. And for a second, beautiful, warm, unexpected doubt ripples through me.

Maybe it doesn't have to be like this after all.

I am still drunk on that thought when there's a flash of heat on my face and the sound of a slap landing on my cheek breaks the silence. When I look at her again the tear has been wiped away and her cold empty eyes are looking through me. I fall back on the bed. There is a ringing in my ears. My rage is hotter than the sun outside. It is volcanic. And watching her march out of my room, I scream: 'You will never do that again ever, I promise you.'

Half an hour or so later I hear the doorbell and Niamh is there before I even move from my bed to answer it. 'The birthday girl,' she shrills, a different person to the one who slapped me thirty minutes before. Those words, saccharine-sweet, float up the stairs and reach me. I feel the bile rising in my throat. I listen to her talking too much, too fast, her voice trying too hard. 'Eighteen and all grown up. Look at you. You're beautiful.' It's just creepy, the way she's going on. There is no end and no beginning to her sentences, just babble. I wonder how many Pimm's and vodkas she's had already. 'And since you are eighteen I thought you could have a special birthday drink, it's only Pimm's, not that your dad would approve.'

You tell her your birthday isn't until tomorrow. 'I'm still seventeen today, Niamh.'

'Twice the celebration then.' She laughs like she's said something hilarious. I hear your footsteps heavy on the wooden floors. You must be wearing something harder than flip-flops, I think. And a dress too? Have you made an effort for the occasion? There is laughter underneath me now. Yours is melodic, hers is louder and more manic. I imagine Niamh is pouring you a Pimm's. A chink of glasses. Collusion. Cheers, you must be saying, although I don't hear that. Aren't you going to ask where I am? Have you even noticed I'm not there?

I lie on my bed and push my face into the pillow so I feel the cold of it on my skin, against my burning cheek. When I sit up I look at the photos on my wall. Me and you, you and me. On the pier, on the beach, up at Devil's Dyke. At school camp in Shropshire, smiling in front of the lake which we thought was a happy place before Lucy Redfern went and drowned and it became creepy and dark. A shared past that binds us together. I get up and look at myself in the mirror. My left cheek is redder than the right but you can't see her hand mark. It still stings. My eyes are red. It is anger, not tears, that makes them bloodshot. More laughter seeps up through the floorboards and penetrates my head. I stir. My body feels like it is twenty stone at that moment; it takes all my effort to heave myself from the bed. But I do. I am coming down to see you, to celebrate with you. It's always just been the two of us. I won't let Niamh get in the way.

She is fanning the flames of the barbecue, or trying to without much success. They are leaping out at her, licking her hands, caressing her face. 'FUUck,' she says in that posh gravelly voice of hers and she turns to look at me. I am a solid mass. My outline must be visible even through the smoke. But she looks through me, beyond me. I do not exist. Her face, distorted by the heat haze coming from the barbecue and the smoke, is crumpled and the mascara she wears religiously is melting on her eyes. She looks like she has just stepped out of hell.

Then I sense there is someone behind me.

'Trust you to keep us waiting, Rach.' You thrust a glass of Pimm's in my hand. 'Have this, I topped it up with vodka when she wasn't looking. Aren't you going to wish me happy birthday?' You are wearing a short orange sundress with a halter neck and at the end of your tanned legs are brown wedges. You've painted your toes orange too. Your hair is tied back loosely in a ponytail so strands of it fall over your face.

'You're not eighteen yet.'

'Two celebrations though, just like the Queen.' You are repeating her words now.

'You look nice,' I say, trying to get that thought out of my head.

'And you look . . .' You take a step back to survey me, wobbling slightly which makes me think the Pimm's has got to you already. I see myself as you see me: baggy linen trousers that are creased and out of shape, legs too fat to show off in a dress, pale skin translucent in the sun. 'You look as good as you always do.' I want to ask you what you mean by that, *as good as I always do*, because I always look fat, Clara. But you teeter off into the garden in your wedges to put the chairs out under Niamh's gaze before I get a chance.

All afternoon the words spin in my head, weaving in and out of the recesses of my brain. I am rehearsing and refining arguments, everything I want to say to you and Niamh, but they stay there, inside my head. There is no opportunity for me to speak, no pause in the conversation for a third person to join in. The only time Niamh acknowledges me is when she thrusts a camera into my hands and demands I take a photograph of you and her smiling into the sun. Apart from that it's just the two of you, talking and joking and drinking, and me the spectator up in the stands watching and listening.

The Pretenders are playing on the stereo (Niamh's playlist) which sounds too heavy in the heat. I don't drink my Pimm's but my head is still throbbing. I focus on my sunflowers, faces raised to the sun, marvelling at their ability to stand tall in the searing heat.

You are on your third jug of Pimm's when I slope off unnoticed. The sounds of the day are giving way to adult chat which drifts through the gardens of our street. The light is dying now; purple and orange have replaced the pale blue of the day. I go upstairs to my room, close my eyes and sink into the bed. My body is swallowed up by its softness. I sit there for a while, trying to read *One Hundred Years of Solitude*. It is my favourite book ever. I've read it twice before but even though I know the story I can't concentrate on the words. All I can hear is your laughter mixing with Niamh's, loud and raucous. You're not used to drinking, Clara, not like this. I wonder if you'll throw up. What a pleasant book end to Niamh's party that would be. The alcohol has also had another, more worrying effect: you seem to be morphing into my mother. I think she is polluting you. If only I could protect you from her.

I want to close my window to block you out but there's no air as it is, so I'm forced to listen. I keep telling myself I don't care if you're having fun without me but finally my curiosity wins and I find myself peeking out from behind my curtain to see what you are doing that is so hilarious.

It looks like a game of charades, each of you taking turns to wave your arms around and pull strange faces in that theatrical way you do, Clara, but Niamh? I've never seen her like this before, carried away by the moment, doubled over when the laughter is too much for her, wiping tears from her eyes, begging you to '*stop, Clara, please,*' as a child might beg for mercy when they're being tickled by a parent. Even in the dimming light I am startled by the change in her, the undiluted happiness that seems to have relaxed her face, softened it, breathed life into it. And never once do you take your eyes off each other. I am still concealed behind my bedroom curtains but it would not matter if I was standing naked in the middle of the garden: neither of you would even see me.

I fall back on to the bed, tears stinging my cheeks. The picture of Niamh's face, transformed, is too cruel a reminder of what is now being stolen from me.

Your attention. Your love.

Ever since that first day at school, when I sat down next to you and the electricity fizzed through me, I knew you had the power to bring people to life, Clara. It's like an energy that radiates from you, a magic that draws people in and makes them never want to let you go. I used to watch other kids try to work their way into your affections and without exception you'd turn away from each one of them and they'd shuffle off, dejected. It made our friendship all the more special. You'd chosen me to bask in your glow. And only once did I contemplate, in a brief chemical-induced moment the night we dabbled with Ecstasy, what life would be like if you turned away from me.

If I lost you, I would lose myself.

Finally the laughter dies and I hear her voice, the tone different, harsh, through the slurred words. 'Rachel, for fuck's sake Rachel, come out here.'

When I don't answer she tries again; this time her words are softer. 'Rachel, where are you? Come and join the party.'

I know I should stay in bed. What does she want from me? But I am propelled by a tiny, pitiful grain of hope that maybe both of you really do want me to join in. So I go down to see you, sprawled on the deckchairs, glasses by your side on the grass. Your eyes are closed. But Niamh's are open. She sees me and sits up.

'I gave Clara a little birthday present from you?' she says, giggling, as she waves her hand in the direction of Clara's deckchair. I follow it and find a pool of yellow on the grass next to you. My sunflowers, each one ripped from the ground. Next to them are the irises, my lovely irises, now wilting and shrivelling in the heat. And the peonies have suffered a similar fate, torn out of the earth and dumped next to the others. Those flowers that I watered and tended and looked after so carefully have been destroyed. I look over to the flowerbed, a riot of colour this morning, now only a few stalks remaining.

'A bouquet for the birthday girl. I knew you'd approve, Rachel,' she says, 'and Clara loves them, don't you?'

'Yeppp,' you slur and you raise your hand drunkenly in the air as if raising a glass to me. The normal sane and sober Clara wouldn't have sat back and let this happen; you wouldn't have let Niamh uproot one single flower, not knowing everything you do about my plants and what they mean to me. Niamh has plied you with so much alcohol she's poisoned you. I have let you get too close to her and now she is destroying the Clara I know and love. She is killing everything that is beautiful.

I can't breathe. Niamh must see my reaction because she is smiling an awful smile which reveals her yellow cigarette teeth. She emits a laugh that is rasping and throaty and echoed by your own. Witches under a burning sky. But you don't know what you're doing, Clara. This is her fault. 'Now are you going to do something useful for a change?' She grabs the empty jug of Pimm's from the table and waves it in my direction.

The fire in my belly has been burning all day long but with that laugh it ignites into a full-blown blaze. I take one last look at the sunflowers, the peonies and the irises and *whoosh* it is raging through me, consuming me. My skin is breaking out in goose bumps, not from cold but from heat.

The flames are in my throat, in my head. I can't control this fire. It controls me.

I grab the jug and go into the kitchen, leaving it on the side for a moment. I'm thinking – *I need her to be quiet, I can't listen to her any more, I need to protect you from her* – and I'm wondering how I can make her shut up, how I can extinguish her just for a little while. And then I have an idea and I'm flying upstairs. I'm in the bathroom and they are there, right in front of me. Two packets, like it is fate or something. I take one of them in my hands, a blister pack cool in my hot palms. The tablets Niamh needs to make her sleep. There is only one missing which means there are eleven left. But I won't use them all, just a few. I'm back in the kitchen bursting them out of the foil, one by one. I keep going. There's a spoon in my hand and I'm grinding them down methodically. There is no hurry. Then before me is a fine white powder. I make up a jug of Pimm's and vodka and pour you a glass and Niamh another. And into hers I spoon the white dust. I watch it float on top and stir. Round and round until it disappears. Then I top it up with vodka.

The grass is cool on my feet as I walk across the garden towards her. I hand you your drink first which you accept, eyes half shut. And then I hand Niamh hers. 'At last,' she says.

At last, I think.

I'm in the kitchen again, watching her gulp. I see each mouthful make its way down her gullet. One after another. She is thirsty, a thirst that burns through her; it must be quenched. And then the glass is empty.

Upstairs in my bedroom, I watch from the window. I hear you chat for a while, the slur of your words. Unfinished sentences linger in the air. A little later I see Niamh lift herself from the chair, and you get up too. 'Time for bed,' she says and you mumble your agreement. You follow her upstairs. And then she asks you to grab her sleeping tablets from the bathroom. You retrace your steps and return a few minutes later, to give them to her.

'Thanks,' I hear Niamh say to you. 'Goodnight, birthday girl.' There's the *mwah* sound of a kiss but then Niamh ruins the moment because I hear her tripping over something and crashing into her bedroom. I think she will be too drunk to take any more tablets.

Ten minutes later I pass by her bedroom, en route to the bathroom to brush my teeth. Her door is ajar. She is lying across the bed fully dressed. Next to her is the blister pack but I can't see if it's empty or not and it's been so long since I heard silence, I don't want to do anything to disturb it.

The next morning I wake to you shaking me. I smell your breath before I open my eyes, rancid and thick with alcohol. You're pulling on my arm. For a brief moment I forget the night before. 'She's been sick,' you say, your voice laced with panic, and then I remember and I'm up and out of bed, in my mother's room. I am standing over her body which is cold and pale beneath the tan of her skin. There's sick on the pillow, red from the Pimm's and regurgitated salad too. I knew having so many salads was a bad idea. You are screaming, your shrieks rattle around the room and pierce my head. I am the child cowering beneath the cushions watching a scary film. I don't want to look and yet I do. I can't help myself. Her body is motionless, so still and quiet, and I creep over to it, half expecting her to leap out at me. I creep closer because I know I need to check her, to see if she is still alive, but the stench is overpowering. I hold my arm up to my nose and then I am next to her. Taking her wrist I put my finger over her veins to check her pulse, just like I've seen them do on TV. Nothing. I watch her chest for any signs that a life might still be in there, beating faintly. Nothing.

There are pins and needles in my head, they're rushing up and down my arms. I'm shaking because no matter how much you don't like your mother it's a bit of a shock to see her cold and dead first thing in the morning. And then amongst the fear and the shock it hits me like a cool breeze in the stifling heat. *She will never hurt me again*. She will never speak to me again or look at me as if I am a piece of shit on her shoes. I don't have to be her daughter any more. I am free of her, forever. That's when the eerie calm descends on me and I feel more in control than I have ever been. A delicious relief washes over me and extinguishes the embers of last night's fire.

The ambulance is on its way, and you are still sobbing, but I'm trying to think practically. Niamh is (was) always so slovenly and it shows in her bedroom. The air is rank, hot and heavy with sick and stale alcohol. I open a window to let a breeze flow through. Her clothes are crumpled up, strewn on the carpet – though I'm grateful she's still wearing yesterday's underwear and I don't have to pick it up. There are half-empty cups of coffee on the bedside table, films of milk floating on top, and the empty blister pack of sleeping tablets too. I take them away and throw them in the bin.

They carry out a postmortem on her body 'It's just procedure,' the policewoman who has been assigned to me explained, nothing to worry about. And I don't worry about it. I am convinced Niamh pickled herself in alcohol; it was simply a matter of her body giving up on her. That was the real cause of her death. Sure enough when the results come through they reveal cirrhosis of the liver and high levels of sleeping pills in her blood. The perfect storm.

We share everything, don't we, Clara? No secret is too great, no truth too heavy. We don't judge. We listen, we understand. That's why I tell you, the week after she dies.

The day starts well – a call from your dad: *Could I help?* he says breathlessly. I can tell he's in a hurry. In my mind's eye I see him running around your house, his dark hair still shower-wet, spraying that aftershave of his, the one we tease him about but really I secretly love, all citrussy and fresh, (It's Issey Miyake, I know because I found it in his en suite one day). Anyway, he said you weren't coping very well. 'I have surgery all day, Rachel, can you come round and make sure she's OK?' I can't imagine anyone ever refuses your dad. I love it when he takes me into his confidence and makes me feel so special, like I alone have the power to solve his problems. At work I imagine him all scrubbed up in theatre, directing an army of nurses and junior doctors, his cool, steady hands, knowing exactly what to do.

I tell him *yes, of course, I'll be there* and he says, 'You're a gem, Rach,' which makes me smile, the way he sounds so grateful.

By ten thirty I'm at your house and we're in the kitchen hiding from the white heat outside. The sunshine isn't a novelty any more. People cross the road to find shade, dart in and out of shops to be blasted by air conditioning. Yesterday I stuck my head in amongst the frozen peas at Sainsbury's. I had no intention of buying them, I hate peas. I just needed to cool my head.

But you don't look like you've seen the sun in a long time. In fact your appearance shocks me: your hair is lank, you look smaller, like you've shrunk two sizes in a week. I want to cheer you up and I don't think talking about Niamh will help so I keep coming up with suggestions: *let's play some music, watch MTV, why don't we go to town?* Even when I share the ripest bit of gossip around, *Shelly Peters shagged Simon Dunstan at the weekend*, you give me nothing back.

Niamh's gone and she's still coming between us.

'I think it's my fault,' you say eventually. We've moved to the living room and are sprawled on the sofa next to each other. I have to hand it to your dad, he has very good taste. The walls are painted in one of those white colours that's not quite white, tasteful paintings add splashes of colour around the room. There are lots of photographs of you alone, and you and him together. There is even one of the two of us sitting under the tree in your back garden. He took the shot with my camera and I had it framed for his birthday last year, suggesting the perfect spot for it in his living-room gallery.

I take a sip of my Lipton's iced tea, which I brought for us because it's your favourite. 'Why would you say that?' I ask.

'I gave her the sleeping pills.' Your lip is quivering and your eyes fill with tears. It's painful to watch, it's like you've disappeared along with Niamh. 'I keep on thinking if I hadn't given them to her she might still be here.'

I want to tell you she's not worth it, all this guilt and grief. Instead I say, 'Don't ever blame yourself, it's her fault, not yours.' I move closer to you so I can comfort you.

'But I gave her the packet. I keep going over and over the moment I did it. I wish I could rewind,' and you press yourself into me so I feel your sobs beating a rhythm against my chest. I want them to stop. I want my old sunshine Clara back. I would do anything to make you feel better. And that's when I think of it.

We share everything. No secrets.

I hold you sobbing in my arms for long enough to convince me it is the right thing to do. I only wanted to protect you from her, make her go away for a little while, so you could see what she was really like. It wasn't supposed to be like this, with you crippled by guilt. That's why I tell you, to absolve you from the pain.

'It's not your fault, she had taken sleeping pills earlier.'

You pull away from my embrace; the sobbing stops, just as I had wanted, and you raise your head to look at me.

'How do you know that?' you ask, hungry for reassurance.

I smile. 'This is just between me and you, OK,' and I watch you nod your consent before I continue. 'I crushed some into the drink I gave her, the Pimm's. And she drank it all.'

I am expecting to see my smile reflected in your face, I want to see the shadow of guilt lift from you. Instead I recognise something and it is chilling. It is a look other people have given me in the past, in certain situations I vividly recall. But you have never looked at me like this, Clara. You are my friend, you've never doubted or questioned. You are loyal. But now you're looking at me like someone has just ripped a mask from my face and you are seeing me properly for the first time. And whatever is there is filling you with horror.

Stop it, Clara, stop it.

But the look doesn't go away. You're scaring me.

'It's OK, Clara,' I say, reaching out to take your hands. 'She used to crush them up in her bedtime drink herself, that's what she did.' It's a lie of course but I think it might calm you down. Instead you push my hands away.

'How many did you give her?' Your eyes are flashing at me.

'I don't know . . . a few, just a few, it doesn't matter does it? They didn't kill her. We didn't kill her.'

Please don't look at me like you're frightened, Clara. You have nothing to fear from me.

'What did you do, Rachel?' you spit. 'What the fuck did you do?' You keep saying it, and I tell you I did nothing. Nothing that she didn't do herself.

'Jesus, Clara, listen to me, I didn't want to hurt her. Don't twist things. It's not your fault. It's not my fault. OK? She died because she was an alcoholic. It's written in her postmortem results, black and white.' But my words don't connect, they can't reach above the screams which are cutting through me.

'Get away from me,' you shout, pushing me, 'GET AWAY FROM ME.' And you keep looking away from me then turning back as if you need to check your eyes aren't deceiving you.

I trusted you.

And now you are turning your back on me. I can see it happening. I can read your thoughts. I know what's turning over in your mind. You have always believed me, Clara. Even when no one else did at school, it was you, and you only who stuck by me. Your loyalty was so unquestioning. But it is ebbing away.

Marching across the room, you get halfway to the door and then, as if struck by a thought, you swivel round and come back to me.

'We need to tell the police. You have to tell them.' You go to the phone hanging on the wall and take it from its cradle and thrust it in my hand.

'You ring them, tell them, Rachel, tell them what happened.'

I always did everything you said, Clara, unquestioning.

And in return you gave me your friendship. Our unspoken pact. But it doesn't work if one person reneges on the deal.

'There is nothing to tell,' I say.

'Tell them what you just told me, what you just said. Tell them. You gave her the pills.'

You are pulling at your hair with one hand and chewing the nails on the other. The funny, calm, confident Clara is being sucked out of you right before my eyes. You keep screaming at me to call the police, but I won't. I can't. I have only just found my freedom from Niamh. I am looking ahead to the future where I can be anyone I want to be. I won't let you do anything to jeopardise it.

'You need to calm down, Clara,' I say and I'm surprised by my voice which seems like someone else's – deep and measured and in control. I think it suits me.

But you don't. 'If you won't tell them, I will,' you shout and try to wrestle the phone from me.

'Tell them what?' I ask you. 'What exactly will you say?' Something in my tone makes you stop in your tracks and you fix me with a watery stare. It gives me confidence to carry on. 'Well?' I ask, 'are you going to tell them YOU gave her the sleeping pills?'

You are shaking your head in disbelief, 'No, no, don't you dare, Rachel. Don't do this. Don't do this to me. It was you, you just told me.' You are holding your head in your hands as if you fear it might burst open.

'Did I? I said she used to do it herself, every night, she'd crush them up in her drink. But of course you weren't to know you shouldn't give her more.'

You look at me like you've just drunk a bottle of poison and realised there's nothing you can do to save yourself. And then you begin moaning and wailing like those people in foreign countries do on the TV news when they've lost a relative, unlike here where we lay cheap teddies and petrol-station flowers at makeshift shrines.

I'm sorry Clara, I'm truly sorry. I wanted you to understand. But you don't. You are not in control of yourself. And if you are not, then someone has to be.

'Don't worry,' I say, 'I won't tell anyone what you did.'

You run crying from the room and I hear your footsteps travelling upstairs. I guess you expect me to leave but I can't leave you in this state so I wait until it is dark and your dad returns. He asks me if I'm staying the night and I say; 'Only if it's not too much trouble.'

'Of course not,' he says, 'it's good for Clara to have you around. No one else understands.'

Creeping into your bedroom I hear your sleep breathing so I pull some pyjamas out of your drawer, slip them on and crawl into bed beside you, just like always.

You see I can't let you go, Clara, not now. Not ever.

A week later; the funeral. The rain has been coming in torrents, short sharp downpours, but the water seems to evaporate before it hits the ground and the grass is still parched and brown.

It's September now, but when the sun sneaks out from behind the dark clouds the heat is still ferocious. We are sitting in the crematorium, our own bodies baking and crackling.

'She always said she wanted a cremation,' Aunty Laura says, which is patently untrue; Niamh didn't organise anything in life, so I'm certain she didn't plan her own funeral.

Laura had asked people not to wear black, an edict all but a few oldies adhered to. I'm wearing a bright green cotton sundress with straps that crisscross my back and brown wedge sandals. I bought them last week, sick of hiding myself away under layers of clothing. *The new me.* And it is strange because I think I already look different; maybe the stress of the last few weeks has helped me shed a few pounds because I can see people looking at me as if they have noticed a change too. They don't say as much of course, telling the daughter of the dead woman she's looking well isn't good form. The same could not be said about you, Clara. Your bones just out from your body. The colour has been stripped from your skin. You are wearing orange again though not the same dress you wore on the day of the barbecue. On any other day I would laugh that we are one colour short of a traffic light but I know today is not the day to make such observations.

The room is full, although not so full you can say it was standing room only. When the vicar talks about Niamh being 'a woman of spirit' I think of vodka and stifle a laugh.

The windows are floor to ceiling in the crematorium and the sun is shining through, bleaching us, washing out the fuchsias and greens and blues of our dresses. It is so bright I can be excused for wearing sunglasses indoors. Every so often, like when Aunty Laura stands up and says Niamh was a 'wonderful mother, sister and friend who fought her demons', I take the tissue that is rolled up, damp with sweat in my palm, and dab my eyes. My eyes are dry but no one notices because I have my sunglasses for cover.

Back at Laura's house in Hove there is a buffet and wine and beer in the garden. You look like a ghost, Clara, like you're not really there, and I am your shadow, following you around, making sure you eat something and drink something to stop you from wasting away. People keep swirling around us, confused by which one of us is the daughter. An older woman with liver spots on her hands and bony fingers gets it wrong and hugs and paws you and says, *You poor thing, just let us know if you need anything,* before she disappears to grab a prawn vol-au-vent. Your grief is so much more obvious than mine, I guess it's an easy mistake to make.

I only leave your side to dash to the loo and on my return, scanning the room, I find you standing next to Aunty Laura, leaning into her as if you are deep in conversation. My heart is racing because I wonder what it is that you have to say to each other, but as I approach there's a lull in the chatter and she turns to me and says, 'Rachel, how lucky you are to have a friend like Clara at such an awful time.' I smile in agreement.

⤙o⤚

Finally, mercifully, the garden empties and it is over. Laura insists on driving us home, dropping you first and then me. She's already offered me a room at her house in case mine is too full of painful memories. But I tell her it's OK, I want to stay there. 'I just think the sooner I clear Niamh's belongings out the better. Not everything,' I say, 'but you know . . . the mess, a lot of the junk.' She nods because she understands her sister, the way she lived. She understands I don't want to live like that.

So I'm only half surprised when we reach my house to see her unload empty boxes from the boot of her car. 'I'd thought I'd help, and well, there's no time like the present, is there?' I am touched, really, because I know it must be hard for her losing a sister, even a drunk, selfish one.

We start in the living room, clearing the horrible ethnic throws and cigarette-burned cushions. The historical romances that fill the bookshelves are boxed for the charity shop. We open the windows to let what little breeze there is flow through. With every wipe and polish I feel like I am being released from my old life. I am meticulous, every skirting board and corner of the room is sprayed and cleaned, the carpets vacuumed twice over. At intervals I stand back to inspect my work and wipe the sweat from my forehead. Yes, the decor still leaves much to be desired but it is beginning to look like a different house, like it could be my house. And her smell, that sickly sweet aroma, is being drowned out by polish and air fresheners. I breathe in lungfuls of it.

Upstairs Laura clears the bathroom of half-empty toothpastes and henna hair dye and gloopy nail polishes. I take the towels and throw them out, except for one which is mine and never touched Niamh's skin. The black bin bags that line the hallways are all that is left of her, and soon they will be gone too.

In the bedroom we are on the final straight. I haven't ventured in here since Laura came to clean it after Niamh died. The smell of sick has faded but still it clings and I am reminded of the image of her lying motionless on the bed. I blink it away. Laura is humming as she removes Niamh's clothes from the wardrobe, the outfits that I have seen her in so many times. I don't want to look at them because if I do I know her body will fill them once more, it will come alive and shout and ridicule me. And she will be wearing that same face that twists with bitterness and disappointment.

The bed is soon piled high with clothes and shoes and Laura starts to take them downstairs, to load them up in her car. We know we both need to carry on until it's finished, to purge ourselves of Niamh, or at least that's what I want. Maybe Laura just wants to finish the job because otherwise it will linger over her like a bad smell.

The wardrobe is almost empty. Only a few boxes. One of them I recognise as the old shoebox, with the picture of ankle boots (twelve pounds ninety-nine) where Niamh kept her photos. It's the same one from all those years before when I was doing my family tree. Inside I find the picture of me as a baby, a crop of ginger hair, and green dungarees. Within the box there is another little album with a few photographs slotted inside One shows a man who looks like he's in his late teens, holding a baby. His hair is long and dark, his face smiling and strikingly handsome. Something within that picture nags me with its familiarity. The next photograph is of Niamh and the man together. She is beautiful, there is no denying it; maybe the beauty comes from the sparkling, smiling eyes. I can't help wondering who stole the young Niamh and replaced her with the old bitter one. The final photograph is taken outside, on a park bench. It looks like winter. The sky bright blue, a child in a red snowsuit in the background. The baby is in it again, wearing a hat, a green coat and a toothless grin, perched on Niamh's knee. I turn it over and see *February 1979,* written in faded handwriting – ten months before I was born.

I go to pull the rest of the photographs out of the box when Laura returns. Seeing me with them I catch something in her eyes and then in a flash it's gone again. 'I was just coming to get those,' she says, 'I'll keep them safe shall I?' And she swoops down and lifts the box with its clues to the past out of my reach.

I must have stored that memory away under lock and key in my mind, choosing on some subconscious level not to acknowledge its significance. Because suddenly it is all so obvious, so utterly, blindingly obvious I wonder how I couldn't have seen it before. And now that I have seen it, in brilliant, flashing Technicolor, there is no going back. Something inside me is unfurling; the layers and layers of lies that made up the story of me, of us, Clara, it is all unravelling.

No one is ever who they appear to be. Not me. Not you.

Chapter Twenty-two

IT WAS UNLIKELY the police were going to make it a priority. You could almost hear the conversations in the control room – *Got something for you, Sergeant, there's been laughter in a house in Kensal Rise* – and even with Jake trying his best to explain the wider context, you got the sense it wasn't exactly blue-light material.

'I still don't understand how the fuck anyone could have got in. It's too fucking weird,' he said when he put the phone down. He started pacing up and down the living room, pulling at his hair. I wondered whether he was beginning to doubt me; it was a fairly implausible scenario after all. I guess that was what you wanted, wasn't it Clara? For me to look like I was losing my mind. 'How can you be sure it is her laugh, Rach, I mean it could be anyone's.'

See that's the thing, no one else understood. No one understood how close we were, the way we knew each other right through to our bones.

'It *is* her laugh,' I said. 'I've never been more certain of anything.' I moved close to him and wrapping myself round his neck I whispered in his ear, 'You can leave if you want to, I wouldn't think any the worse of you for doing it. I'd understand.'

He pushed me off him like I'd given him an electric shock. 'Don't ever fucking say that to me again,' he said and stormed out of the room. That was the first time I had ever seen him angry.

The police sauntered up to see me a few hours later: a young officer in his mid twenties with dirty blond hair accompanied by a woman who looked like she'd been on the beat too long. Her dark hair was cropped in a no-nonsense mum cut (we used swear we'd never have one, didn't we?), her narrow, make-up-free eyes surrounded by crow's feet and a frown line that sliced through the middle of her forehead. She introduced herself as DS Richardson. I showed them in, sat them down and offered them coffee, which they (she) declined.

'Miss Walsh,' she said, wasting no time on pleasantries. She managed to speak through her nose and look down it at the same time. 'I understand you think someone has been in your flat, presumably while you were otherwise engaged with our colleagues in Sussex?'

I don't know why I was surprised to learn that my name came with a back story these days. My arrest had been all over the news the previous night. Your disappearance alone had been a big story; now a semi-famous crime reporter had been thrown into the mix' it had *all the right ingredients* as we said in the business. I hadn't read the papers that morning but I knew they would be screaming *TV Girl in Murder Probe.* In years to come reporters would put me on their CVs: *I covered the Rachel Walsh story.*

A few days ago people believed everything I said, I had that sheen that comes with being successful, well known. Now here I was trying to present a story that most sane people would find questionable. *Someone broke into my house and played laughter. What a fucking lunatic.*

'She found a CD playing in the stereo. It was on a timer,' Jake said. 'It's still in there.' Thank God for Jake. At least one person found the story credible.

DS Richardson walked over to the stereo and paused. 'You say it's a recording of someone laughing?'

'Yes. It woke me up in the middle of the night. Someone wanted me to hear it, to spook me.' I hated how ridiculous I sounded.

DS Richardson leant forward and peered at the stereo as if it would offer up some clues. 'May I?' she said, her finger hovering over the play button.

I nodded and raised my hands to my ears to block you out. I didn't want to hear your laugh again. Not ever, but it filled the room once more, ricocheting through me. Then mercifully it stopped.

'It's sick, really, just sick with everything else going on,' Jake said. DS Richardson made a point of ignoring his outburst and turned to me.

'Do you have any idea why someone would want to do this?' she asked in such a calm, even voice I wanted to shake her.

'It's her laughter,' I said and waited for a reaction. But her face gave nothing away. I wondered if she'd practised the blank look for so long she'd actually lost the power of expression.

'Whose laughter?'

'It's Clara's. I'd know that laugh anywhere.' Finally her face moved, a flicker of surprise and disbelief escaping from behind her mask. And then she caught it and froze her features once more.

'We are talking about the same Clara O'Connor who has been missing for two weeks, who has been the subject of one of the largest inquiries Sussex Police have ever conducted. You're saying someone has recorded her laughter, broken into your flat without any signs of forced entry and placed a CD in your stereo to play to you in the middle of the night?'

'Yes,' I said, wondering whether I should add, *I know it doesn't sound very plausible but it's true*, before deciding it would make me look even more desperate.

The sidekick was taking notes, looking up occasionally to glance at DS Richardson – *you really want me to write this crap down?* – then carrying on with his scribbling.

'We understand you have reported instances of stalking,' she flicked back through her notepad, 'as long as a year ago.'

'That's right.'

'And you think the two could be connected?'

'No, I think that's what I'm supposed to think.'

'Would you care to explain what you mean?'

'What I mean is the stalker, if you can call him that,

well, he used to send me e-mails and letters, all fairly low-level, harmless kind of stuff. Then suddenly Clara goes missing and I'm getting texts and letters and someone is getting into my house changing things around and leaving me things like that.' I pointed to the stereo. 'It's not the same, it doesn't feel like the same person.' I walked over to the window to peek through the shutters and sighed, a heavy sigh. Outside the street was quiet; the reporters and camera crews had packed up, leaving their takeaway coffee cups in the road.

'With stalkers we often see their activity start like that and then escalate, it's quite common,' DS Richardson told me.

She wasn't listening to me, she didn't understand what I was trying to say. So I made it clearer.

'I don't think Clara is dead.' I focused on a black mark on the wall, just below the mirror, a fingerprint; anything to avoid their faces, and then turning to face DS Richardson I said, 'I think she is stalking me, I think she is trying to set me up.' The words echoed around the room, loud and unbelievable. No one looked at me, no one said anything until I broke my own rule and filled the silence.

'I'm sure of it,' I said.

They stayed for another hour, asking all the obvious questions like: how do you suppose she got in? Do you think someone is helping her, and the most difficult one to answer: why would she want to frame her best friend for murder?

That was a whole dissertation's worth of an answer – *Why did Rachel's and Clara's friendship turn toxic? Discuss* – and I didn't think DS Richardson or her sidekick were up to it so I palmed them off with the usual *she is certifiably mad* line. It wasn't a tag you'd like but to be honest you hadn't left me many options.

The question that troubled me the most was how you had got in. Not initially, I mean, swapping the photographs was easy – you still had a key to my flat. But I had changed the locks since then. Knowing you could enter the flat freely, unseen, was more unnerving than you could ever imagine. The sound of the ice in the freezer, a dripping tap, a voice outside, I jumped at them all. I couldn't sleep. I needed to do something to feel safe again.

'What's freaking me out,' I said to Jake, 'is that I think she's watching me and I can't see her.' We were sitting in the kitchen, jittering from the fifth coffee of the day, wondering what the hell to do with ourselves.

Silence hung over us for moment until Jake got up and walked out of the room muttering something about setting up an undercover shoot for Monday.

And the thought blinded me.

Cameras.

If I caught you on camera, they'd have to believe me.

I opened up my laptop and Googled security cameras. I could buy a package: one for the kitchen, one for the living room and watch the pictures on my laptop when I was out of the house.

Watching you, watching me.

I called Jake back in and told him my idea.

'Genius,' he said and planted a kiss on my forehead. 'How soon can you get them?'

The website said seven days which meant a whole week not knowing who was in the house.

'Leave it with me,' said Jake, 'the guy we use for the hidden cameras in Clerkenwell owes me a favour.'

'Thank you,' I said, letting my head fall on his chest. 'Thank you for taking care of me.' And he squeezed me in a bear hug.

'It's the alpha male in me.'

'Do you know,' I said, extricating myself from his grip and looking up to him. 'When all this is over, I want to go away for a long holiday, somewhere about as far away from here as you can get.'

'Australia, the other side of the world,' he said.

'I'm not sure that's far enough.'

'Do I get to come with you?'

'You don't get off that easily,' I said, my mind already transporting me to a place far away from here.

Next, I phoned Mickey the locksmith to check he had changed *every* door- and window-lock. He sounded mildly irritated by the interrogation.

'Every single one was changed luv, just like you asked.'

'I'd like them done again,' I said, cupping a set of keys in my hand.

'Something wrong?'

'I just want to be absolutely sure, that's all. And I want an extra bolt on the front and back doors.'

'Well, if that's what you want.'

'I need them done today,' I said.

'I only work a half-day Saturday . . .'

'I need them today.'

'OK, I get the picture, luv, I'll be round in half an hour. Cost extra, mind you, for such short notice. I take it you want me to cut you four this time in case your boyfriend loses his again?'I stopped still. From the living room I could make out Jake's voice on the phone talking cameras, reeling off his shopping list of requirements, 'I need them soon as you can, mate,' he was saying but his voice was growing faint, drowned out by the clamour in my head. '

'What did you say?' I asked, finding my voice.

'I said I'll cut another set for your boyfriend. He said he's always losing his.'

For a moment I let myself pretend. I still had a boyfriend. How typical of Jonny to lose his keys. And then the pretence came crashing down on top of me.

'My boyfriend died.'

A cough and the sound of papers being shuffled at the other end of the line.

'But he came in here the other day, said he was locked out and you were at work. I wouldn't normally do it but he had a letter with his address on, and it was getting late, I thought I was doing him a favour.'

My whole body stiffened, the blood was pumping in my head.

He.

A man.

Not you, Clara.

Just when it was all clear in my mind.

I gripped the receiver and shouted down it: 'What did he look like?'

Mickey cleared his throat. I could hear his breaths, deep, deep, through the line.

'Late twenties, wearing a green parka coat. He had a hat on, I couldn't see his hair. Has something happened, luv?' His voice was pleading, shaky. 'I'll be round right away to change them, free of charge of course.'

The thoughts clunking in my head created such a noise I could barely hear him.

I don't believe it is Bob the stalker.

I think it is you.

And somehow you've persuaded someone to help you.

'I'll just grab my things and be with you in ten,' said Mickey, trying to reassure me.

Chapter Twenty-three

JONNY WAS BURIED in the ground three weeks after his body was found. It was a miserable, sodden day where not even a sliver of sunlight poked out from behind the grey clouds.

The thought of him lying cold and wet forever in the soil of a St Albans graveyard haunted me. The burial was Sandra's choice. If she had asked me (she didn't) I would have told her Jonny would have wanted to be free somewhere, but I didn't have the stomach to fight her. The truth was we'd been too wrapped up living our lives to plan our funerals. And Sandra obviously wanted somewhere physical to be with him, to visit and lay carnations and chrysanthemums, all the flowers he would never have chosen.

I don't feel like going into any detail about Jonny's funeral. I don't think it's right to let you in on it, not after what you did. But I'm not afraid to tell you that in those moments standing at his graveside, cold tears on my face, wind whipping my body, I truly believed I hated you. I thought I hated you more than I ever thought possible. I hated you for the years of lying, for the blame you placed at my feet, the way you tried to destroy me but ended up destroying the person I loved the most in the world. I hated you because I had trusted you and you betrayed me.

That's how far you had driven me away, Clara.

And yet the weight of grief pressing down on my shoulders, crushing me into the ground, gave me some insight into how you must have felt when Niamh died. When part of you was taken away.

Whereas before your grief at her death was unfathomable, now I understood it. But there were many other questions that needed answers and only one person who could provide them. It was time to return Laura's calls.

Her voice was a softer version of Niamh's without the rasp and rattle of years of Marlboro Light smoking or the close-to-the-edge emotion that my mother's always carried.

'Rachel, darling, how are you my dear . . .' She let her sentence trail off for a moment and coughed. 'I'm so glad you called, I've been trying desperately to get hold of you. What a ghastly thing, and the papers, I don't know how they get away with printing such nonsense, I really don't.'

'Can we meet? I need to speak to you. In person,' I said abruptly.

'Well . . . of course, Rachel, I have the ladies' tennis tournament tomorrow but I'm free the day after. We could do lunch somewhere, my treat, or I tell you what, you come here and I'll cook your favourite meatballs.'

They were my favourite when I was ten. I am twenty-seven years old.

'I need to see you tomorrow.'

'Darling, that's just not . . .'

Fuck the tennis, Laura, and fuck your meatballs.

I took a deep breath and spoke slowly and deliberately.

'It's about Clara.' Your name sent a charge down the line.

'It's a terrible thing that she's missing, poor girl. Such an awful, awful thing. I'm just devastated by it, I know you must be too.' Her voice was shaking. 'You must be in a dreadful state, darling, and the police, for them to even think you could have done something, well they'll look bloody stupid when they realise their mistake. I hope someone gets the sack for this. Really I do wonder about policing these days, Ethel up the road was mugged the other day and they couldn't have been less interested—'

'Laura, please,' I said, cutting through her monologue. 'I need to know.'

She still lived in the same large double-fronted villa in Hove where Niamh's wake was held a decade ago. She put it up for sale once and the estate agents described it as elegant, *a stone's throw from the beach,* although who could have thrown that far I never did find out. I was glad when she decided to keep it; it had been a place of refuge from the chaos of life with Niamh, where the kind of order and tidiness I craved ruled. In the summer the wisteria would creep up the doorway in a flush of pink and the smell of Laura's sweet peas would hang in the air. She'd hurry me out into the back garden leaving Niamh behind and whisper all the Latin names of the plants to me as if they were secrets for our ears only. Niamh rarely sauntered out in the summer, the sun too bright for her night-time eyes, but on the few occasions she did I'd block her out of my eyeline just so I could keep up the pretence that Laura was my mother for a few moments longer.

I didn't trust my memories, now. I'd clung to Laura in those days because she was different from Niamh, not realising how similar they really were. Sure, Laura's house was more ordered, her cooking edible, she talked to me, she indulged me. But she had also been complicit in hiding the truth from me, in guarding Niamh's lie. At their core there was very little difference between the two sisters after all.

The bell was old and large and gold and rang as if it was sending a message to the servant of the house to answer. Laura opened the door in her tennis gear. Was she hoping to squeeze me in between matches? She wore a smile on her face that didn't reach her eyes.

'Rachel.' She pulled me towards her and hugged me tight. An older, bonier version of her previous self. Her skin was a deep shade of brown, despite the winter, and wrinkled beyond her years. *Too much time on the tennis court*. But the eyes, the pale blue of them, the way they looked deep into you, all-knowing. They were Niamh's. I felt myself recoiling from her embrace.

Walking into the living room we exchanged comments

about the weather before she turned to look at me properly.

'You're tired, Rachel, I can see it in your eyes. They are sparkling just like they used to when you were little and needed to go to bed.'

I swear she never made such an observation when I was younger. It was as if she was trying to create some blissful, Enid Blyton childhood memories for me. All made up because it wasn't ever like that.

I looked around me. The flowers on the patterned wallpaper had lost their colour, bleached by the sun over the years, and the green carpet, fashionable no doubt in the eighties, was dated and worn. She hesitated for a moment, as if there were words sitting on her lips waiting to be spoken. Then she must have decided against it. 'I'll get us some tea, shall I?' she said too loudly.

Laura didn't have children of her own, so there were no photographs of graduations or weddings or christenings to flaunt to her friends. Only images of John, my uncle, her husband who died when I was little. It struck me that hers might be a lonely, sad existence, and I wondered why I hadn't made more of an effort to visit her more often. But when she came back into the room with a tray of tea and biscuits I was reminded why I kept my distance. In her face I could see my mother's.

Taking a seat in the armchair opposite me, she poured the tea and handed me a cup and saucer. She had always seemed so big when I was younger, in the role of my protector. Now the armchair looked ready to swallow her up. Instead of sinking into it she perched on the edge, waiting to be interviewed.

'I know about Clara,' I said. She didn't look up so I couldn't see her expression. 'I know, Laura, but I still have a lot of gaps. You have to tell me everything. I think you owe me that at least.'

Laura sighed and spooned the sugar into her tea and stirred.

'I'm sorry,' she said, 'Niamh should have told you long ago.'

'Niamh should have done a lot of things,' I said. 'When did Clara find out?'

'Oh Rachel, what good is it going to do now, dragging all this up . . .' I felt my cheeks heat with anger. After everything she still assumed she knew what was best for me. I gritted my teeth and spoke.

'I asked you how long had Clara known? Did she know when we moved here, to Brighton?'

'No darling, they wrote to each other, well your mother wrote to her, but they hadn't seen each other in years. There was no way Simon, Clara's dad, would have agreed to them meeting, not after everything that happened.' She stopped, wondering no doubt about how much of the story I was actually familiar with, how much she could get away with glossing over. 'Then of course he turned up one day to collect her from a friend's house and found out it was actually Niamh's house. That was a bit of a problem, I don't mind telling you. Simon took a lot of convincing that it was just one of those inexplicable coincidences, which it was, Rachel, I hope you know that. No one was more surprised to find out you and Clara were friends than Niamh.'

'Anyway there were lots of arguments after that. Simon had a job offer in the States and was all for taking it and moving Clara over there but Niamh begged him not to.' She took a little sip of tea and placed her cup gently back on the saucer. 'So they came to an arrangement. He insisted that as long as Clara was a child Niamh would never tell her she was her mother. But once she was an adult, old enough to make her own decisions . . . well, he knew he couldn't keep it from her forever.'

'And she agreed to it, just like that?' It seemed so uncharacteristic of my mother to adhere to anyone's rules.

'What choice did she have? She'd walked out on them after all, no judge would have given her custody. Clara was only a baby at the time and Simon, well it was terribly hard for him, he was barely an adult himself when it happened. But he wouldn't let Clara go. He would have done anything for that girl.' Her gaze moved towards the window. The sun was streaming in, hitting my face and making me squint. I shifted in my seat to avoid it.

I thought of your dad who had always put you firmly at the centre of his universe. You used to tease him. *When are you going to find a girlfriend, Dad?* And he did have them, but the relationships were fleeting, never serious. You filled up so much of his world there wasn't room for anyone else. It made sense now, the struggle to take care of you and carve out a career, to make a life for you both. Why would he have done anything to jeopardise it?

'Poor Simon, it was such a difficult time for him and then the worry that he might lose Clara altogether.' Laura sighed.

I was trying to take it all in slowly, memorise what she was telling me, so I could leave her with the facts clear and ordered in my mind.

'I don't understand,' I said. 'Why would he have lost her?'

'You never knew your grandfather did you?' Laura asked. I thought of the blurry image I had of an older man with white hair and a beard that always held a crumb or two of what he had eaten for his last meal. The smell of pipe smoke. That was all I remembered.

I shook my head.

'Hmmm,' she said as if the story of her father held the key to everything. 'Well, your mother was always his favourite, she could do no wrong even when we were children. He gave her everything. And I mean everything she wanted. He ruined her, we could all see it. And then she went and got pregnant and we thought he would hit the roof because he was strict but no, he told her not to worry, that she always had her family for support. And then Clara came along, his first grandchild, and he doted on her; he'd take her out for hours in her pram at the weekend, sit her on his knee and sing her lullabies, he'd tell her stories, tickle her and make her chuckle. He was smitten with his little Clarabel,' she said, the resentment towards her dead father still sharp in her voice.

'When Niamh walked out he was devastated. He couldn't understand how anyone could do that, let alone his own daughter, his favourite daughter. He insisted on giving Simon all the help he needed, looking after Clara at weekends, organising childcare so Simon could study. But that wasn't quite enough for my father and he decided it would be best for everyone if Clara came to live with him and my mother. The man had taken leave of his senses.'

'I assume Simon wasn't exactly receptive to the idea?' I said.

'Good God no, he was enraged and who could blame him? He thought my father was trying to be kind by offering him support, not angling to steal his baby daughter from him. My father threatened to fight for custody, lawyers' letters were sent backwards and forwards, but then suddenly he dropped it. I think he was taken aback by how protective Simon was of Clara. I don't think he expected a man who was barely twenty to put up such a fight. Besides, he'd never have got custody anyway. Simon was a model dad. But he did make sure your grandfather never saw Clara again. First he lost Niamh and then Clara too. It killed him in the end.'

She took a breath and sighed. 'So you see, Rachel, your mother didn't doubt Simon when he threatened to take Clara away. And if it wasn't that job in the States he could easily get another one; he was a successful consultant, in demand. At least if she played by his rules she still got to see Clara through you.' Laura saw the look on my face and lowered her eyes, shamed by her own words. 'Oh, I didn't mean it like that, I meant—'

'Don't.' I held my hand up. Niamh had exploited the thing most precious to me and then kept me in the dark when everyone else knew. I wanted to pick up Laura's china tea set and hurl it across the room.

She must have read my mind.

'She was going to tell you, Rachel, how could she have kept it from you? Simon agreed that she could tell Clara a few months before her eighteenth birthday and she was supposed to tell you afterwards.'

'Supposed to . . .' I laughed. 'When did Niamh ever do what she was supposed to do?'

'Well now, Rachel, I don't want to makes excuses for your mother but she was in a difficult position. It was a shock for Clara, an enormous shock for a young girl to be told her friend's mother is actually her mother too. And she begged Niamh just to give her a few weeks to get her head round the idea, to let it sink in, before she told you.'

The room was spinning, the tea tasted like tar in my mouth. I closed my eyes but I could see colours jumping about beneath my eyelids. You knew, Clara, you knew and you kept it from me, begged her not to tell me and all the time you acted as if nothing had changed. I thought of the day of your birthday barbecue, the way you both ignored me. You wanted her all to yourself, to erase me from the picture.

Best friends who tell each other everything but the truth.

'Ten years,' I cried, 'ten years she's been dead, Laura, and you haven't told me. Everyone else knew and still you chose to keep me in the fucking dark.'

'Oh darling, you just seemed to be doing so well for yourself, it was like you didn't want to be reminded of the past. You were so focused on the future. I always admired that in you.'

What a weak, lame excuse.

'Hang on,' she said and got up and left the room too quickly, eager to escape. I heard her footsteps climbing the stairs, then overhead. Five minutes later she returned carrying the ankle-boot shoebox I recognised immediately.

'I shouldn't have taken this from you after the funeral, but at the time I thought it was for the best.' I heard the strain in her voice. 'You deserved better. You always deserved better.'

Her eyes were wet with tears as I took the box from her. I wondered if she expected me to comfort her. I didn't have it in me. All those years I thought she was protecting me. I thought she was better than Niamh. I believed she loved me where my own mother didn't. Now I realised it was just pity disguised as love. *Poor little know-nothing Rachel.* All those memories: the flower names, the baking, they were all so false and empty now.

Opening the box I let the photographs spill out on to the floor. I saw the one of Niamh with the gumsy, smiling baby. I turned it over to read the name. Five faded letters.

CLARA.

They met when she was seventeen and your dad was nineteen. Niamh was still in the sixth form taking her A levels at the local private school. Childhood sweethearts, everyone said. And then she fell pregnant. It was 1978 and they thought they should do the right thing and get married. 'They were in love,' Laura said, staring out of the window, anywhere to spare her from looking at me. There was no part of her that wanted to tell me this story. The red blotches creeping up her neck, the sound of a dry mouth talking. She did it though. I think she must have known I would have beaten it out of her if I had to.

'Clara was born at the beginning of September. I think Niamh had loved the attention of being pregnant, you know she always wanted to be different from everyone else and no one else she knew was having a baby. But the reality of being a mother soon hit her.'

'Did she live at home with your parents?' I asked. Laura allowed herself a dry laugh.

'Your grandfather told her she would always be welcome in his house; she could have brought the baby up there if she'd wanted. But that wasn't Niamh's style – she craved independence, so he paid for a wedding and set her and Simon up in a flat. Not that she ever thanked him for it.' I let her words hang in the air for a while, before I breathed them in. My mother, the woman with no redeeming qualities. 'She was given everything and then she went and messed it up again.'

'You mean she messed it up by getting pregnant with me?'

'No, I . . . that's not what I meant. Niamh threw everything my father did for her back in his face. We'd all been telling him for years that she could twist him round her little finger. We warned him to let her make her own mistakes.

I think he thought we were jealous. And then she started leaving Clara in the flat on her own and going out. God knows where she got to. She couldn't handle the responsibility, she'd never had to. And when she left, abandoned her baby and husband without so much as a goodbye, he shrank right before our eyes. My mother tried to contact her, to get her to come back, or speak to him at the very least. But she wouldn't. She thought he would try to persuade her to come back to Brighton and back to Simon and her old life. So in the end she stopped taking the calls. I think that's why your grandfather was so fixed on keeping Clara, that way he wouldn't have lost Niamh entirely.' Laura's words were laced with anger and reproach. I allowed myself a wry laugh. All those years I had mistaken a sense of duty for sisterly love. I had believed their relationship was harmonious, if frustrating. But now I saw Laura had been jealous of Niamh, jealous of the undisguised, undeserving favouritism their father showed her. And now she was angry, that ten years after her sister died she was still dealing with the consequences of her sister's behaviour.

'Tell me about Clara,' I said, 'as a baby,' I added, before she told me I knew you better than she did.

I heard her huff, and realised she thought she'd already told me more than enough to satisfy me. She had no idea what it was like to find out your whole life story has been fabricated and built on layers of lies. She didn't understand the insatiable hunger to consume every single detail that has been kept from you.

'She was difficult. Any mother would have found her hard work, let alone a teenage one. She didn't sleep, she cried all the time.' It sounded like Niamh's description of me as a baby. I wondered whether she had deliberately swapped our stories.

Apparently your first home, Clara, was a one-bedroom flat on Lewes Road, where the noise of the buses thundering past would keep you awake. Laura said Simon gave Niamh lots of last chances, even when he found out she had gone out and left you alone in the flat. He must have really loved her to put up with that.

When Laura reached the point in the timeline of my conception, she began to squirm. I let her stew for a while, watching her struggle to come up with a palatable form of words to deliver the blow, before my impatience got the better of me.

'For God's sake, Laura, just say it: it was a drunken fuck against a pub wall.' She blinked, startled by the language, and then nodded slowly.

'Well I wouldn't have quite put it in those terms, Rachel, but sadly that is roughly what happened.'

It was the one detail of my life Niamh had never tried to hide from me.

I wanted to know about the letters, when and how Niamh had begun sending you little missives of her love. Laura rubbed her head as if to staunch off a headache.

'She'd always sent them, ever since Clara was at the age she could read. Before that she sent cuddly toys and cards, on her birthdays and at Christmas, but Simon wouldn't give them to Clara. He said she was too young to be disappointed by her mother again.' I wondered when Niamh wrote these tender messages of motherly love, cards that said *all my love, Mum* xxx. Would she pour her heart out to you and then turn to me, the daughter she lived with, and tell me I disgusted her? It was all so clear now, the absence of love: she was starving me of her affection to store it all up for you. I felt like I was sinking again, back into the past I had tried so hard to bury. My mother loomed so big in that room I felt her ghost was ready to consume me.

'So how did they finally make contact?' I asked and watched with horror Laura's face colour. She couldn't look me in the eye.

'Oh God, it was you. You were her fixer.' The pain ripped through me. So many betrayals.

'Rachel, you're making it sound so sordid. She promised me she was sorry, genuinely sorry for what she had done; she told me she regretted walking out on Clara every day of her life. She said she had changed, she wanted another chance. Your mother was so persuasive, she could make you believe anything. That was her power. She had it over my father. And she could turn it on whoever she wanted to. She begged and begged me.' Laura stopped and took a tissue from her pocket to blow her nose. 'So yes, in the end I . . .'

'You agreed to do her bidding,' I said, finishing her sentence.

'I'd always kept in touch with Simon and seen Clara the odd time as she was growing up. So when she was a bit older I asked if we could spend some time together. She'd come here one Sunday a month and I would give her Niamh's letters. She never once told Simon, she knew it was to be our secret. All the poor girl wanted to know was that her mother still cared for her. You should have seen her face when she read them, Rachel, she devoured them. Her eyes would light up. Every girl wants a relationship with their mother.' Laura carried on, the irony of her words lost on her.

Every girl wants a relationship with their mother.

'She was fourteen when I gave her the first letter.'

'A real coming of age,' I said, doing the calculations in my head. 'And your little introductions must have gone well because we moved down to Brighton the following year.'

'Niamh didn't expect you to become friends. Clara was older after all, we had no idea you'd end up in the same class. I didn't want to be involved after that. I didn't want Clara to find out that I was your aunt and make the connection. It was all so tangled.'

Tangled. The word didn't even come close to encapsulating the twisted mess Niamh had created.

'Do you know what it was like for me?' I spat. 'While you were passing fucking letters to Clara, have you any idea? Niamh didn't give a fuck about me; Jesus Christ, you must have seen that. Every day she'd tell me how I was fat, or ugly, or stupid, how she wished she'd never had me. She was inventive, I'll give her that, she always found a different way of telling me I was a piece of shit. You must have known, and yet you believed her when she said she'd changed? How could you have been sucked in by her promises, how could you have believed she was truly sorry when you saw how she treated me?'

Laura was sobbing, polite little stifled sobs that sounded like hiccups.

'Rachel, please, please don't do this, I never wanted you to find out like this.' I watched her get up from the armchair and come over to me, her tanned, leathery arms outstretched.

'Oh Rachel, I'm sorry. I'm so, so sorry.' She was very close to me, kneeling next to me so I could smell the same lavender smell that was once comforting. But today it was heavy and sweet and made me gag. I felt her cold, clammy hand reach out to me, trying to clutch at forgiveness. I pushed her out of the way and watched her fall back. Then after grabbing my bag I ran out of the room, through the hallway. She was calling my name: 'RACHEL, RACHEL, PLEASE.' Again and again. As I glanced back I saw her pathetic figure pulling itself up from the floor, following me to the door.

'You disgust me,' I said and turned and left.

Halfway down the street I heard the sound of the waves, and her words reached me, carried on the wind.

'I was only trying to help her, Rachel. She was my sister.'

And you are mine, Clara.

Chapter Twenty-four

On the beach, the only place to go to clear my head. It was February-freezing, no warmth in the sun, but I didn't mind, I couldn't feel anything anyway. Sitting close to the water the waves rolled up towards me, stopping just short of my feet. I imagined a huge one taking me by surprise and dragging me in. Would I put up a fight? This person, this successful, polished creature I had created with her magazine-perfect life – she was slipping away. I wasn't sure I cared enough any more to save her.

That feeling again of being on the outside, separate, the way I had felt most of my life, the way I had felt when you and Niamh ridiculed me the day before she died. It was rolling over me. Jonny had gone, you were against me. No one was left who cared. I was alone again.

In my head the tick-tick-ticking of a clock. You were out there planning and plotting, creeping closer and closer.

Coming to get you ready or not.

What else did you have in store for me, Clara? Or would you wait to see if I was charged with your murder before you stuck the knife in again?

Then the phone rang and Jake's voice came at me through the wind.

'I have something for you,' he said. 'A name.'

'Surprise me.'

I grabbed a handful of pebbles from the beach and threw them one by one into the sea.

'The *Crimewatch* caller, the one who called twice. Does the name James Redfern mean anything to you?

James Redfern, Lucy Redfern.

My stomach twisted, a shimmer of nausea. I thought I might be sick.

Names from the past I'd never forgotten. Names that made everything slot into place.

Amber's description of your boyfriend came shooting back to me – *he's called Jim or something, I think she knew him from years back.*

Jim, James. The same person. A man who wanted revenge as much as you did.

'It rings a bell,' I told Jake, as I lay back on the pebbles and looked up to the sky, wondering when it was going to swoop down and swallow me up.

You might have been acting out of spite and jealousy and misplaced blame, but you weren't acting alone, Clara. My instincts were right. James was on your side, the man in the locksmith's I presumed, the same person who broke into my flat twice. I was whizzing back through our conversations, our meetings, the rare fun times and laughter we'd shared since you came back, dizzied by the thought that everything had been a lie.

And who else had you recruited into your coven? How far and wide and deep did your plot reach?

Who else was smiling and talking to me one minute and planning my downfall the next?

Sarah.

Suddenly I heard her voice echoing in my head: the too-chirpy calls, the chats peppered with questions as to my whereabouts and plans. I thought she was showing an interest in my life because hers was so boring; I'd fallen for her line, *'Oh my life is so dull, I won't bore you with it, tell me what you've been doing.'* Jesus, I'd even come to look forward to her calls in a strange masochistic way.

I'd allowed myself to slip into the trap; I thought she liked me and I was flattered. Even after all these years, after all I had achieved when *she* had achieved so little, I still wanted her to like me, and you'd known that hadn't you, Clara? You had ruthlessly exploited my schoolgirl insecurities.

Anger pulsed through me. Even in the cold my skin began to bubble with sweat.

You knew me too well.

And then I laughed, a hideous crazy person's laugh that was carried away on the waves.

You know my weaknesses. But I know yours too.

I left the beach, walking quickly up Queen's Road, the outline of a plan taking shape in my head. I dipped into a Starbucks, ordered a hot chocolate and a muffin and found myself a table at the back of the café. Sitting down, I pulled my phone out and scrolled through to find her number.

It rang twice before she answered.

'Oh hi doll,' she said – babe and doll were interchangeable in Sarah's lexicon. 'How you coping?'

Not very well actually, I've just found out my whole fucking life is a lie.

'OK,' I said. 'It was Jonny's funeral the other day and that was hard. And everything is still hanging over me with Clara and the police.' I paused for a moment and then decided to go ahead. 'Oh, and to top it off lots of weird stuff keeps happening.'

'Like what?'

'Just texts and letters, you know, threatening kind of stuff, and then the other night I woke up to the sound of someone laughing in the house.'

'Fucking hell—'

'Turned out someone had got into my house and stuck a CD in the stereo with someone's laughter on it, how fucking spooky is that?'

'Do the police have any idea who it is?'

'They think I'm crazy, no sign of anyone breaking in, and then I told them I recognised the laugh; you should have seen the way they looked at me. But I'd know it anywhere.'

She hesitated before saying: 'Tossers, they should take

you seriously.' I heard a doorbell ring in the background. 'Oh babe, sorry, that's a delivery at the door, I need to go. I'll call you later OK, this afternoon, take care.' And she rang off.

I sat and finished my hot chocolate, wincing as I drank a mouthful of sugary residue at the bottom of the mug. Then, picking up my coat and bag, I headed back out into the cold.

Sarah hadn't once asked whose laugh I thought it was.

She hadn't asked because she already knew.

A shopping list in my head: food supplies – chocolate, sandwiches, biscuits, more than I thought I would need but you could never be too sure. Flask, sleeping bag, torch, tick, tick, tick. Then back to Starbucks for coffee to fill the flask.

Packing the car when I had finished, I called Jake at work.

'Can you do an electoral roll search on James Redfern?' I asked him.

'You worked out if you know him yet?'

'No, but I figure if I see him it might jog my memory,' I lied.

'By the way,' he said. 'I have a surprise for you when you get home.'

But I was too focused on finding James to ask him what it was.

James lived in Applesham Avenue in Hove, a wide tree-lined street of 1950s semis. His house was a few doors down from a parade of shops. I parked up outside a motor supplies store giving me a clear view of his garden without looking too conspicuous. The afternoon light was fast disappearing into an early-evening gloom. I turned the engine and my lights off and covered my legs with the sleeping bag. The car thermometer read two degrees, but I couldn't afford to keep the engine running; I knew I had to stay there for as long as it took.

Hours went by, the shops closed, people in suits made their way home from work. Every man who walked past I sized up – *could that be him?* – until the sheer concentration of it made my eyes heavy with sleep. I opened my flask and poured some coffee to stay awake, careful to ration it in case I needed the loo.

Still, his house was in darkness. I toyed with the idea of phoning a pizza to be delivered to his door, just to check he was actually there, but I didn't want to arouse any suspicions so I just sat in the car, drinking lukewarm coffee from the flask and eating an egg-and-cress sandwich, waiting, waiting.

Just after eight o'clock, a silver BMW pulled up outside his house and a figure emerged from the driver's door into the glow of the streetlights. It was a man at least, dressed smartly in a suit, but more than that I couldn't tell. He pointed his keys at the car and the lights flashed to lock it. Then he walked at a pace up the garden path and disappeared. A current of excitement flowed through me before passing as quickly as it came.

Now what?

I didn't have to think for too long because ten minutes later he emerged again. He'd changed clothes, swapped the suit for jeans and trainers and a parka coat. He was carrying one of those supermarket 'bags for life'. There was a click and his car lights flashed again. He was inside, the engine humming.

I flung my sandwich on to the passenger seat and cast the sleeping bag aside. Having been so tired I pinged awake. Blood pumped through me and pulsed in my head.

I turned the keys in the ignition and watched him drive away. He was halfway down the street when I pulled out and followed him up Old Shoreham Road, then out on to the A27 heading west. I had no way of knowing if the man in the car was James, let alone if he would lead me to you, but it was like a fairground ride: once you're on, you're on for the duration.

As every signpost or turning approached a rush of adrenalin flowed through me. *Is he taking me closer to you?* Worthing, Littlehampton, Bognor Regis, as we passed each one I ticked them off my list of possible destinations. It was like a game of elimination.

He was careful not to speed, hovering just above or below seventy the whole way. I kept my distance but never took my eyes off his car.

Fifty minutes later as we approached the turn-off for the Witterings I noticed him indicating. Five seconds later I did the same.

The road was dark and unlit and much quieter than the

dual carriageway. I slowed right down and hung back in case he became suspicious. We weaved down towards the village and then through it, to West Strand. Ahead, the sea, a carpet of black.

Even at night the village seemed familiar, like a fading memory. And then it came to me; I had been here before with you and your dad on one of those English summer days where the air is filled with suntan lotion and fish and chips. When we were still smiling and joking. A lifetime ago.

The BMW pulled over and I decided to carry on past it, fighting the urge to snatch a glimpse of the driver as I went by. I was 100 metres ahead when I saw the figure in the parka get out of the car, Sainsbury's bag in hand, and walk a few metres along the street before dipping down on to the beach.

I had rehearsed the finding-James part of my plan, imagined tailing him like a character in a film and in my head I'd gone over the moment when he would reveal you to me. But I hadn't planned for this scenario: exposed on a dark beach with nowhere to hide. And yet any doubts it was actually him had now evaporated. I had no choice but to follow him.

I pulled on my hat, buttoned my coat, grabbed my new torch, my phone and headed out into the night.

The squally weather was a blessing and a hindrance – the noise of the wind drowned out my footsteps but made it impossible for me to hear anything else. I traced the same path as I'd seen James take five minutes earlier, turning down to the beach at the same point where he had faded into the night.

As I reached the beach my feet hit the soft sand, slowing my pace. I felt the burn in my legs, the exertion taking the breath out of me. Ahead white foam sprayed off the waves. I stopped to rest for a moment, breathing in the mineral-scented air, and looked up to see a blanket of dark sky pierced by pinholes of brilliant light.

I knew from the heavy thumps of my heart that I was terrified, and yet I'd never felt more alive than on that beach. The sense of danger, the promise of discovery, being exposed to the rawness of nature on the dark, desolate stretch of sand, it was as if suddenly I felt the force of life pumping through me. I wasn't dead yet.

I scanned the beach ahead for moving shadows. There were none. In the distance, I saw a row of weather-beaten beach huts sitting in darkness and I thought he must have gone into one. But as I approached there were no sounds, no signs of life. The wind chilled me; I looked around, aware that you or James could see me and pounce. What then? No one knew where I was. No one would know where to look for me.

Then, my eyes caught sight of a smaller row of huts set back into the sand dunes. At the very end, one painted in yellow. An orangey light seeped out from underneath the door. As I approached I realised I had seen it before. The photograph of your dad sitting over a camping stove, the framed picture from your bedroom. It was your dad's hut. How poignant it had become your chosen hiding place.

⁂

I edged closer, the chatter finally drifting out towards me, broken up by the scream of the wind. Unmistakably, it was your voice, and his too. Even after all those years, I could still hear his words:

You fucking bitch, Rachel.

I turned, suddenly craving the safety of the car, and began the walk back, the wind whipping the sand up into my eyes. I don't know how far I'd got – not far enough – when I heard the sound of the door creaking open, voices – yours and his – saying goodbye and I was aware that he was walking behind me, in my footsteps. My blood rushed to my head, dizzying me; the drip-drip of cold fear ran down my spine.

My body screamed at me to run but I had to fight the urge. If he hadn't seen me in the pitch dark, running would certainly attract his attention.

He was moving quicker, quicker, the noise of sand shifting underfoot deafened me. He was gaining ground and his breath, a wheezy rattle, tingled through me –

Stay calm, don't panic.

And then I reached the turning.

There was a black industrial bin, wide enough to hide me. I ducked down behind it. All the time I could hear his footsteps closer and closer, vibrating through me.

One, two, three, four . . . I counted.

. . . nine, ten seconds.

He passed me at thirteen.

I waited, unable to move, until finally the sound of a car door opening and an engine starting flooded me with relief and I sat back and inhaled greedy breaths of air for the first time in minutes.

Back at the car I ripped a sheet of paper from my pad and wrote you a note.

> Dear Clara,
> The truth, once and for all.
> No lies.
> Just you and me.
> I'll be waiting, at home, alone, for you.
> Rachel

I read it over to myself, folded it and crept back along the beach to the yellow hut. There was no light on now but I was sure you were still inside and I slipped it quietly under the door.

Chapter Twenty-five

IT WAS THE end of the world today, or that was how it felt – don't plan anything, don't look to the future, just wait for it all to come crashing down.

Jake phoned from work – 'Out on a shoot until evening in deepest Essex, I'll call when I'm finished,' he breezed, offering me a snapshot of my old life. And then he paused as if he was going to tell me something.

'What is it?' I asked irritably.

'Nah.' He gave a little giggle. 'I'll save it for later, it's a surprise.' He sounded pleased with himself.

'You'll come round tonight, won't you?' I asked.

'It'll be a late finish.'

'I don't care. I don't want to be alone.'

'I'll be there. But Rach . . .'

'Yes?'

'You're going to be fine, you know. I'll make sure of it.' And then he hung up. I pictured him at work directing the shoot with another reporter and here was me with no idea when (if) I would return to work. An undetermined period of compassionate leave had been thrust upon me. My bosses had insisted I take time off *until everything sorted itself out,* when what they really wanted to say was *stay away until we know you're not a psychotic killer.*

Where work had kept me busy I was now held hostage by my thoughts, imprisoned by the constant churn of them, preparing for endless, ever-changing scenarios and consequences. The planning and plotting and thinking created a relentless whirr of noise that hammered into my skull. I would have given anything for a moment of silence, to be set free from my mind. But you were the only person who could give me a way out, Clara.

Would you show your face today?

I turned the TV on to still my head. It worked for a while, sucking me into *This Morning* and a slot on erectile dysfunction. There was a man in his forties, *a case study,* admitting he had suffered from it for a decade. I found myself hoping they paid him well to do it, because however much it was it couldn't have been enough. Then it was over and next up was a couple whose son went missing two years ago. They were on the sofa talking to Fern Britton, holding hands, tissues wiping tears, Fern's head cocked to one side in sympathy. I turned it off, choosing to wander through the flat instead, watering my plants, lighting scented candles, dusting, making coffee I wouldn't drink. The minutes dragging, stretched out, time never ending.

At midday, the news. Richard Goldman's slimy face all

over a terrorism story that should have been mine. I watched him, willing him to fuck up.

It was word-perfect.

It's a sign.

Nothing will go my way today.

I tried to drive the thought away. Too late. It slid down through me like liquid mercury, settling deep in my stomach.

Outside my door, chatter, mums on the way to the park with whingeing children, *Arthur darling don't do that, Tilly sweetie don't be rude otherwise there will be no treats after Tumbletots.*

Lives moving on, but not mine: stuck here on rewind, being dragged back into the past.

Hours later, the doorbell. A ring, an intake of breath, the sharp stab of panic. *It's you.* I walked to the door, *slowly, no rush, take it easy. Breathe deep.* Then I unlocked it and saw a young bloke in tatty jeans and a shell top waving cloths and ironing-board covers in my face. He flashed an ID card, a smile, and started on his sob story.

Fuck off.

I shuffled back inside, every sound amplified; the creak of the pipes were your footsteps, the draught from the door your breath sneaking up on me. Cortisol flushing through my blood. I wondered how long I could take this.

You are not coming

But I knew you would.

The truth, it's what you've always wanted.

It's all anyone wants.

⊸o⊷

At some point in the afternoon the light disappeared, the way it does in winter: one minute it is day and then you blink and night has fallen too soon. I peeped out through the shutters, the inky blackness broken up by the lights of the city. I needed air.

Food, fresh air, I was calculating in my head. Ten minutes. I could be out and back in ten minutes. Then my coat and keys and phone were in my hands and I was heading for the door, leaving my world of waiting behind, stepping out into a different one of movement and bustle and change. The cold slapped my face. I steadied myself for a moment on the gate before marching ahead.

The headlights and streetlamps cast shadows that danced on the path. Horns and sirens went off, erupting in my ear. I was walking forward but looking back all the time, scanning the street for you.

In the takeaway, a woman in front of me. Fat enough to be a regular customer: *Sausage and chips, no make that fish and chips . . . actually throw in another portion of chips. And a Coke, make that two.*

Hurry the fuck up.

I asked for chips, open, and sprinkled them with extra salt and vinegar. They were too hot to eat, but walking back home I shovelled them in anyway, mouth half open, *huh huh huh* blowing air to cool them.

Turning into Kempe Road I saw two figures walking in the distance, moving away from me. One, a man, crossed the road to the other side. The second person carried on past my door as if heading down towards Queen's Park. Then suddenly my view was obscured; I was on the ground, chips sprayed out in front of me. I looked around and saw a stray paving slab.

'Fuck.'

On my feet again I scanned the street once more. Then, a jolt surged through me, as if my eyes had sent the message to my body before I understood what was happening. The figure that had been moving away was getting bigger now. It was coming towards me, edging closer.

Closer and closer still.

Someone in the darkness, collar pulled up against the cold. Hair covered by a hat. But the walk, that strange lollop, I would have recognised it anywhere.

I stopped outside my flat, the beat of my heart coming up through my throat, banging in my head. I swallowed hard. And then I looked up and saw your face.

'You'd better come inside.'

We didn't breathe. There was silence, even our feet were soundless on the floorboards, as we floated like ghosts through the hallway.

The air was stretched, taut, my heart thumping, *boom, boom, boom*. Or maybe it was yours I could hear too. Stereo sound.

In the living room we sat on the sofa. There were two to choose from but you sat on the same one as me. We did this without exchanging a word. *Who blinks first?*

I'd had enough of the games, Clara. I wanted to hear

it all, to shake it out of you. You killed Jonny: *why, why, why*?

'Welcome back from the dead,' I said, looking at you properly for the first time since you'd gone. You looked like a ghost. How fitting.

You said nothing, but your staring eyes didn't stray from me. They had a strange reflective quality to them. I could see myself in them. Could you see yourself in mine?

You removed your hat slowly to reveal bottle-blond hair, telltale dark roots beginning to creep through. You'd cut it short, or hacked it to be precise. I wondered if you'd done it yourself, or if James had done it for you. How romantic, your little game of playing dead.

In other circumstances I would have told you the colour made your skin look sallow and tired and highlighted the dark circles under your eyes. It made you look like a hooker, Clara, but I didn't want to provoke you. Besides, I was mesmerised by your appearance. You had loomed so large in my head, this powerful mastermind of my downfall. And now? Now I saw you for who you were. The skin around your face was pinched, your eyes still heartbreak blue but tired and beaten. Under your fingernails, thick rims of dirt. Life was eating away at you. I wondered how many more bites it would take to finish you off completely.

'Jonny,' I said. It was a question, a statement, an accusation all rolled into one. You looked down at the table, shaking your head.

'Later . . .'

'Tell me.'

'You get to go first, and when you've told me everything, I will tell you about Jonny,' you said. I felt the heat prick my face, my anger frothing to the surface. My reward for telling you what you want to hear was to find out how my boyfriend died. In my head I counted, one . . . two . . . three. *Don't rise to the bait.* You were in control, that's what you wanted to think. I would play your game. For now.

I was focusing on that thought, *control, stay calm,* when I saw your hand slip down and fumble in the pocket of your thick black coat. When you pulled it back out I saw the glint of metal.

My eyelids clicked. I blinked. I was staring at the object in your hand. The light bouncing off the metal.

The glint of metal on a knife.

Something slipped in my head. My plan, so tightly woven, began to unravel. My plan to lure you here and keep you talking until Jake came back and found us. My plan for him to call the police. My plan to clear my name and prove my case. Because only when the police saw you here, alive and breathing, could I finally convince them I hadn't killed you.

But now you were sitting in my living room where I watched TV and read the papers and drank wine and relaxed, and you were sitting here with a knife.

Everything had changed.

Your fingers skimmed the top of the blade. You smiled.

The thought of you smiling as you closed your eyes and sank it into me sent waves of icy panic through my body.

You could still surprise me, Clara.

I found myself smiling back because if I didn't I might have laughed, manically, or screamed in fear and frustration. I felt the momentum slip away from me. I thought I was in control but you had wrested it from me.

I needed to clear my mind, to think of a way through.

And then your voice pierced my brain like a hot needle.

'You think I won't, but I will, trust me, Rachel. I've got nothing left to lose.'

I nodded slowly.

I understand.

'Where shall we start?' I asked, at pains to steady my voice.

'Tell me the truth about Niamh.'

Everything always started with Niamh.

I sat for a moment thinking of what you wanted me to say, before you said it for me.

'You killed her,' you told me.

'So why all this,' I said, pointing at the knife, 'if you're so sure you know already?'

'I'll tell you what I know, what you tried to cover up for years. You gave her the sleeping pills and you killed her and then you let me believe I had done it. You twisted it all and made me think I had killed my own mother,' you said, your voice rising to a shriek.

'I didn't know she was your mother. I'm sorry about that.'

'Sorry?' You sounded surprised to hear the word come from my mouth. 'Sorry?'

'I'm sorry she was your mother. I'm sorry she was mine.'

'You fucking bitch. You cold-hearted fucking bitch. She loved me.'

I couldn't help it; rich, ironic laughter was escaping from me. *She loved you.* I tried to bring it under control as your eyes burnt into me.

'She loved you so much she fucked someone up against a wall and then left you. Some love,' I said.

'If she could have turned back the clock she would have.'

'And not given birth to me? Is that what you mean?'

'She was going to tell you, you know, that day before my eighteenth, before everything happened. I'd made her promise. I felt so wrong keeping it from you. That was why she was so nervous, so uptight, she was working up to it. She was trying to make everything perfect that day and then you argued with her and spoiled it and she couldn't do it then. She hated you for spoiling the moment. And then you killed her.'

I remembered Laura's words; *you* begged Niamh not to tell me, Clara, to give you time to let it sink in, and now you expected me to believe your lies. I thought back to that morning of the barbecue before you came round, the crackling heat of the day hanging heavy in the house. Niamh chopping and humming and talking too fast, her eyes darting around. On edge. It was because she wanted to make everything perfect for *you*, not me. Even a decade later I saw it as clearly as if it were happening right now in front of me. You were lying. You were trying to torment me with your twisted version of the past; you wanted *me* to think I had got it wrong.

'We both know that's not true. You can't come here and expect the truth from me and still spin me your lies,' I said.

It was your turn to laugh. You threw your head back, your hand still resting on the knife.

'Jesus, what the fuck do you know about the truth, Rachel? You have no concept of it. Everything that happens to you is moulded to fit your own ends. You killed your fucking mother so you need to cast her as this evil villain to absolve yourself from what you've done. Poor little Rachel, poor unloved, neglected Rachel. But it wasn't like that. She wasn't like that. She tried hard with you, Rachel, she tried to make you love her but she couldn't. She didn't live up to your expectations, she wasn't quite good enough so you wrote her off. Literally. You got rid of her like some unwanted fucking baggage because you got it in your mind you would be better off without her. And then you moved on to me.'

I let you continue with this monologue of yours, the torrent of accusations, the raw fury you'd suppressed for so long finally finding its outlet. You had no idea what it was like to have Niamh as a mother. All you had was a two-month-long honeymoon that would have turned sour and destructive if she hadn't died.

You were in full flow and with every sentence I watched the flush on your face grow deeper, the beads of sweat on your top lip multiply, the tremble of your hands become more pronounced. I was watching, watching, never taking my eyes off you for a moment.

'That day,' you spat, 'that day when you told me what

happened – and don't dare, don't fucking dare deny you told me – you said you'd given her the sleeping pills and then you saw my reaction, you knew you'd made a mistake by telling me. Didn't you? You knew you'd totally misjudged it. You revealed yourself to me that day, all the things people had told me about you and I had never believed. Well, I started believing them then.

'You knew it had all changed, that all of a sudden your best friend had become your biggest threat because I wanted to go to the police. I wanted you to tell them what you had done. I wanted you to face up to it. But you would never do that, would you, Rachel? So you did what you always do, you turned it round and made me think I had imagined what you said, like I was going fucking crazy. Oh God, I was such an easy target, my mother had just died and I was literally collapsing with grief and guilt and I came to you with it, this guilt I had about giving her one fucking sleeping tablet, and you made it grow inside me. You fed my fucking guilt every day, always there, watching over me, suffocating me. *Don't worry, Clara, I won't tell anyone,* you'd breathe into my ear, *your secret's safe with me.* It all became so clouded, so foggy, I didn't trust myself to think any more, let alone remember clearly what had happened. You'd created this fucking nightmare for me. How could you do that?'

You stopped to wipe fat tears away from your face with the back of your dirty hands, streaking your face as you did it. You looked so pitiful, I wanted to reach out to you, but I knew I couldn't. Not yet.

'Going away, even knowing you had persuaded my dad to have me fucking sectioned, even knowing he believed you over me, that was nothing compared with the relief I felt just to escape from you.' You jabbed your index finger at me, as if you were going pierce me with it.

'I thought I never wanted to see you again but when I came back I realised I had to see you to prove to myself you had no power over me any more. And then we met and you were so nice, so fucking lovely, it broke my heart. I thought maybe, just maybe, I'd got it all wrong. I'd come back hating you and wanting revenge and yet you'd do things that were so wonderful and kind and you'd make me laugh and I'd feel this love for you seep into the hatred again, diluting it.'

'And then you changed your mind,' I said.

You started laughing again, a horrible, empty cackle that echoed in my ears, and your tears were mixing with the snot on your face but I didn't dare move to offer you a tissue.

'Jesus Rachel, are you for fucking real? I changed my mind when you tried to push me off a mountain.'

I closed my eyes. We were living in parallel worlds; there was no use in trying any more because somehow, whatever I did, whatever happened to you would always be my fault. I let my head slip down into my hands as your words kept coming at me.

'That day, you know in the mountains, it was so beautiful, the sky and the powder, all of us peeling down the slopes. I thought I'd died and gone to heaven. You reminded me why we'd been friends, the fun, your ridiculous beer-drinking party trick. And then we went for that one last run. We were climbing the mountain on the chair lift and I thought, *I need to know*. I needed to know if I'd dreamt it all up in my mind and you really were my friend. Because I couldn't stand the doubt any longer. I needed to get everything straight in my head. That's when I asked if you killed her. I was watching your face all the time and I saw it, just a beat, a tiny ferocious flash of anger, and then you hid it again. But you knew, didn't you, that you'd let your mask slip. You knew that all your efforts at friendship had been in vain because I'd seen it. Oh God, we used to joke that we didn't need words to communicate. Well I didn't need you to say anything that day because your eyes told me everything.

'The next thing we're on a black run, of course it was quiet, we were literally on our own, the last run of the day, and I was trying to go fast to get away from you and you came at me with your poles, so close to the edge, and you pushed me. That's all I remember; the next thing I was waking up in hospital.'

There was nothing really to say to all of this, no point in defending myself because it was all so fanciful, the work of a 100 per cent fucked-up mind.

I let you take a breath.

'That's some theory you've come up with, Clara. I guess you found a kindred spirit in James? After all, he convinced himself it was my fault his sister drowned, my fault she capsized in the lake. And who made him believe that? Sarah of course. What a coincidence that you've all become such good friends.'

Your eyes bored into me. 'Sarah knows what she saw in the lake. Even after all these years she knows what she saw. Lucy's canoe capsized and you were the only one close to her. You shouted you were helping. But you didn't help, did you? You kept your oar just out of her reach and Sarah saw it all but she couldn't get to Lucy on time, and when she told the teachers, you were so convincing in your lies that no one believed her. No one believed that you would deliberately let someone die just to get your own back. Lucy pushed you in the water one day and made everyone laugh at you and the next day she was dead. Because you can't stand people making a fool of you, can you, Rachel? You can't stand the shame of it, so she had to pay.'

I couldn't believe you were throwing this at me now, the oldest story, the one we had gone over so many times and every time you told me you believed me.

'Fuck, when I think of how I stood up for you at school when everyone else was against you. I didn't want to believe you could do that. You are so fucking evilly persuasive, the way you cast your spells and make people believe anything.'

'Is that so?' I asked, unable to sit back and take your accusations any longer. 'So let's get this straight: I am the crazy person here, am I? Well let me ask you this: do I have a whole county's police force looking for me? Have I lied and plotted to frame my friend? I'm not hiding out in a beach hut with filthy nails and bleached hair. Look around, Clara, look for fuck's sake,' I shouted, rage surging through me. 'I am successful, I have a great job, I have this flat, I *had* a boyfriend who worshipped the ground I walked on. Everything in my life was so fucking perfect, so clean and ordered, and you . . . you couldn't stand it, could you? So you had to destroy it. You went and killed Jonny to get back at me for something I haven't done.'

'No,' you screamed, 'don't you dare turn this round. I did not kill Jonny. I didn't fucking kill him. He wasn't supposed to die.'

'Well he's dead, Clara, so whatever was *supposed* to happen doesn't matter much now, does it?'

You scratched your head with the hand that wasn't holding the knife as if you were scratching a drying sore.

'He wasn't meant to die,' you said, your head rocking back and forth gently like you were repeating a mantra. 'We just needed him to get to you. Can't you see that? You deserved to be punished, Rachel, someone had to punish you for what you did. Someone had to stop you.

'It was James's idea to play dead and frame you for my murder, at least that way you would finally pay the price for what you did to his sister and Niamh. We had it all planned. I arranged to meet you on Friday night and then I'd vanish. I wanted to get away from everything here anyway, James did too; we were going to India to start with. So what did it matter if everyone thought I was dead.'

'So why involve Jonny,' I spat, my mind reeling at your cunning. 'Why not leave him alone and he'd still be alive?'

'Because I needed the police to think I was having an affair with Jonny.'

My motive.

The penny dropped.

There was no air to breathe in the room. I was too hot, flames licking my head, fire in my stomach.

'And the picture . . . the laughter?' I could barely get my words out.

'I wanted you to know it was me, to be so sure of it but have no one believe you. I wanted you to know how I felt all those years ago. To know the truth but have no one believe you. I wanted it to send you crazy.' You looked pleased with yourself for a moment.

'I told Jonny we were all meeting up as a special surprise for you. He was reluctant at first, but he would have done anything for you. We arranged to meet at my flat.'

'That's when you gave him the sleeping pills?' I asked. 'Of course it had to be sleeping pills.'

You nodded in agreement.

'After that we drove along to Cantina Latina and we waited for you to leave.'

I remember how he looked on the CCTV, leaning into you, eyes closed. I thought it had been a trick of the camera.

'Sarah called us as you were leaving to warn us. She said you were pissed, which was always part of the plan, to get you as drunk as possible, so we waited until we saw you walking along the promenade and dragged Jonny out of the car. He wasn't totally out of it by then, he could walk. We just needed to be seen in the same area as you.'

'And you'd checked where the CCTV cameras were, I take it. So it all worked out beautifully,' I said. 'Except Jonny died and you didn't make your getaway after all.'

'James left him near Preston Park; he was clothed. It was cold I know, but Jesus Christ, we didn't expect him to die – he was wearing a jacket when he left him. He must have stripped it off, you know people do that when they've got hypothermia. It wasn't our fault.' The words came out shakily, without conviction, because you knew that it *was* your fault, didn't you? The unavoidable truth that you had killed him.

'Well whose was it? It wasn't his fault he ended up dead in the mortuary, his mother wailing because she's lost her only son, ripped apart by grief. It wasn't his fault he was so full or life and he had it stolen from him so fucking needlessly.'

'Don't, Rachel, don't. I swear we didn't mean it. I would never ever do that. I would never ever have tried to kill him.' You wiped your nose with the back of your sleeve. 'James heard they'd found his body when he was driving to see me, it was in the headlines on the radio. He had to pull over, on to the hard shoulder, so he could throw up. And then he told me.' You were wailing now. 'I didn't believe it at first, I couldn't believe how it had all gone so wrong. And then I just wanted it all to end. James had to hold me back from running into the sea because that's all I wanted to do. Disappear into the waves, sink down somewhere cold and still and never resurface again.

'He should still be alive, I should be thousands of miles away from here. It all went wrong,' you said needlessly.

'Why didn't you leave, make your getaway?'

'Amber,' you told me. 'Amber went to the police to report me missing so fucking quickly. We couldn't believe it. I didn't think they'd start a missing person's inquiry so soon but there I was, all over the news, my face in every fucking newspaper. We couldn't try to leave when all that was happening. We thought we'd let it die down – these things do, don't they, we thought everyone would get bored with me after a few days and then . . .' You still couldn't say his name.

'And then they found Jonny's body,' I said, finishing your sentence. Poor dead Jonny, the final nail in your coffin.

You opened your mouth, staring at me, unable to speak, like something was shattering within you. Every piece of you breaking up.

You were trapped, Clara, nowhere left to go.

James, Sarah, Debbie: they couldn't help you now.

There was only me left to protect you.

Suddenly, a new plan was forming in my head.

'Where do you go from here, Clara?' I asked, gently this time.

You opened your mouth but no words came out. A look of horror crept across your face.

There was nothing to say.

'All those people who've been searching for you, giving up their time, putting up posters, you've tricked them all. I can see the headlines now. You'll be the most hated woman in Britain. You're still breathing, Clara, but you're already dead.'

You let out a cry, and then started sobbing the pathetic sobs of someone who had nothing left. I wondered if I was pushing you too close to the edge, unsure of which way you would jump. I imagined I was walking a tightrope, above a bottomless gully. One wrong move and it could be the end of me.

'Look at you,' I said softly. 'Niamh caused all this, it's her fault. She tricked you into believing she loved you and ever since you've been paying the price. She didn't love you, not real love where you'd do anything for someone. She loved herself. She loved drink. You were just a novelty, a plaything that made her feel she could make amends. Given the time, she would have cast you aside when she got bored with you. She didn't love you in the way I did.'

I watched as your hand clenched around the knife, it's blade directed at me. I felt my breaths coming irregularly, I tried to concentrate on breathing through the fear that was expanding in my lungs, suffocating me.

'Shut up, shut up, Rachel.' You were shaking your head to dislodge my words.

Gently I stretched my hand out to you, turning my palm up to the ceiling, a sign of peace. 'When I realised what you had done, how you had set me up, I thought I hated you, I tried to hate you. But this thing we have, it's too strong, it keeps pulling us back to each other. We're friends, Clara. Remember, friends, forever. Even after everything you've done I still love you.'

Your sobs echoed round the room, one following the other, leaving you gulping for air. But you didn't let the knife fall from your hand.

'I'm the only one who can help you now, Clara.'

You wailed, raw pain seeping out from you, your face blotchy and puffed. You were like an animal writhing in agony, a creature that needed to be put out of its misery.

'It's so black,' you said finally. 'Everything is so black.'

The knife in your hand still pointed my way.

'Killing me won't make it go away. I'll be the last person you see before you sleep at night and the first person you look at in the morning.' You were sinking, Clara. Those waves you wished would wash over you and drag you out to sea, they were coming for you now, squeezing the breath out of you. You were drowning in life. You looked at me with desperate, dying eyes.

'I . . . don't . . . know . . . I just don't know anything any more. I don't know how I got here.' You cast your eyes down to the knife and I watched as your hand loosened its grip on it. 'I've tried, I've spent years trying to make sense of it all, but it's all so murky. And every time I think I have it straight in my mind something happens to make it twist out of shape again.

'Do you have any idea what it's like not to trust yourself? To question every word you hear, every thought that goes through your head, to not know what's real? I used to be so confident, Rachel, so certain of everything before Niamh died.'

You stopped for a moment, your sobs dying down into little puffs of air. I was looking at you, looking at the knife, thinking, thinking.

And then I saw you raise it in the air again, towards me, a final show of strength.

'You did this to me, Rachel, you broke me with your lie. It's you, it was always you,' you screamed but by the end of the sentence the conviction had gone from your voice.

'No, Clara, I didn't.' I spoke the words as softly as I could, so they'd soothe you like a balm.

The sobbing started again, your body shook as if it was shutting down.

'Clara,' I whispered. 'Let me help you.'

Slowly you looked up and our eyes locked just as they did that very first day we met. A spark between us momentarily reignited. And we didn't need to speak, we understood each other without words, just like we used to. It made me want to cry.

'You can escape, Clara.'

Your eyes were wide, staring, filled with tears.

'Help me,' you mouthed. It wasn't a question, was it? It was a plea to the only person who loved you enough to save you.

I will help you, Clara.

You let the blade of the knife slip downwards, your sign of surrender.

And I knew then there was no fight left in you.

I breathed deep.

Slowly, with both hands, I reached out for the knife. Your grip still loose on it, your fingers cold around the handle. I placed my hands on top of yours and let them rest there for a moment. Your whole body quivered.

The room was silent, hushed, the light dim. A candle flickered on the mantelpiece.

Your eyes were closed as if in prayer, waiting, for some kind of intervention to lift you out of your pain.

Gently, by degrees, I moved my hands upwards with the knife. Your breath irregular, hot on my skin.

'Don't be scared, Clara,' I whispered.

Your eyes clicked open. Questioning.

'It's your way out,' I breathed. 'Don't be scared.'

I knew I had to be quick then. Little time left. The blade touched the skin on your neck. A sharp blade against soft skin. The shock made your body twist, your hand tried to push the knife away, to stop me, but mine were too strong. Your face full of surprise, of fear.

'Be brave,' I whispered. And then I couldn't look at you any longer so I closed my eyes.

I closed my eyes as I pushed the knife deep into your flesh.

Everything stopped, frozen in a moment.

We were next to each other, very close, closer than we had been for so long. All around us still and quiet and calm.

When I opened my eyes again I saw blood running everywhere, pools and patterns and swirls of red, beautiful, crimson red, spilling over the white sofa and floorboards.

Drip, drip, drip.

I let the knife fall. From my hands and yours.

I told you I would do anything for you, Clara. I was the only one who could. I saved you by ending it all.

Then finally my gaze came up to meet yours.

And in your eyes I saw something was wrong.

A movement.

Two words on your lips. 'Help me.'

I tried to think, think clearly, empty my head. It had to end. I had to finish it. But before I could do anything, it was too late. A bang followed by shouts, loud voices screaming, and then the door was kicked open and armed police were running through the hall, a swarm of black, heading towards me.

Coming to end it all, before I could end it myself.

In my statement I told the police you'd threatened to kill me. I told them of a struggle to wrest the knife from you, how we fought and it went into your neck.

'Thank God you arrived when you did,' I said with all the conviction I could muster.

I gave them that version, Clara, because no one would ever understand the lengths I would go to in order to help a friend. No one would believe I was simply trying to help you find the peace you craved.

When my statement was finished and signed, I asked them the question that had been on my lips since the moment they burst into my home hours earlier.

How did they know you were there? How did they know to come to my aid?

'The security cameras,' they said, smiling. 'The ones your friend fitted for you yesterday. He had them rigged up to his computer, a feed from your house. He called us when he saw she was there.'

I didn't breathe, I just listened to the sound of thunder

in my head, the sound of my life crashing down around me.

⤙o⤚

I staggered out of the police interview room to find Jake waiting for me, his face a picture of concern.

'Thank God,' he said, 'thank God you are all right.'

'The cameras?' I asked, my voice stretched and tight.

He smiled and kissed me.

'It was supposed to be my surprise.'

After

September 2007

IT'S BEEN WEEKS now, months since I started writing to you, Clara, and I've almost reached the end of our story.

In the beginning, in those first days, the summer sun would slant through the window casting its shadows, filling the room with a brilliant white light. That's when I could lift myself out of here and pretend I was far away. I could see it all, the vast sky, the expanse of sea drawing me in. I could almost taste the salt air on my lips.

But it's autumn now. The light is changing, deserting me. No matter how hard I try, all I can see are the four walls of my cell, the painted brick, the bars, a bed and a desk. The room where I have been locked up for months facing trial for your attempted murder.

I am here because I love you.

I am imprisoned because my love for you is so powerful I was prepared to hurt you in order to save you.

Sometimes you have to be cruel to be kind.

If only we had learnt to hate each other, stayed away, cut all ties, it would have been much easier. But that magnetic force that pulled us together was always too strong to resist. We are each other's weaknesses and our bond is tight.

So tight it might destroy me.

Because you are the star witness for the prosecution. Their case will stand or fall on what you say, on how convincing you are, and how far you are prepared to go to damn me. They will have offered you a deal, I know that much: *save your own skin, sacrifice your friend*. Without you, they only have the footage of a struggle. I say it was self-defence, you claim I was trying to kill you. My truth and yours. The police believe you, but ask yourself this: who will a jury believe?

You tried to frame me for your murder, you stalked me, broke into my house and then you came for me with a knife. It's enough to rile the saintliest person.

Of course the police won't tell you their case is hanging by a thread. They need to keep you on side, Clara. Nor will they prepare you for the force of what is coming your way. The press will feast on every moment of the trial, TV cameras from here and abroad (our appeal is global I'm told) will follow your every move, study your expressions, dissect your words. The most high-profile reporters from the BBC, NNN, Sky News and ITN will pack the courtroom to listen to your evidence. The rest will fill the overflow room where they'll be drip-fed your testimony to parcel and package into something sensational.

And then there's the cross-examination. My barrister will tear you apart, chew you up and spit you out. It's brutal. I've seen it done so many times. It's like a blood sport. And you're not a reliable witness.

You killed your mother and now you want to put your sister away for life. What kind of person are you, Ms O'Connor?

Is it true you were sectioned in your late teens? Why should I believe someone like you?

Rehearse your answers, they'd better be good.

But worse, Clara, just when you think you can't take any more, when you feel like your soul has been ripped out and you want to run away and hide from the men in wigs who twist your words and the police who lied to you and the press vultures who hound you, that's when the jury will return a not-guilty verdict. I will be free to walk away. And Jake, who has never doubted me, will be there waiting for me. What then for you? The woman who faked her own disappearance and played the public so cruelly.

The intensity of public outrage will rain down on you like an erupting volcano. It'll be ferocious, merciless, fanned by a press frenzy. No one will save you from it. Not the police; they'll want to forget all about you and the case they should never have brought to court. They'll behave like you never existed. You'll be cast out to face the heat alone.

There will be nowhere to hide.

You could go anywhere, travel thousands of miles, and still you wouldn't escape it.

I'm telling you this because I care for you in a way no one else does. I am the only one who understands you. I'm telling you this because even after everything you've done to me, I can't stop loving you. I want to protect you.

I'm sure you're scared, Clara. I imagine the darkness is

circling and enveloping you. You can't see a way through, can you? There is no light ahead.

I could have saved you from all this; it's all I ever wanted to do.

I was trying to help you because I knew it was what you wanted, before you even knew yourself.

It's a gift I have.

You wanted out.

If I offered you the choice now, if I breathed it quietly into your ear, you'd take it, wouldn't you? You'd snap my hand off, just to be free from all this. From your racing, tormented mind. From the pain that will never end.

But I can't help you now. I can only send you this letter. I've been passing it to Jake every week when he visits, when the prison officers aren't looking. He's been waiting for this, the last instalment, before he gives it to you.

Read it, Clara, read it and then destroy it. Destroy it so no one ever finds out what you did to Niamh, your mother. And I promise I will tell no one. Our secret, safe forever.

You know what you have to do, Clara.

Be brave.

Friends, always,

Rach

X

Two weeks later

Press Association news snap

1 PA Missing

A young artist who faked her own disappearance has been found dead in her flat in an apparent suicide.

Sussex police were called to the home of Clara O'Connor, 29, in the early hours of yesterday morning. It is thought her boyfriend James Redfern called paramedics after finding Ms O'Connor's body. In a police statement DCI Roger Gunn said they were not looking for anyone else in connection with her death.

Acknowledgements

The idea for *Precious Thing* came to me in 1998 but it took fifteen years of procrastination before I finally began to breathe life into the story.

The wise words, critique and support of many people have helped shape this novel. I am grateful to them all but in particular my thanks go to Richard Skinner at The Faber Academy. I may have written a novel without your input, but it wouldn't have been this one. To my agent Nicola Barr, I am still amazed you got it so early on. Your gentle cajoling forced me to write better and bolder than I could have imagined. I am indebted. To Imogen Taylor, Sam Eades, Jo Liddiard, and all the wonderful team at Headline, I have been blown away by your enthusiasm and drive. I really couldn't be in better hands. To the Faber writing class of 2011, thanks for the laughs, criticisms and ridiculous email streams. To Dr Niamh Power and Chris Johnson QC, thanks for your professional generosity and insight. To Liz and Danny McBeth, who always believed, thank you. I don't need to tell you that your support, childcare and home cooking has made all the difference. Thanks also to Jacqueline McBeth, James Waters and John and Margaret

Cuman, and to Haylee, for keeping the kids entertained when I couldn't.

Precious Thing is a story about the destructive force of friendship but it has been the encouragement of many great friends that has kept me going. You know who you are, thank you. A special mention goes to Helene Graham, my oldest friend, for providing the inspiration for the classroom scene, thankfully we are nothing like Rachel and Clara.

Finally, my love and thanks to Finlay, Milo and Sylvie for the smiles, cuddles and putting it all into perspective.

And to Paul, for everything. Thanks doesn't seem enough.